BRIAN

FEAR AND

BRIAN FLYNN was born in 1885 in Leyton, Essex. He won a scholarship to the City Of London School, and from there went into the civil service. In World War I he served as Special Constable on the Home Front, also teaching "Accountancy, Languages, Maths and Elocution to men, women, boys and girls" in the evenings, and acting in his spare time.

It was a seaside family holiday that inspired Brian Flynn to turn his hand to writing in the mid-twenties. Finding most mystery novels of the time "mediocre in the extreme", he decided to compose his own. Edith, the author's wife, encouraged its completion, and after a protracted period finding a publisher, it was eventually released in 1927 by John Hamilton in the UK and Macrae Smith in the U.S. as *The Billiard-Room Mystery*.

The author died in 1958. In all, he wrote and published 57 mysteries, the vast majority featuring the super-sleuth Antony Bathurst.

BRIAN FLYNN

FEAR AND TREMBLING

With an introduction by
Steve Barge

DEAN STREET PRESS

Published by Dean Street Press 2020

Copyright © 1936 Brian Flynn

Introduction © 2020 Steve Barge

All Rights Reserved

The right of Brian Flynn to be identified as the Author of the Work has
been asserted by his estate in accordance with the Copyright, Designs
and Patents Act 1988.

First published in 1936 by John Long

Cover by DSP

ISBN 978 1 913527 55 6

www.deanstreetpress.co.uk

INTRODUCTION

"I believe that the primary function of the mystery story is to entertain; to stimulate the imagination and even, at times, to supply humour. But it pleases the connoisseur most when it presents – and reveals – genuine mystery. To reach its full height, it has to offer an intellectual problem for the reader to consider, measure and solve."

BRIAN Flynn began his writing career with *The Billiard Room Mystery* in 1927, primarily at the prompting of his wife Edith who had grown tired of hearing him say he could write a better mystery novel than the ones he had been reading. Four more books followed under his original publisher, John Hamilton, before he moved to John Long, who would go on to publish the remaining forty-eight of his Anthony Bathurst mysteries, along with his three Sebastian Stole titles, released under the pseudonym Charles Wogan. Some of the early books were released in the US, and there were also a small number of translations of his mysteries into Swedish and German. In the article from which the above quote is taken, Brian also claims that there were French and Danish translations but to date, I have not found a single piece of evidence for their existence. Tracking down all of his books written in the original English has been challenging enough!

Reprints of Brian's books were rare. Four titles were released as paperbacks as part of John Long's Four Square Thriller range in the late 1930s, four more re-appeared during the war from Cherry Tree Books and Mellifont Press, albeit abridged by at least a third, and two others that I am aware of, *Such Bright Disguises* (1941) and *Reverse The Charges* (1943), received a paperback release as part of John Long's Pocket Edition range in the early 1950s – these were also possibly abridged, but only by about 10%. These were the exceptions, rather than the rule, however, and it was not until 2019, when Dean Street Press released his first ten titles, that his work was generally available again.

The question still persists as to why his work disappeared from the awareness of all but the most ardent collectors. As you may expect, when a title was only released once, back in the early 1930s, finding copies of the original text is not a straightforward matter – not even Brian's estate has a copy of every title. We are particularly grateful to one particular collector for providing *The Edge Of Terror*, Brian's first serial killer tale, in order for this next set of ten books to be republished without an obvious gap!

By the time Brian Flynn's eleventh novel, *The Padded Door* (1932), was published, he was producing a steady output of Anthony Bathurst mysteries, averaging about two books a year. While this may seem to be a rapid output, it is actually fairly average for a crime writer of the time. Some writers vastly exceeded this – in the same period of time that it took Brian to have ten books published, John Street, under his pseudonyms John Rhode and Miles Burton published twenty-eight!

In this period, in 1934 to be precise, an additional book was published, *Tragedy At Trinket*. It is a schoolboy mystery, set at Trinket, "one of the two finest schools in England – in the world!" combining the tale of Trinket's attempts to redeem itself in the field of schoolboy cricket alongside the apparently accidental death by drowning of one of the masters. It was published by Thomas Nelson and Sons, rather than John Long, and was the only title published under his own name not to feature Bathurst. It is unlikely, however, that this was an attempt to break away from his sleuth, given that the hero of this tale is Maurice Otho Folliott, a schoolboy who just happens to be Bathurst's nephew and is desperate to emulate his uncle! It is an odd book, with a significant proportion of the tale dedicated to the tribulations of the cricket team, but Brian does an admirable job of weaving an actual death into a genre that was generally concerned with misunderstandings and schoolboy pranks.

Not being in the top tier of writers, at least in terms of public awareness, reviews of Brian's work seem to have been rare, but when they did occur, there were mostly positive. A reviewer in the Sunday Times enthused over *The Edge Of Terror* (1932), describing it as "an enjoyable thriller in Mr. Flynn's best manner" and Torquemada in the *Observer* says that *Fear and Trembling* (1936) "gripped my interest on a sleepless night and held it to the end". Even Dorothy L. Sayers, a fairly unforgiving reviewer at times, had positive things to say in the *Sunday Times* about *The Case For The Purple Calf* (1934) ("contains some ingenuities") and *The Horn* (1934) ("good old-fashioned melodrama . . . not without movement") although she did take exception to Brian's writing style. Milward Kennedy was similarly disdainful, although Kennedy, a crime writer himself, criticising a style of writing might well be considered the pot calling the kettle black. He was impressed, however, with the originality of *Tread Softly* (1937).

It is quite possible that Brian's harshest critic, though, was himself. In *The Crime Book Magazine* he wrote about the current output of detective fiction: "I delight in the dazzling erudition that has come to grace and decorate the craft of the *'roman policier'*. He then goes on to say: "At the same time, however, I feel my own comparative unworthiness for the fire and burden of the competition." Such a feeling may well be the reason why he never made significant inroads into the social side of crime-writing, such as the Detection Club or the Crime Writers' Association. Thankfully, he uses this sense of unworthiness as inspiration, concluding: "The stars, though, have always been the most desired of all goals, so I allow exultation and determination to take the place of that but temporary dismay."

Reviews, both external and internal, thankfully had no noticeable effect on Brian's writing. What is noticeable about his work is how he shifts from style to style from each book. While all the books from this period remain classic whodunits, the style shifts from courtroom drama to gothic darkness, from plotting serial killers to events that spiral out of control, with Anthony Bathurst the constant thread tying everything together.

We find some books narrated by a Watson-esque character, although a different character each time. Occasionally Bathurst himself will provide a chapter or two to explain things either that the narrator wasn't present for or just didn't understand. Bathurst doesn't always have a Watson character to tell his stories, however, so other books are in the third person – as some of Bathurst's adventures are not tied to a single location, this is often the case in these tales.

One element that does become more common throughout books eleven to twenty is the presence of Chief Detective Inspector Andrew MacMorran. While MacMorran gets a name check from as early as *The Mystery Of The Peacock's Eye* (1928), his actual appearances in the early books are few and far between, with others such as Inspector Baddeley (*The Billiard Room Mystery* (1927), *The Creeping Jenny Mystery* (1929)) providing the necessary police presence. As the series progresses, the author settled more and more on a regular showing from the police. It still isn't always the case – in some books, Bathurst is investigating undercover and hence by himself, and in a few others, various police Inspectors appear, notably the return of the aforementioned Baddeley in *The Fortescue Candle* (1936). As the series progresses from *The Padded Door* (1932), Inspector MacMorran becomes more and more of a fixture at Scotland Yard for Bathurst.

One particular trait of the Bathurst series is the continuity therein. While the series can be read out of order, there is a sense of what has gone before. While not to the extent of, say, E.R. Punshon's Bobby Owen books, or Christopher Bush's Ludovic Travers mysteries, there is a clear sense of what has gone before. Side characters from books reappear, either by name or in physical appearances – Bathurst is often engaged on a case by people he has helped previously. Bathurst's friendship with MacMorran develops over the books from a respectful partnership to the point where MacMorran can express his exasperation with Bathurst's annoying habits rather vocally. Other characters appear and develop too, for example Helen Repton, but she is, alas, a story for another day.

The other sign of continuity is Bathurst's habit of name-dropping previous cases, names that were given to them by Bathurst's "chronicler". *Fear and Trembling* mentions no less than five separate cases, with one, *The Sussex Cuckoo* (1935), getting two mentions. These may seem like little more than adverts for those titles, old-time product placement if you will – "you've handled this affair about as brainly as I handled 'The Fortescue Candle'", for example – but they do actually make sense in regard to what has gone before, given how long it took Bathurst to see the light in each particular case. Contrast this to the reference to Christie's *Murder On The Orient Express* in *Cards On The Table*, which not only gives away the ending but contradicts Poirot's actions at the dénouement.

> "For my own detective, Anthony Lotherington Bathurst, I have endeavoured to place him in the true Holmes tradition. It is not for me to say whether my efforts have failed or whether I have been successful."

Brian Flynn seemed determined to keep Bathurst's background devoid of detail – I set out in the last set of introductions the minimal facts that we are provided with: primarily that he went to public school and Oxford University, can play virtually every sport under the sun and had a bad first relationship and has seemingly sworn off women since. Of course, the detective's history is something not often bothered with by crime fiction writers, but this usually occurs with older sleuths who have lived life, so to speak. *Cold Evil* (1938), the twenty-first Bathurst mystery, finally pins down Bathurst's age, and we find that in *The Billiard Room Mystery*, his first outing, he was a fresh-faced Bright Young Thing of twenty-two. So how he can survive with his own rooms, at least two servants, and no noticeable source of income remains a mystery. One can also ask at what point in his life he travelled the world, as he has, at least, been to Bangkok at some point. It is, perhaps, best not to analyse Bathurst's past too carefully . . .

> "Judging from the correspondence my books have excited it seems I have managed to achieve some measure of success for my faithful readers comprise a circle in which high dignitaries of the Church rub shoulders with their brothers and sisters of the common touch."

For someone who wrote to entertain, such correspondence would have delighted Brian, and I wish he were around to see how many people enjoyed the first set of reprints of his work. His family are delighted with the reactions that people have passed on, and I hope that this set of books will delight just as much.

Fear and Trembling (1936)

'If anyone on the verge of action should judge himself according to the outcome, he would never begin.'
Fear and Trembling (1843), Søren Kierkegaard

IT's not entirely clear where Brian Flynn took the title for *Fear and Trembling* (1936), the nineteenth Anthony Bathurst mystery, from, but perhaps the mostly likely source is Kierkegaard, who himself took it from the Bible – it occurs in both Psalms 55:5 and Philippians 2:12 (the second possibly being a reference to the first). Kierkegaard was writing in part about fathers and sons, notably Abraham and Isaac, and the Somerset family, David and his two sons, Geoffrey and Gerald form the centre-piece of Flynn's *Fear and Trembling*. You will have to ask a philosopher about how much of the story of the Somersets mirrors Kierkegaard's theory, but of course, there's also every chance that Brian chose the title because it was a familiar phrase that sounded sinister. It's a little clearer where the US title, *The Somerset Murder Case*, came from.

Fear and Trembling is notable for two things above all. First of all, this is a mystery involving twins. The use of twins, especially a twin who is only revealed to exist at the denouement of the tale, has long been used in fiction, so much so that it was one of the rules in Ronald Knox's Decalogue, a good-natured set of ten rules for mystery writers, including rule 10: Twin brothers, and doubles generally, must not appear unless we have been duly prepared for them. Needless to say, since the Decalogue was written, writers have been trying to circumvent these rules for their own (and their readers') entertainment, culminating with a set of ten short stories, *Sins For Father Knox*, by Josef Škvorecký, where each tale breaks one rule, and a chapter in the collaborative Detection Club novel *The Sinking Admiral*, where L.C. Tyler manages to break all ten in the space of about ten pages . . .

Father Knox didn't prohibit the presence of twins in detective fiction, just *unannounced* twins. There are essentially three sorts of ways in which twins are used in mysteries. The first is where the twins are the central point of the tale, such as in John Rhode's masterpiece, *The Robthorne Mystery*, centred on the question, or so it seems, of which twin killed the other. The second is where the twins are part of the cast of suspects, and their duality may or may not be important, such as in Christopher Bush's *The Case Of The Flowery Corpse*. Finally, there is the rare case where the twins have nothing to do with the mystery. A somewhat extreme example of this is Ellery Queen's *The Siamese Twin Mystery*, where the presence of the characters seems to do little but inspire the title of the book. Needless to say, I'm not going to spoil which sort of twin mystery *Fear and Trembling* is . . .

The second notable thing to mention is that in this book, Bathurst finally notices an attractive woman! After we discovered in *The Padded Door* (1932) that Bathurst's oblivious celibacy has ruined certain women's lives, in this book he, almost out of the blue, falls head over heels for a mysterious femme fatale. Bathurst in love – or in infatuation at least – is an extremely entertaining change of pace for the reader. Alas, this does not ultimately mark much of a change for him, back to normal as he is in the next book.

Fear and Trembling is one of those books that, in my opinion, should have made Brian Flynn a much better-known author. There's misdirection a-plenty and yet the alert reader just might work out what's going on, and, if they do, feel very pleased with themselves, i.e. the sign of a great mystery.

Steve Barge

Chapter I
THE "GOLDEN LION"

DAVID Somerset fumbled in a pocket, gave his ticket to the collector at East Brutton station, and passed through the barrier. As he was destined to become a figure of public interest for at least a month, a description of him, as he was at the time, may not be out of place. He was fifty-five years of age. Of middle height, he had square shoulders, a strong, well-formed body, wore horn-rimmed glasses, had thick dark-brown wavy hair that he brushed well away from his forehead, light-coloured blue eyes, prominent ears, a full-lipped mouth, and a chin that betokened both obstinacy and determination. The time of the year was mid-March. A day or so prior to the Ides. He wore a bowler hat, dark overcoat, dark lounge suit, and carried an attaché-case.

Coming to the outside of the small railway-station, he paused on the pavement and looked somewhat contemptuously down the narrow street that he saw in front of him. He had never been to East Brutton before, and from what he had so far seen of it he had little wish to come there again. Also, if he told the truth, he felt a certain amount of misgiving concerning his journey. Had he not, perhaps, taken too much for granted? Been too trusting in the matter? On the other hand, the offer was a good one, and there were his wife and his two boys to be considered, no matter which way you looked at things. After all, there came times in life when to refuse to do business because the other party was unknown to you would be the height of folly, and might result in opportunity being turned from your door.

He crammed his hat more tightly on his head and set off briskly down the narrow street which he had already found so unattractive and so uninviting. Argue as you might, an opportunity of this kind came only once in a lifetime, and it must be faced and dealt with, firmly and courageously. Halfway down the village street, he stopped and took a letter from his pocket.

"May as well refresh my memory over the details," he muttered to himself as he stood and read.

One cannot be too precise as to your instructions. At 2.15 p.m. in the smoke-room of the "Golden Lion", High St., East Brutton. Inasmuch as it would be a blazing indiscretion for you to come by car, the 10.22 train from Paddington will suit you admirably. It is timed to arrive at East Brutton at 1.57, which will give you a margin of eighteen minutes to reach the rendezvous. You will find that this is ample. Actually, the walk from the station will not take you more than four minutes at the outside, so that you will be in no way pressed for time and can take matters comfortably.

When you reach the hotel, don't ask for me by name. With so much at stake, from the point of view of each of us, you will readily see the soundness of the reason behind this precaution. When you arrive, go at once to the smoke-room. I shall be there waiting for you. I shall be wearing a dinner jacket with white vest, black bow, black studs and links, and a white gardenia. For my own part, I could never understand why His late Majesty, King George the Fifth of Blessed Memory, preferred the carnation to the gardenia for the purpose of sartorial decoration. But there you are: de gustibus non disputandum est. Till next Thursday, then, and in the very strictest confidence, I remain, your cheerful but unwilling victim, Adam Antine.

Somerset replaced the letter in his breast pocket, gave a hurried glance at his wrist-watch, saw that he was still well within his time, and started off again on his journey to the inn of assignation. He was not long in coming to it. The message that had been sent to him had not erred. Four minutes had been ample. The inn of the "Golden Lion" was, to all appearances, an old-time posting-house. It stood at four cross-roads in the middle of the little town. As he approached it from the railway-station, it faced him on the opposite left-hand corner. There was a wide cobble-stoned yard on its farther side that seemed almost an anachronism, and towards this, David Somerset made his way. His instinct proved sound. On the right of the cobbled turning was a door marked "Saloon", which door he opened, to see immediately, and directly facing him, an indication in large lettering, "To the smoke-room".

Somerset passed up a winding staircase, narrow and with old-fashioned stairs. Evidently, he judged, many centuries old. A sharp turn at the top brought him to the room that he sought. He pushed the door open and entered. The room, low-ceilinged, was warm and cosy. But, save for himself, empty. He glanced again at the time. It showed to be eleven minutes past two. That explained his solitude. The man whom he had come to meet was, no doubt, as precise in character as had been his instructions. He would not arrive until a quarter past two. Neither before that time nor after. As he surmised thus, David Somerset heard a noise behind him. Somebody had entered and closed the door. Turning, he saw a young fellow, clad in grey flannel trousers and a pullover.

"Your order, sir?" the man asked.

"Ah, yes. Bring me a Black Label, will you?"

"Water, or a splash, sir?"

"Neither," returned Somerset curtly. "I like my whisky neat."

"Very good, sir." The barman disappeared, to return surprisingly quickly with Somerset's whisky. The latter took his drink to a near-by table, sat there and waited. For a few minutes only, however. A voice behind him caused him to turn. A man had entered the room, who, from his attire, must be the person with whom David Somerset had made this unusual appointment. Somerset rose from his seat and bowed. He desired to waste no time.

"I presume that I am addressing Mr. Antine?"

The short, dark, foreign-looking man, in the dinner jacket with gardenia, smiled and showed his white teeth.

"And I, Mr. David Somerset. Yes?"

"That is so. I am David Somerset. I hope that our interview will not take too long."

"A most commendable desire. Naturally. Be seated, I beg of you."

The man coughed, and then a most extraordinary thing happened. Before the sound of the cough had died away, the door of the smoke-room opened again, and four more men entered. They were, as may be readily imagined, of varying physical types. But they had one thing in common with the man whom David Somerset had called "Antine". Each was dressed in the same fashion. That is to say, in complete accordance with the terms that had been nominated in Somerset's letter. Somerset looked round this strange company with an expression of bewilderment that he made no attempt to conceal.

"I don't think that I . . ." He paused, but every sense of him was on his guard. Taut and at full tension. Into what hornets' nest had he been foolish enough to stray? How he wished now that he had brought his revolver!

The five men took five chairs, and arranged themselves in a semi-circle that faced him. Antine had two of them on each side of him.

"You're just a little surprised? Yes?" The man whom he had called Antine was the speaker.

"Certainly I am surprised! How else can I feel? There is no mention of such a contingency as this in the letter that you sent to me. I understood that I was to meet you, and you alone. May I inquire the meaning of the procedure?"

"You may. But you must content yourself with the answer that I give you. You must not ask the same question, or what is tantamount to being the same question, more than once. You understand, yes? Well, the answer to the question that you have just asked is—'Five heads are better than one.' I'm positive that a gentleman with the good sense and general intelligence that Mr. David Somerset is known to have, will not be disposed to argue as to the truth of that." Antine's eyes gleamed through his gold-rimmed spectacles. His voice was soft and unattractively sibilant. There was rather more than the suggestion of a lisp about it. To Somerset, as he listened, it was distinctly unpleasant, if not menacing. He resolved, however, to put as bold a face on the situation as possible.

"Of course. I will not dispute what you have said. Shall we get to business? I am a busy man, as I presume you know, and time means money to me."

"Ah—money! What a thrice-blessed sound that word always has to English ears."

"I don't know that the English ear is unique in that respect. Indeed, my experience teaches me otherwise."

"Mr. Somerset shows a little pique. Don't you agree with me, César?" Antine shot the question at a tall, thin, dark man with an aquiline nose, seated immediately on his right.

"Perhaps. It is, though, a little understandable—but have a care! You are forgetting, I think."

For a moment David Somerset thought that the warning was meant for him. To his surprise, though, it had been addressed to Antine. The latter took the rebuke with peaceful composure.

"You're right, *mon ami*! The lapse shall not occur again, I promise you. It shall be my one ewe lamb of lapses. Have I not put that well?" Again he smiled through his glasses.

There were nods of assent from two or three of the black-coated company.

"We will not strike an acrimonious note," said Antine, "so early in the proceedings. It would be most regrettable. Mr. Somerset naturally has certain national sympathies and inclin-ations that are understandable. Who amongst us shall blame him?" He turned to either side of the semi-circle of seats, as though inviting criticism or approbation.

"You are our spokesman." The voice was that of the last man seated on Antine's right.

"Thank you. That is undeniably true. We are prepared, Mr. Somerset, to make you a most handsome and generous offer . . . for what you possess, and what we want of you. We trust"—he emphasized the word "trust"—"that you will see your way to accept it."

"That depends. What is the offer?" Somerset's reply was brusque and blunt.

"Do you mean 'how much', Mr. Somerset?"

"That's exactly what I do mean." The tone he used was still uncompromising.

Antine bent towards the man whom he had addressed as "César", and conferred with him in a low voice. There were head-noddings and hand-gesticulations. Although he strained his ears Somerset was unable to hear anything of what was being said. At length the conference ceased. Antine nodded to his companion and looked directly at Somerset.

"The offer is one hundred thousand pounds! If you can satisfy us as to the strength of your claim. One hundred thousand pounds. A truly noble sum, if I may say so. A truly magnificent gesture on our part, Mr. Somerset."

"The offer is refused." Somerset was curtly precise.

There came a period of silence. The room was so still and the atmosphere so tense that Somerset could hear his wrist-watch ticking. Antine broke the silence.

"Mr. Somerset will think again. Yes?"

"Undoubtedly. But not at the figure which you have offered me."

Antine shook his head deprecatingly.

"Mr. Somerset is the last person to act indiscreetly. I am convinced of that. We are all convinced of that."

"And the last person also to act foolishly, and without due regard to his own interest."

"There might be an extraordinarily narrow margin between indiscretion and foolishness. I should hate Mr. Somerset to over-step that margin. In fact, there could be nothing that I should like less. Because . . ." Antine paused and watched Somerset narrowly.

The latter was imperturbable. "Because what?"

"Because it might cause the breakdown of our little confer-ence and put an end to our mutual condition of understanding. I could not bear that to happen. It would desolate me." Antine smiled, but Somerset knew that behind the smile there lay, already banked up, the fires of malevolence.

"I am sorry."

There ensued another silence. Somerset had not, for a second, shed any of his sangfroid. With some ostentation, which he intended all of them to see, he glanced at his wrist-watch. Antine's four companions rose and gathered round their spokesman. There were murmurs and mutterings. Some of the phrases used, Somerset decided, were in French, others in German. Every now and then, his ear caught the snatch of a tongue with which he was totally unfamiliar. He made no comment, however, allowing them to find a solution of the "impasse" that had presented itself which would be satisfactory to both sides. Eventually Antine broke away from the group. He held up his hand. The movement had the nature of a command. Somerset felt that the moment of acute crisis had arrived.

"I have been instructed to ask you, Mr. Somerset, what is *your* price?"

"Thank you. That's a lot better. I've been expecting you to ask that. It shows cool sense on your part. My price is one million pounds paid in notes—as I bargained. Neither a penny more nor a penny less, gentlemen! And, considering all the circumstances, a most reasonable offer."

Antine's face changed as though a mask had been suddenly jerked from it. "T'cha!" he snapped, bitterly. "What you ask is ridiculous! Utterly absurd."

"I think not. Let me point out that it all depends upon the point of view," countered Somerset. "Your price is ridiculous to me, my price is nonsensical to you. Therefore, gentlemen, we have reached a deadlock. A condition of stalemate. I will not take up your time any longer, gentlemen."

He rose deliberately and pushed back his chair.

"Stay!" cried Antine. "Not so fast. This is indeed regrettable, but there may yet be a way out. It is for us to find it, for I am convinced that it can be found. Be seated again, please. And you, too, my friends. Let Mr. Somerset see that we are all still willing and ready to talk business with him."

Somerset, half-regretfully, resumed his seat. The five others followed his example.

"There is a way out," cried a harsh, guttural voice from Somerset's right. That is to say, it came from a man seated on Antine's left. Murmurs of assent greeted the remark. The voice continued. "Why parley with him? I have always been against it! We are fools—all of us. Brainless idiots."

Again there were sympathetic cries. Antine stroked his chin reflectively. "Murder is an ugly word." He paused, to continue, however, at once. "But I take it, gentlemen, that that is your meaning. I have not misunderstood you?"

Somerset rose and faced them, his teeth and his hands clenched. His outraged feelings showed in words of burning indignation. This condition mastered any fear that he might have felt.

"You can't talk like that!" cried Somerset. "You're in England—not in Chicago! Murder! Because I differ from you on a question of price? Let me tell you that you won't put the wind up me like that. You'll have to pull a faster one."

"Be seated," returned Antine peremptorily. Somerset had the sense to take the hint, and obeyed.

"We are five to one. *And*, moreover, you are unarmed."

Somerset half rose, either in protest or attempted denial. Antine silenced him again.

"I *know* that you are unarmed. You have shown us that much unmistakably. Do not waste your breath in denying it. And I feel that I must repeat my previous statement—we are five to one. Heavy odds, Mr. Somerset, even making allowances for the Englishman's proverbial superiority to the—er—'dirty foreigner'. I believe that I am using the correct expression for a situation of this kind."

"A question!" The interruption came from the man "César". Antine raised his eyebrows and nodded. "If we pay Mr. Somerset's price—will he hand over to us what we require here and now? I should like that question answered, gentlemen, before I am called upon to decide on any further step."

Somerset saw the trap that had been set for him and evaded it adroitly. He saw how he could do so, too, without giving away the material point of knowledge that his antagonists were seeking. He replied immediately:

"I naturally did not come here prepared to hand over what you want at once. If, however, you are ready to accept *my* offer, the exchange can be effected in a proper business-like way at a time and place upon which we can agree now. I appeal to you! We are dealing, I suggest, with the sale of something more than a box of kippers."

The five men to whom he had spoken left their chairs and gathered together again. After a few moments Antine emerged from the others and advanced towards David Somerset.

"Mr. Somerset," he said, excessively softly, "my colleagues and I are agreed upon this. There must be a condition of absolute confidence between you and us. That is a vital necessity as a basis of agreement. Will you join us at the table there and listen to our terms? I may say our *new* terms."

Somerset nodded.

"As long as there is no more stupid talk of murder, or threats of any kind. If you are reasonable, you will find me ready and willing to be equally reasonable."

The company moved to the table which Antine had indicated.

"Briefly, Mr. Somerset," said the latter, "our revised terms are these. We are prepared from our standpoint to meet you. Our figure will be as high as we can go. . . ."

David Somerset bent his head to listen.

CHAPTER II
THE NEWS COMES TO SCOTLAND YARD

BRIGADIER-General Sir Austin Mostyn Kemble, K.C.V.O., D.S.O., Commissioner of Police, turned sharply in his revolving-chair in his room at the "Yard" and regarded his companion somewhat whimsically.

"Well, Bathurst, what have you to say to all of it? Why so disinclined to discuss it? You don't seem too keen to give me your opinion. Unlike you, my boy."

Anthony Bathurst flicked the ash from a cigarette. A humorous gleam showed in his grey eyes.

"'Tis better, sir, to be silent and to be thought a fool, than to speak and leave a doubt upon the point."

"As bad as that?" returned Sir Austin, with a suspicion of mockery in his voice. "Good lord, you surprise me!"

"Every bit, sir. I have no data. Not a shred, sir."

"It's a most extraordinary occurrence, I agree, Bathurst. From many points of view. But Mr. Gerald Somerset should be with us in a very few minutes now and you will be able to hear what he has to tell us. As you've always preferred first-hand information to any other, your preference will be gratified. You can find no fault with that."

Sir Austin looked at his watch.

"If he keeps to the time of his appointment, Bathurst, he should be here at any moment."

"Good!" Anthony Bathurst walked to the window. "Thank God we're destined for a fine summer."

Sir Austin stared at his companion in some perplexity.

"I don't know that I . . ."

Anthony turned to him and smiled.

"Today is St. Patrick's Day, sir. And a fine day, at that. In Ireland they would say today, as they met each other, that 'the Saint had turned the fine side of the stone up!' Which is the harbinger of the summer that is to come. A wet St. Patrick's Day—vice versa—that is to say, a wet and sunless summer as a consequence. As you know, you can count me in with mad dogs and Englishmen—I love to go out in the midday sun. I believe that you English people cherish a somewhat similar belief with regard to the 28th of January and its relation to the summer that follows. But, personally, my money's on St. Patrick as against Paul of Tarsus. I never did care overmuch for the Levantine."

The Commissioner coughed. "Ah, yes . . . quite so. . . ."

Mr. Bathurst permitted himself the luxury of another smile. Sir Austin's limitations were always so obviously and so easily exposed. Anthony walked back from the window to Sir Austin's table in the middle of the room. Before he could reach it, the telephone-bell rang and the Commissioner answered it.

"Good. Send Mr. Somerset up," Anthony heard him say. "I'll see him at once." He replaced the receiver. His face held a look of satisfaction. "He's here. I told you that you wouldn't have to wait long. I was pretty certain he'd be punctual."

"Excellent," returned Mr. Bathurst. "I shall listen to his statement of the case with the greatest possible attention. I began to think that you had let me alone too long."

An official brought his charge to the door of the Commissioner's room, tapped on that door, and within the space of a few seconds Gerald Somerset was seated facing Sir Austin Kemble. Anthony, from his position at the side, saw a tall, clean-shaven, slim young fellow with blue eyes, longish face, and rather pointed chin. A sensitive mouth, a trifle weak, perhaps, for the more fastidious psychologist, a long nose, and long pointed fingers, all united to give an impression of length and agility and gracefulness.

"Now, Mr. Somerset, tell us your story, will you? Mr. Bathurst and I will listen to you most attentively."

Gerald Somerset flushed appreciatively at Sir Austin's statement.

"Thank you, sir. I will endeavour to tell you my story as simply as possible. I am more than grateful for your kindness in giving me a private interview, and I appreciate intensely the fact that Mr. Bathurst is here, to hear me, with you. My mother—my stepmother really, she is my father's second wife—was insistent that I should come to you. She has been insisting on this procedure for two days. At first I will admit that I was inclined to wait a little longer, in the hope that there might be news come to us at any moment. But no news has come, and I think now that my mother was right, and that I should have come to Scotland Yard with my story before. But I'm telling the yarn badly and not starting in the right place. I mean—in the beginning."

The young man stopped. He was nervous and overwrought. Anthony noticed how he continually passed his hand backwards and forwards over his knee.

Sir Austin offered him encouragement.

"Tell us everything, Mr. Somerset, in the order in which everything occurred."

"I will do my best, sir. My father is David Somerset. He is an analytical and manufacturing chemist, who, after working in the service of Raleigh and Osborne for several years, started a business of his own about twelve years ago. Our offices are in Boot Lane, E.C. We—that's my father, his wife, my brother Geoffrey and I—live near Brentwood, in Essex. Between Brentwood and Ingatestone. Our address actually is 'Urswick', Clutton Chase, near Brentwood. My father left home in his usual manner on the morning of Thursday last, the 12th of March, for our offices in the city. I say 'our offices' for the reason that my brother Geoffrey and I assist in the running of the business, which is now styled 'Somerset and Sons'. On that particular morning my father issued certain instructions to my brother and me before he left the house, which meant, in effect, that we should not arrive at Boot Lane until after midday. Couldn't possibly. When we did arrive there, we found that my father had left the office fairly early in the morning and had not returned. He had left no information with any of the staff there as to where he had gone, or even as to when he expected to be back."

Again Gerald Somerset paused. But not for long.

"Sir Austin Kemble," he said gravely, "my father has never been back. He has never returned. For all we know, my stepmother and I, my father, David Somerset, might have vanished into thin air."

"Most extraordinary," commented the Commissioner of Police. "Can you tell us what—"

Gerald Somerset held up his hand courteously. Sir Austin saw what his intention was and broke off with his sentence unfinished.

"That same night, the night of Thursday, the 12th of March, our troubles increased still more. My brother Geoffrey did not come home! In fact, neither my father, nor he, my brother, has ever been seen again. That is, of course, as far as we have been able to trace."

"The 'absences' were reported, of course?"

"To the local police, do you mean?"

"Yes."

"Yes. They were reported. On the thirteenth, on the Friday. I telephoned to them today, to the local police, I mean, and told them straight out that I was coming up here to you at the Yard. I'm afraid that I took this course whether they liked it or not."

Sir Austin Kemble nodded. "Don't worry about that. Matters can be arranged."

"Thank you."

"You haven't the slightest reason, of course, Mr. Somerset, to advance to us, as to why your brother and father should have absented themselves from home?"

"Do you mean a reason of which I have definite knowledge?"

"Yes, exactly."

"I know of no reason at all, sir. From what I know of both my father and my brother, neither of them would stay away from us deliberately of his own free will. I haven't the slightest doubt in my mind that they have been the victims, in some way, of foul play. My stepmother agrees with me."

"Who would wish to harm either of them?"

"I don't know. I really haven't the slightest idea. I wish that I could make a reasonable suggestion in that direction to support my opinion, but frankly, I can't."

"But, Mr. Somerset, there must be a reason behind what you have described as 'foul play'. You must see that. It doesn't arise wantonly. I will amend the terms of my question. Why should anyone desire to hurt your father and your brother?"

"Again, sir, I haven't the least idea. I can conceive of no reason why anybody should wish to do such a thing."

Anthony Bathurst glanced across at the Commissioner and nodded. Mr. Bathurst turned and put a question to young Somerset.

"Revenge a possibility?"

"No. We have no enemies in the business world. The firm is respected and admired everywhere."

"How about such a possibility, privately? That is to say, away from business interests? Is there any chance of that?"

Gerald Somerset shook his head decisively. "To my knowledge, none at all."

Sir Austin Kemble came in again. "I understand, then, that the Essex police have had no success at all?"

"That is so, sir. They have discovered nothing. Since my father walked out of the office on the morning of last Thursday not a trace of him has been picked up anywhere."

Anthony turned to the Commissioner.

"They have been in touch up here, of course?"

"Oh yes. Mr. Somerset reported it locally, naturally, but Mr. Somerset senior having been known to have been in his office that morning meant that the police up here had to look into things."

"Who was the last person who is known to have spoken to your father?"

"The chief clerk in the office. Leonard Digby, by name. One of the firm's most reliable servants. Been with us for years. You can almost call him my father's confidential clerk. It appears that my father told Digby that he was going out and might be away some little time. But he told him nothing that might have indicated in any way where he was going. At the same time, there is one little point that emerges from the talk that I've had with Digby, and that is this. It's disturbed me considerably, Sir Austin. There was a revolver on my father's desk when he called Digby in to tell him that he intended to go out. Digby noticed it and was utterly surprised to see it there."

"It wasn't usual, I take it, from that statement, for your father to have a revolver in the office?"

"I have never seen one there. Never in my life! That is all I can say about that."

"Thank you, Mr. Somerset. As you say, a most remarkable and significant point. Now—your brother Geoffrey. Who was the last person known to have seen him alive?"

"His fiancée, Irene Pearce. The Irene Pearce. Pictures—you know. Miss Pearce lives at Chiswick, Braundway Avenue. Geoffrey spent the evening with her, which was quite a normal occurrence, and, according to her statement, left her to come home about half past ten. From the moment of leaving her house at Chiswick he, like my father, has simply vanished from the face of the earth. Stepped off the edge of it."

Anthony Bathurst paced the room. Here was a problem indeed.

"Which way would your brother have returned home? In the ordinary way."

"If he hadn't used his car, we have two cars, to go to town that morning, he would return either by Green Line coach from Aldgate as far as Brentwood, or by the Eastern National Service which runs through to Chelmsford. Probably by the latter, which actually passes through Clutton Chase. The odds are that way. I know that he didn't go up by car that morning, because of carrying out the instructions which my father had given to us."

"The police, you say, have made no report at all?"

"Up to the moment they have drawn a blank in each case. As far as I know, up to the time of coming here today, they have discovered nothing whatever."

Anthony came across and looked at him intently.

"These instructions that your father gave you to carry out on the morning of the day that he disappeared, were they extraordinary, or, shall we say, unusual, Mr. Somerset?"

"Not in the least, Mr. Bathurst. I called upon Breckenridge and Co., the manufacturing chemists at Stratford, and my brother Geoffrey called similarly upon Holmes, Hayes, and Waterson, the chemists at Canning Town. The two appointments were absolutely necessary ones. Each concerned important business and had been on the board for some little time. They were certainly not manufactured or trumped up by my father for the purpose of getting Geoffrey and me out of the way. You can be quite easy on that score. But at the same time . . ." As he approached the end of his statement Gerald Somerset had begun to speak more slowly and suddenly he paused.

"I am interested, Mr. Somerset, to hear what you were about to say." Anthony Bathurst's tones were eager.

The young man took his time. He refused to commit himself hurriedly. Eventually he found the words for which he had been mentally searching.

"I was going to say this, Mr. Bathurst. I want to make myself perfectly clear. That was why I hesitated. I shouldn't like either you, or Sir Austin Kemble here, to misunderstand me. That although I stated just now that the interviews which my brother and I had with the firms I mentioned were certainly not 'deliberately engineered' by my father, I am not at all sure, now that I look back on things, that he did not seize the opportunity that they presented for getting Geoffrey and me out of the way. I mean that they came *opportunely* for him."

"Ah!" The exclamation came from Mr. Bathurst.

"With what idea, do you think, Mr. Somerset?" The question came from the Commissioner of Police.

Gerald Somerset shook his head.

"I can't say. But there's just this—our absences *might* have prevented questions being put to my father during the morning that he might have found awkward to answer . . . if he were keeping us in the dark with regard to anything. That's the point I am trying to make."

Sir Austin nodded that he understood and agreed. "Yes, I follow that. It's feasible, I grant." Anthony Bathurst intervened again.

"Are you and your brother in your father's confidence? Generally speaking, that is."

Gerald Somerset answered with an excess of frankness.

"Had you asked me that, Mr. Bathurst, before this trouble of ours had occurred I should have unhesitatingly answered in the affirmative. In the whole of my business career I cannot remember an incident of the slightest consequence to occur to make me think otherwise, but—now!" He broke off and shrugged his shoulders. The gesture was eloquent.

"Which means that you can throw no light whatever on either of these two disappearances?"

"None at all, Sir Austin. I have racked my brain in all directions, but with no success. I feel helpless and hopeless in the matter. Because of these feelings I have come to you for your advice, and, as I hope, your help. Both my stepmother and I appeal to you."

Sir Austin Kemble hummed and hawed. The damned problem looked pretty nasty, look at it which way you would. He drummed on the table with his finger-tips. Anthony Bathurst came in with yet another question.

"Your father's never been away before, I presume—without warning? A merely temporary absence?"

"Never. He always let us know where he was and how long we might expect him to be away. If I may say so, for a business man with numerous calls upon his attention and upon his time, he was singularly considerate in that respect. Much more, I should say, than most men in a comparable position."

"No recent correspondence has come to disturb him or worry him, or throw him out of the run of his usual routine."

"If there has been correspondence of that kind, I haven't seen it or been informed of it."

"Were your brother and yourself regarded as equal in importance in the business? Nothing senior or junior about your posts? What I mean is this. *Might* your father have shared confidences with him that he wasn't prepared to share with you?"

"How can I say? Especially now that this has come to pass. It's a possibility, of course, but I really don't think so. Nothing has ever happened in the business to give me cause to think such a condition existed."

"You are positive of that? If you test your mind on the point, most thoroughly, search it intensively, you can still think of nothing? It is important—you realize that, Mr. Somerset?"

Gerald Somerset shook his head slowly.

"I can think of absolutely nothing, Mr. Bathurst. As a possible factor in the case, you may dismiss that idea immediately." The man's tone was so emphatic and so decisive that Anthony Bathurst felt certain that he could rely upon the statement being true.

While Mr. Bathurst was registering these particular thoughts, young Somerset leant over towards the Commissioner of Police with intentness.

"You will take up the case on our behalf, Sir Austin? May I rely upon that?"

Sir Austin Kemble pursed his lips.

"Rest assured, Mr. Somerset, that we shall endeavour to assist you as far as lies in our power. We have no option."

"Thank you, sir. Will Mr. Bathurst himself take the case?"

The Commissioner shook his head with a genial smile.

"I have no jurisdiction over Mr. Bathurst. He is a free lance in these matters, and more or less pleases himself. Whether he takes the case or not is a matter that lies between you and him."

Gerald Somerset turned to Anthony.

"Will you take the case, Mr. Bathurst?"

Mr. Bathurst came over and stood by him.

"I will take the case, Mr. Somerset. It appeals to me rather. But don't be too sanguine about my success with it. At the moment, I haven't the glimmer of an idea. That is perhaps chiefly why it appeals to me. As a singularly knotty problem and of a rather different kind from any that has come my way before."

Somerset held out his hand.

"Thank you tremendously. I can't tell you how much I appreciate your kindness. The mere fact that you are interested, gives me hope." He paused, but almost immediately continued. "Would you answer me a question, Mr. Bathurst?"

"Certainly. If I am able to do so."

Gerald Somerset began to speak with an earnestness that was unmistakable. Both Sir Austin and Anthony were impressed by it. Each watched the speaking man intently.

"Do you think that my father and my brother are dead? Frankly, Mr. Bathurst?"

"Frankly, Mr. Somerset, I do not. But don't build too much hope on that opinion of mine. I have so little data at present that it's worth nothing."

"You think that they are being held somewhere, under restraint?"

"Yes. That's just what I do think."

"So that, if that be the case, it would be as well for me if I watched *my* step? Yes?"

"I entirely agree with you. In fact, you have anticipated my intentions and taken the very words from my mouth. I was on the point of warning you. I consider that you are in a certain amount of danger."

"Of death? Of attack?" Somerset's lips went white and blood-less.

"Say, rather, of—abduction."

"I feared as much. What can I do?"

"Take extra care of yourself, everywhere. And I've no doubt that, having heard your story, the Commissioner will let you have the services of a couple of men as a protection. Will you, sir?" Anthony turned to Sir Austin Kemble.

"Of course. That shall be attended to today. You'll hear from me."

Somerset expressed his gratitude.

"Thank you, sir. In the meantime, is there anything else I can do?"

"Yes. Let me know immediately *anything* that occurs, that you consider in the very least unusual or abnormal. Anything away from your general routine."

"I shall do that at once, Mr. Bathurst. I had already made up my mind to do so. You can rely on it. Good-bye."

"Good-bye."

Somerset shook hands with the Commissioner of Police and with Anthony Bathurst and left them.

"Well, what do you think of it now?" questioned Sir Austin.

Anthony was silent for a moment before replying.

"Only one thing, sir. That I wouldn't care to be in that young man's shoes. No, sir. All I hope is that we haven't sent him to his death."

Sir Austin Kemble pressed the bell.

"That reminds me. I'll see to that bodyguard of his that I promised him. At once. Delays are proverbially dangerous."

Anthony Bathurst was gazing into space.

"They most certainly are, sir," he murmured. "But, on the other hand, we are advised to look before we leap. The English have a knack of reversing their proverbs."

CHAPTER III
MISS MASTERS REMEMBERS

ANTHONY Lotherington Bathurst stood outside No. 22 Boot Lane and looked up at the block of offices which showed on their front the name of "Somerset and Sons". The surroundings were definitely those that belonged to the City of London. The hard, enduring industry of the trader, of the merchant, and of the supporting agencies were easily discernible. The scene at which he looked was also typical. The traditions of the city, almost of the city that Dickens knew and painted, were all there in the forefront of the picture at which Anthony Bathurst looked. He entered the offices in question briskly and handed his card across the flap of a counter that he found upon his immediate right. A youth with tousled hair took it.

"Mr. Gerald Somerset? You want him?"

"If you please. I take it that he is in the office?"

"Yes, sir. Mr. Gerald is here. I saw him come in this morning. We were all glad to. Things here aren't quite normal. Recent events have upset us a bit, you know, sir."

"I expect they have. Understandable."

"Come this way, sir."

Anthony followed his guide upstairs to the private office of this firm of the three Somersets.

Gerald Somerset sat therein, intent upon a mass of correspondence. His face flashed pleasure as he saw Anthony Bathurst standing on the threshold.

"Oh, come in!" he cried.

The youth who had conducted Anthony up the stairs disappeared almost as though by magic, and Anthony passed into the room. Somerset waved him to a chair.

"Sit down, Mr. Bathurst—do. I can't tell you how pleased I am to see you. I wasn't expecting you quite so soon after my interview with you and the Commissioner of Police yesterday."

"Thank you. There is no news, I suppose? You know no more than you knew yesterday, I presume?"

Somerset shook his head. "There is no development of any kind."

"I see. That's not too good, is it? Was this your father's room?"

"Yes. This is my father's private room. The next one along the corridor was used by my brother and me. He used one side of it and I the other. Digby's on the other side of the landing. I'll take you into my room in a moment or so, if you'd care to see it."

"Thank you. I should." Anthony walked round the room that had been David Somerset's. Gerald Somerset watched him.

"Anything I can do for you?"

"Yes. There is. May I see the letter-book for, say, the last two months?"

"With pleasure." Gerald Somerset used the departmental telephone. "Miss Masters? Bring me in the current letter-book. At once, please." He turned to Anthony. "It'll be here in one minute. The girl's bringing it in."

A thin girl with sharp features and pale-blue eyes was as good as his word. She arrived a minute or so later with the letter-book which Mr. Bathurst had requested permission to see, and placed it in front of young Somerset.

"Thank you. That's all just now."

The girl favoured Somerset with a look into which Anthony read the epitome of contempt. Evidently Miss Masters regarded Gerald Somerset as a poor substitute for his father.

Without troubling to open it himself, Gerald Somerset pushed the book over to Anthony.

"Here's the book that you want. It covers the period you asked about. Help yourself and look at what you like. I won't worry you. So you can be as quiet as you like. Of course, if you want any information on any point, don't hesitate to ask me and I'll let you have it."

Anthony thanked him and turned to the book. He examined letter after letter, going back, in point of time, over a period of two months. But he found nothing that rewarded him. There wasn't a letter in this book that, as far as Anthony was able to see, could by any stretch of imagination have anything whatever to do with the disappearance of David Somerset or his son Geoffrey. Anthony tested everything, the ordinary and commonplace business letter and the more unusual specimens that might relate to "something unusual". None yielded him the slightest satisfaction. Every letter in this book that had been brought to him was a purely business letter which in its own terms explained itself. Eventually Anthony surrendered the letter-book to Gerald Somerset.

"Thank you, Mr. Somerset. There's nothing here. It was only an idea on my part, of course, but it's failed. I've drawn a blank. Ah, well—we're no worse off than we were, even if we aren't any better."

Somerset nodded, took the book from him, and took up the departmental telephone again.

"Miss Masters! Come in for the letter-book, will you? We've finished with it."

The thin, sharp-featured girl reappeared. Somerset handed her the letter-book. She took it, gave Anthony a quick darting glance, turned away towards the door, almost reached it, and then turned back to face the two men again.

"Mr. Somerset," she said nervously, and then stopped as suddenly as she had begun.

Anthony looked up at her with interest. What was coming? Did this girl know anything or was it merely . . .

"Yes?" replied Somerset. "What is it, Miss Masters?"

"If you're inquiring into your father's trouble, Mr. Somerset—please forgive me for interfering, won't you?—I think, perhaps, that I might be able to help you. It's just an idea on my part, but somehow I feel that there's something in it. May I say something?"

The words left her lips in an uncontrolled rush. Gerald Somerset's face took on a puzzled expression. Anthony watched keenly. What revelation was he about to hear? The girl did know something! That seemed a certainty.

"To what do you refer, Miss Masters?" asked Somerset.

"Come and sit down," suggested Mr. Bathurst sympathetically, "and take your time. Then you can tell us what you want to tell us easily and comfortably."

The girl looked askance at her employer. He nodded his permission for her to act on Anthony's suggestion. She brought a chair and sat between them. They waited for her.

"It was on the day that your father was last here, Mr. Somerset. On that morning—you know! He sent for me and dictated two letters to me directly he came in. This gentleman has seen the copies. Nothing in that. They were ordinary. When I brought them in for signature, your father had asked for them to be done at once, he signed them and then asked me to bring him the A.B.C. 'At once,' he said."

Mr. Bathurst rubbed his hands.

"Miss Masters, you're a treasure."

The girl frowned. It was evident that she was unable to distinguish between compliment and flattery.

"Thank you, I'm sure. But I merely try to do my duty, that's all. And to be fair and just to everybody."

"I'm sure you do. But go on."

Miss Masters recollected her thoughts and herself. Her personality was not cradled in subtlety and she was by no means sure of the stranger who sat there close to her, and who spoke to her with such scant regard for convention. She decided to tell her story plainly and to avoid every temptation that she might feel towards decoration.

"I did as I was told and brought the A.B.C. into Mr. Somerset and I left him looking at it. About a quarter of an hour later, he rang for me again. I came in, of course, and he dictated another letter. To Holmes, Hayes, and Waterson, of Canning Town. Nothing startling in it—just ordinary. Now I come to the part that I feel I must tell you about. As I sat in this room and took down Holmes, Hayes, and Waterson's letter I noticed that the A.B.C. was lying open at Mr. Somerset's elbow. I also noticed something else." She paused and looked at the two men with her. If she lacked degrees of subtlety, Miss Masters, at least, had a mind for dramatic recital.

Anthony Bathurst took swift advantage of the pause.

"You are more than a treasure, Miss Masters. When I gave you that word I damned you with faint praise. You are very nearly my heart's delight."

She flashed him a look of severity and reproof.

"Thank you—but you've made a mistake, I am not that sort of girl. If you have no objection, I'll go on with my story. The 'something else' that I noticed was the number of the page that the A.B.C. was open at. I just couldn't help seeing it. It was number one hundred and fifty-six. The top place—that is to say the first 'name' on the page on the left hand side was Eastbourne," Miss Masters recited in triumphant conclusion.

"Thank you, Miss Masters," said Mr. Bathurst quietly. "I congratulate you most heartily on your powers of observation."

Miss Masters flushed with pleasure. There was no doubting the stranger's sincerity on this occasion, whatever he might have said before. Anthony Bathurst turned to Gerald Somerset.

"This is splendid work on Miss Masters's part. It may help us out from what looked to me uncommonly like heavy going. I suggest that you send for your office copy of the A.B.C. at once. We'll see what we can see."

Somerset nodded.

"I agree. That's no sooner said than it will be done."

The ever-ready Miss Masters rose from her chair.

"Shall I bring it in for you, Mr. Somerset?"

Somerset shook his head.

"No. You stay here, Miss Masters. You will be of more use to us here. When we get the book, no doubt you will be able to help us still more."

He spoke again on the departmental telephone. Within a moment a lad brought in the A.B.C. Somerset opened it at the page to which the absurdly competent Miss Masters had made reference. Anthony Bathurst came to his side and leant over his shoulder.

"Read out the various places," he said, "covered by pages one hundred and fifty-six and one hundred and fifty-seven. Then we can see where we are."

Somerset nodded and obeyed the instruction.

"Eastbourne, followed by several hotels there and house agents' advertisements. East Brixton. East Brutton. East Budleigh. Eastbury. Eastchurch. Eastcote. East Dulwich. Easterhouse. East Farleigh. East Finchley. East Fortune. East Garston. Eastgate. East Grange. East Grinstead. And more hotels. East Halton, and East Ham. That's the last place. East Ham."

"I can well believe it," remarked Mr. Bathurst. "I've been there. I shall never forget it."

Somerset began to count.

"How many are there?" queried Anthony Bathurst.

"Eighteen," replied Somerset.

"H'm. Eighteen places." Somerset indicated the counties. "In Sussex, London, Devonshire, Gloucestershire, Berkshire, Kent, Middlesex, London, Lanarkshire, Kent, Middlesex, East Lothian, Berkshire, Durham, Fifeshire, Sussex, Lincolnshire, and Essex respectively. Pretty hopeless—what?"

"Oh, I don't know. Not more than a seventeen to one chance. Might have been considerably worse than that."

"Yes—but they're so far apart—that's what impresses me. On the points of the compass. Devon in the west. Sussex and Kent, south, Lincolnshire in the east, and no fewer than three Scottish counties to represent the north. Good lord!—it's like looking for a needle in a haystack, and that's assuming that the book wasn't open at the page by pure accident."

Anthony Bathurst carefully considered this last statement.

"You think—" He raised his eyebrows at Gerald Somerset.

"I can't exactly 'think' anything. I mean that I have no definite idea which I'm working on—but it struck me, as I thought things over, that if my father had something on that morning which he wished kept secret, some venture, shall we say— he *might*, mind I only say 'might', have deliberately altered the page in the A.B.C. at which he had been looking. You see my point, Mr. Bathurst?"

"Oh, yes. There is always that risk, though, to be taken when a book is found opened at a certain page. Is the page the one that's wanted or is it a pit digged for the unwary? One is forced to treat every case on its individual merits. With regard to the present instance, I think that perhaps Miss Masters might be able to help us yet once again." He turned to the girl. "What do you think about it yourself, Miss Masters? You heard the point that Mr. Somerset made?"

"My mind is already made up," returned Miss Masters, without the slightest hesitation. "I can understand what Mr. Somerset means, but I certainly don't think that it applies in the case under our notice. I am absolutely certain in my own mind that the page at which I saw the A.B.C. open was the same page that Mr. Somerset senior had been looking at before I came in. I am fully aware that I cannot support this opinion by any display of reasoning, but that doesn't concern me. You see, I am willing to be satisfied with what I may call my feminine intuition."

In Anthony Bathurst's opinion the girl was right. He put his opinion into words.

"I'm inclined to agree with you, Miss Masters. As I visualize the scene that you depicted to us just now, I don't somehow see your employer turning to that page deliberately and with malice aforethought. I rather fancy that he had too much on his mind for calculated subterfuge at that moment."

Somerset intervened with a quick gesture.

"You think that seriously, Mr. Bathurst?"

"Yes."

"Why—particularly, may I ask?"

"The use of the A.B.C.—which suggests most strongly to me that your father was contemplating a journey, some features of which at least were not familiar to him."

Gerald Somerset tapped on the desk with the butt-end of his fountain-pen as he thought over Mr. Bathurst's statement.

"Well, if that's the case," he said at length, "it remains for us to discover what *was* the journey, if we possibly can. That brings us again to your seventeen to one chance, Mr. Bathurst. Which are pretty appalling odds, to my mind."

"Not too good, I admit. But don't you think that they may be reduced almost immediately?"

"How?"

"Think, Mr. Somerset."

Gerald Somerset wrinkled his brows. There was a silence. Miss Masters's face was flushed. Her lips were parted as though from the keenest sense of expectancy. Somerset eventually broke the silence.

"I must confess that I *don't* see."

"Can't we reduce that figure seventeen to thirteen? Fairly logically?"

Somerset scanned the two pages of the open book. "I don't see. How can you do that reasonably?"

"By deleting four of the names, of course. Don't you see now what I mean?"

Somerset was still puzzled. He looked and then spoke his bewilderment.

"I know that if you subtract four from seventeen you are left with a remainder of thirteen, but *why* delete four, and which four? How can you be guided? That's the part of the arrangement that I can't get over."

Anthony smiled.

"And yet when you hear my suggestions, you'll realize how eminently sensible and simple they are. I said 'four', didn't I? Well, 'four' it shall be. Now look here." He took the book. "Can't we reasonably exclude such places as East Brixton, East Dulwich, East Finchley, and East Ham? Don't you think so? I can't bring myself to believe that your father would require an A.B.C. for the purpose of getting to any one of those four places. Now, Mr. Somerset, I put it to you—can you?"

Miss Masters uttered an exclamation of approval and almost crowed with delight. The performance was mid-way between a crow and a gurgle. Somerset looked at Anthony Bathurst and slowly nodded his head.

"Good lord! Why, yes. I was slow. Of course, he *might* look up a train from a terminus—that's just on the cards—but I must say that I think you're almost bound to be right. And it never struck me at all. And that reduces our odds to thirteen to one, as you say. Working on similar lines, can we eliminate any more?"

"That's just what I've been thinking," returned Anthony Bathurst. "Let's have a look at the list again. Perhaps the names may help us still further." They looked at the book that lay between them. There ensued another period of silence which Anthony eventually broke.

"This second line tends more towards guesswork pure and simple, I admit, but I think that we might reasonably rule out Eastbourne and East Grinstead. I shouldn't imagine that your father would need to know very much about either of them. There are frequent trains from Victoria to each of them." Miss Masters leant forward eagerly. Words trembled on her lips. Her moment was coming. Anthony Bathurst was quick to notice that she desired to enter the lists again.

"You have thought of something else, Miss Masters. I am sure of it. What help have you for us this time?"

"Help that you shouldn't need. I regret saying so—but there it is."

Somerset looked a trifle perturbed. He immediately questioned her.

"How do you mean, Miss Masters? I'm afraid that I don't quite follow you."

Anthony's grey eyes twinkled. This girl interested him.

Somerset spoke again.

"Tell me your point, Miss Masters—and let me see what I've missed."

Her lips were set and her mouth was prim.

"Give me the A.B.C., please."

Somerset handed her the book.

"Look here!" she said sharply. "Let me prove to you how you can eliminate Eastbourne with perfect safety. It won't take me a moment." She pointed to the top of the left-hand page. "If you look here you will see that this page contains only a *continuation* of the information that the timetable holds in respect of Eastbourne. For instance, to show you what I mean, if you look, you will see that there are no trains to Eastbourne shown on this page at all. What you have about Eastbourne on this page is simply a list of hotels and house-agents. Nobody who wanted to pick out a train to Eastbourne would be found looking at this page. Now would he? He would examine the previous page. Therefore, I say that Mr. Bathurst is perfectly sound when he is prepared to take out Eastbourne from the list of likely places. But I think too, if you'll pardon my saying so, that I have made the point much more clearly and strongly than he did."

She paused for breath. Anthony looked at the time-table and saw both the force and justice of Miss Masters's remark. He paid her a graceful tribute.

"You are undeniably right, Miss Masters. The honours are yours. I am more confident than ever that we can lay Eastbourne on the shelf. I regard it as twenty to one against Eastbourne. I am positive that Mr. Somerset senior never searched in here for either an Eastbourne hotel or an Eastbourne house-agent. I take it that you agree, Mr. Somerset?"

"Yes, I suppose so. As it's been shown to me. But what does that leave us with?"

"An eleven to one shot. In the terms of the book-makers it's always a hundred to nine. We are left to choose between East Brutton, East Budleigh, Eastbury, Eastchurch, Eastcote, Easterhouse, East Farleigh, East Fortune, East Garston, Eastgate, East Grange, and East Halton." He checked the names over again. "That's right. Twelve of 'em. As I said just now. Eleven to one against us picking the right one."

Somerset rubbed his cheek. "Still a pretty hopeless proposition, or so it seems to me."

"Wait a minute. Hold your horses. Perseverance is what's wanted when you're on this game. Tell me, Miss Masters—what was Mr. Somerset wearing when he left the office? Did you actually see him leave?"

"I did, Mr. Bathurst. He was wearing ordinary clothes. Just his hat and his overcoat over his everyday suit of clothes. Just as you'd see him leave here nine times out of ten."

"He had no bag, for instance?"

"None."

"No case?"

"No suit-case. Just his everyday attaché-case. It wouldn't have held clothes, for instance."

"Certain of that?"

"Positive. Absolutely positive."

Mr. Bathurst rubbed his hands. "Good. I deduce therefrom, Mr. Somerset, that wherever it was that your father intended to go that morning, it was not his intention to stay the night there. A reasonable deduction of mine, don't you think? A man doesn't carry his razor, tooth-brush, and pyjamas in a small office attaché-case."

Somerset nodded his head.

"I agree with you."

"So that we can add to our list of already eliminated places, East Budleigh, 169 miles, Easterhouse, 430½ miles, East Fortune, 373¼ miles, Eastgate, 263¼ miles, East Grange, 417¾ miles, and East Halton, 217½ miles. That's six more of 'em gone. Never to return, let us hope. Devon, the three Scottish towns, Durham, and Lincolnshire. Now, what have we left?"

"Six. Five to one against now."

"What are they?"

"East Brutton, Eastbury, Eastchurch, Eastcote, East Farleigh, and East Garston."

"H'm! I'm afraid that we can't expect to reduce the number any more. Our field has become Gloucestershire, Berkshire, Kent, Middlesex, Kent and Berkshire. That's strange! Two Berkshires and two Kents."

Anthony turned to the girl who sat there watching them.

"Well, Miss Masters, any more inspirations for us?"

Her face again set in prim lines.

"What are the various termini for those six places? To know that might help a bit."

Somerset read out the answers to the question. "Paddington, Paddington, Victoria, Baker St., Charing Cross, and Paddington."

"Delete Eastcote then," she replied promptly. "A man doesn't have the A.B.C. to look up a train from Baker Street. That is to say, a man used to London doesn't. Besides, the trains to East-cote aren't shown on this page. They're on a page at the back of the book. It tells you so if you look."

"Excellent," said Anthony. "I shall take you with my razor, pyjamas, and tooth-brush wherever I go! Well—this leaves us with five places, three of which have the same terminus—Paddington. Inquiries at Paddington *should* produce results. I fancy the law of probability would have it so."

"You will go?" inquired Gerald Somerset.

"I shall go," returned Mr. Bathurst. "Without a doubt I shall go. Also, it seems to me, I want a further piece of information from you. The full address, if you please, of Miss Irene Pearce."

"With pleasure. '"Antigua," Braundway Avenue, Chiswick.' As you turn down the avenue from the main road, it's the third big house on the left-hand side."

Anthony rose to go.

"I won't detain you any longer, Mr. Somerset. If any news reach you from any quarter, please acquaint me immediately. Of *anything*, please, no matter how trivial or unimportant it may seem to you. Good-bye. Good morning, Miss Masters. Many thanks for your most valuable assistance. It has helped me tremendously." Anthony Bathurst lingered for a moment by the door. "By the way, Miss Masters," he said quietly, "there is perhaps just this. Eastbury and East Garston, those two places in Berkshire served by Paddington, have no train service of their own. The service in each instance is to Lamborn, where a certain Mr. Cottrill rubs cheeks with a Mr. Templeman. So I really think that, after all, East Brutton in Gloucestershire is worth a searching inquiry. Congratulations, though, on all that you have done. For one thing, consider what an apt pupil you have made of me."

Miss Masters gasped as Mr. Bathurst closed the door behind him. Her cheeks crimsoned with annoyance. A minute later, she rose and, with an eloquent toss of the head, returned to her own room. Gerald Somerset frowned wearily, watching her every movement.

CHAPTER IV
CONCERNING GEOFFREY SOMERSET

Miss Irene Pearce of Antigua, Braundway Avenue, Chiswick, had been so staggered by the march of events, that life with its various activities had been to her, for the past few days, but a purely mechanical process. For it must be admitted that she was by way of being a celebrity. Her success in the "British-produced" picture, *The Proof of the Pudding*, had brought about this (to her) pleasing condition. The "Dailies" that were sold for a penny constantly contained her portrait. Photographers corresponded with her concerning free sittings. Their studios ached for her coming. Advertisers of commodities of all kinds, from face-cream to silk stockings, vied with each other for the sovereign grace of Irene's almost illegible signature underneath their various advertisements. The day before the disappearance of Geoffrey Somerset, her fiancé, had been her twenty-second birthday. The *Morning Message* of that day had shown her latest photograph in the full glory of her raven hair, and had printed also stories of her qualities and personal characteristics which, if the truth be told, were but legendary. The picture of her that the *Message* published showed her small head with its shining black hair covered with a broad band of scarlet.

Now that this shock of Geoffrey's disappearance had come to her, she sat on her divan with its cluster of cushions, clasped her dark head between her beautiful hands, and rocked her body in the throes of her distress. For, incredible though it may seem, she had been genuinely fond of Geoffrey Somerset, and this attraction for him had come to her some time before she had been touched by the wand of success. The recollection of the last evening which Geoffrey Somerset had spent with her was so real and still so vivid that she was unable to escape its ever-recurring image.

When Anthony Bathurst came into her presence, at her request, after seeing his card that her maid had presented to her, there was a moment's silence after the initial greeting, which neither she nor Mr. Bathurst seemed at all desirous of breaking. Anthony found himself carefully considering her. He felt, when she had spoken upon his entrance, that her voice had sounded sincere and had been touched by a poignant accent of genuine regret. He looked at her, straight in the face. She was intelligent, he found, responded to his question and told him the story that he wanted to hear. Of how Geoffrey Somerset had spent that last evening of his known existence, with her. Here in this same room that now housed Mr. Bathurst and her. Of how Geoffrey had said good-bye to her quite normally and left her. She paused. A fierce gust of rude and rough March wind shook the windows. The fire in the grate took its cue from it and spluttered.

Irene Pearce, in her concise way, had given Anthony Bathurst a clear picture of this young man whom he had never seen, and of this last companionship that she, Irene Pearce, had known with him. The sound of Miss Pearce's fresh, pleasing voice was in his ears. She rose from the divan with an impatient, almost abrupt movement, went to a cigarette-box and took a cigarette. She lit it with admirable self-control. Her fingers were perfectly steady.

"You know of nothing, then, Miss Pearce, that you consider at all likely to help me?"

She shook her head sadly.

"Nothing at all. If Geoffrey wasn't entirely normal all the time he was with me and when he left me, then I have never seen him normal. And nobody knew him as well as I did."

Her eyes seemed to soften at the reminiscence, but there was, nevertheless, a certain courage in that softness. She went to the window and stood there with her back to him. Anthony watched her. He made no sound. It was some time before she turned to him. Her small face was uplifted like a flower. She had her feet together. Her slim arms were outstretched and her fine nose uplifted. Her small firm breasts were outlined clearly. He understood her attractiveness and her allurement. Her lips parted in speech.

"I have been thinking, and there is one thing that I perhaps might tell you. I think that I should. The one thing about Geoffrey that evening that was not normal. The only thing."

She advanced towards Anthony from the window where she had been standing.

"Yes?" said Mr. Bathurst in invitation.

"He carried a revolver."

Anthony stared at her.

"Why did he carry a revolver?"

"I do not know."

"Didn't you ask him why he carried it? If it were such an unusual procedure for him, I mean?"

"No. I didn't. You are surprised? Let me explain. Perhaps I didn't make myself too clear before. Geoffrey didn't *show* me the revolver. Don't think that. I felt the outline of it in his pocket. I am certain of what I say."

"Yet his manner and his spirits and his demeanour generally were all absolutely normal, you say?"

"Yes," she replied, simply. "Quite."

"Tell me, Miss Pearce," said Anthony Bathurst in a gently persuasive tone, "have you ever heard any mention from Geoffrey Somerset of a place called East Brutton?"

"Never," she replied emphatically.

"Of any place with a name similar to East Brutton?"

"Recently, do you mean?"

"Yes."

She wrinkled her brows. "No. I have not. I'm certain of it. I should have remembered it, if he had. Why do you ask?"

Mr. Bathurst finessed the answer.

"Mr. Gerald Somerset fancies that a letter came from there to the office some little time ago. But we've nothing definite on which to go. He's not absolutely certain of it. He has no more than a hazy idea; nothing beyond that. I flung the name at you with the scantiest of hopes."

He turned the subject.

"Now help me again, if you can. Have you a recent photograph of Mr. Geoffrey Somerset? If you have, I'd be interested to see it."

Irene Pearce touched a bell. The maid who had opened the door to Mr. Bathurst answered the summons from her mistress.

"Bring me the photograph of Mr. Somerset that stands on the small table in my bedroom, Lilian."

"Yes, ma'am."

Irene Pearce turned again to Anthony Bathurst. "The photo that I'm going to show you was taken last Christmas. It's a splendid likeness of Geoffrey. The best that he's ever had taken. This is the only copy, apart from what the photographers themselves have, in existence. Geoffrey had it taken specially for me as one of my Christmas presents."

"Good. It should give me just what I want." The maid entered with the photograph.

"Thank you, Lilian. Give it to me, will you? That is all I want."

Miss Pearce handed Anthony the photograph. While he examined it, Miss Pearce stood with a foot upon the fender, her back towards him and her hands resting on the rim of the mantelpiece. Anthony looked up and saw her there. He saw also that there was a mirror in front of her. He found himself wondering whether Irene Pearce had assumed that particular position out of deliberate design. But she was not to remain there for long. She turned, moved swiftly across the room, and sat at Mr. Bathurst's side again. She stretched out an arm towards him and touched the photograph of Geoffrey Somerset.

"Well," she questioned, "are you satisfied?" Anthony was looking hard at the face in the frame. The likeness to Gerald Somerset was almost uncanny.

"I can't judge its merits. I never knew Geoffrey Somerset. I have met his brother, Gerald, but recently. This might even be he. The likeness is amazing."

"You think so?"

"It is almost incredible."

"But they are twins, Mr. Bathurst. Twins are always alike."

"Scarcely as much as these two brothers are."

"I can tell them apart quite easily."

"How do you do it?"

Her uplifted eyebrows showed that she was at a loss to understand him. He amplified his question.

"I mean this, Miss Pearce. Have you any *special* way of your own of distinguishing them?" He smiled. "You know! 'Then you are Box'. The absence of the strawberry mark on the right arm, for instance."

She understood and wrinkled her nose in an attractive grimace.

"Oh no. Nothing like that, Mr. Bathurst. I am just able to, that's all. There's just this—perhaps. Geoffrey's eyes are a shade lighter in colour. The blue of them is lighter. It's the same shade as his father's. Gerald's are—well—a little darker. That's all I can say. But their manners are quite different. That's how it's easy to know them. Geoffrey's far more lively. Gerald's always been the quiet one."

"What of their voices, Miss Pearce?"

She looked straight in front of her, her face thoughtful and grave.

"I know of nothing that's quite so vitally personal as the human voice," added Anthony Bathurst.

She nodded. "I know. My own work has helped to teach me that. That was why I didn't answer your question immediately."

Anthony watched her carefully. What was moving and stirring behind this girl's intelligence?

"Well?" he prompted her.

"There is a likeness about their voices. An undoubted likeness. But, of course, *I* could always tell the difference between them, as I told you just now." She coloured a little. "I suppose that, as regards Geoffrey, I must consider myself a specially privileged person. That statement doesn't need elaborating, does it, now?"

Anthony shook his head. "I understand that."

Irene Pearce went on.

"Both Geoffrey and Gerald are good-looking. Judged, that is, by ordinary standards."

Anthony made a quick movement of the head. Irene Pearce smiled sadly.

"Oh, I know what you men think of one another's looks. But women are different in that way. We don't possess your lofty detachment towards looks in a man. Looks mean more to us than they do to you. Both Geoffrey and Gerald have faces which are faces. Not just something under their hair which suggests an empty soup plate." She made a quick movement and picked up a paper. "Look at that, now."

Anthony saw a vacant face at the top of a column.

"That man's a librarian," said Miss Pearce, "if you can believe it. I think he looks more like a tureen. Isn't it dreadful? Looks are a lot, Mr. Bathurst, for a young man to have these days. In addition, each of the Somerset brothers is clever, in a business-like sort of way—persistent and industrious. Geoffrey, too, has the gift of conversation, quick-tongued and quick-witted. Sometimes I teased him and called him a conversational sensualist. That's where, possibly, he was always so distinguishable. Gerald hasn't that gift."

Anthony made no answer to her. But he leant forward in his chair with his eyes fixed upon her face. Not for a ransom would he have interrupted her at this moment, lest he should check the valued utterances that were coming to him from her. Hints at psychology! Pointings and indications towards the personal equipment of these two brothers who had become entangled in this mesh of mystery. Gestures that might very possibly guide him to the truth. Irene Pearce began to speak again.

"I will tell you something now, that, when you came in, I had no intention of telling you. I have made something of a 'name', as you know. Yet I would have sacrificed it all to be Geoffrey Somerset's wife. If he is dead . . . as I fear . . . I feel that I have no desire to face the world. I don't think that I can. I don't know what I should do. I feel alone. Stripped and bare to pain and suffering."

The misery of the thought encircled her. She shrank in positive terror from the mere envisagement of her distress. Anthony sat quite still. He was unused to meeting emotion of this kind in a woman. He had thought her too modern, too sophisticated altogether, too successful as an individual, to have felt as she did. After a time he rose and walked to the window, where he stood with his back to her. The sky was heavy with threatening clouds. Rain was but a short time away. March would shortly be at its mordant worst. Suddenly Irene Pearce called to him.

"Mr. Bathurst." He turned and moved towards her. "I want you to find Geoffrey. I want him back. I want you to do this for me, at all costs."

"Miss Pearce," he said, "I hope to be able to. I shall do my best, believe me."

"You don't think that he and his father are dead?"

"No, Miss Pearce. Frankly—I do not."

"Why don't you?"

"I can't see the motive for them to be killed. I have traced no *enmity* against them. People aren't murdered in sheer wantonness. Murder here, in this case, it seems to me, would be so needlessly wanton."

"I hope and pray that you are right."

Anthony added a statement.

"I should find it easier to believe, indeed, that they had disappeared of their own accord."

All at once Irene Pearce seemed to become desperately afraid. She looked as though his hand had drawn back a curtain and disclosed something there, behind that curtain, which horrified her.

"Of their own accord," she repeated after him. "Geoffrey! Of his own accord?"

He nodded.

"You frighten me, Mr. Bathurst. Why should Geoffrey disappear of his own accord?"

"I don't know. If I knew that, I should probably know all the rest."

She shook her head.

"You're wrong! That's another thing that I'm certain of."

"Why? What makes you so certain?"

"Because if that had happened, Geoffrey would have been bound to have written to me. Or at least communicated with me in some way. If he were alive, and at liberty to do as he pleased, he would have been in touch with me somehow by now. I know Geoffrey, you see. You don't."

He smiled at her. "I thought that I was beginning to know him."

The colour had drained from her cheeks. She steadied herself. He saw that his suggestion, despite her denial, had been a tremendous shock to her. Consternation still reigned in her face in spite of herself and the control that she was exhibiting.

"I am a little different from most women. Perhaps my experience is the cause, the *chief* cause of that. It has made me see things, I think, a little more clearly than most women of the present day. Because of this, I feel that Geoffrey is lost to me for ever. That I shall never see him again. To use a cliché—'that the worst has happened'. I know, quite surely, within my heart, that I shall never speak to him again."

Anthony Bathurst wondered at the way in which she spoke. Without any impressive lowering of the voice, that she might well have used for effect, but in the steady, level tone of one who merely states the simplest imaginable fact. The fact that is both relentless and inevitable. Moreover, she kept her eyes upon his face as she spoke, and the glance was both frank and fearless. She continued:

"You see, Mr. Bathurst, I care a little more than most people, as I told you a few minutes ago. Not a lot of people count with me—just a few. But when they count, they *really* count. A few friends whom I should hate desperately to lose—and Geoffrey." Her voice had changed. It now held passionate obstinacy. She rose and walked restlessly about the room as though she were endeavouring to school her mind to much against which it instinctively rebelled. She picked up a cushion, only to throw it down again with an air of complete weariness and distaste. She turned to him.

"What are you going to do?"

Anthony shrugged his shoulders at the question. "Now, do you mean?" he asked.

"Yes."

"I am seriously inclined towards the West country. To a place called East Brutton in Gloucestershire."

She showed puzzled eyes.

"That's the name of which you spoke before."

"Yes."

"Tell me, then. What takes you there?"

"A hunch? A whim? Shall we call it that? No—a little more than either. I have some slight grounds for thinking that David Somerset *may* have gone there."

"Yes. You hinted at it." She gave him her hand. "I will drive you back to town, if you will let me. I have a call to make which I can't miss."

"Thank you."

"In ten minutes, Mr. Bathurst."

She drove well, Mr. Bathurst discovered. The rain had stopped and a thin mist now swirled in the wind. Places looked dim and seemed strangely distant. Commonplaces took on glamour. Anthony and Miss Pearce came into the heart of London.

"I must leave you here," she said.

Anthony saw a look of despair in her eyes. For a moment she let her hand rest lightly on his sleeve and did not speak to him. "I cannot tell, Mr. Bathurst," she said very gently, "when I shall see you again."

He alighted from the car and looked through the space of the lowered window to say good-bye.

"I cannot tell either, Miss Pearce. But I'll make it my business to bring you good news. I'll promise you that."

She shook her head.

"You're saying that on purpose to encourage me. It is kind of you, and I appreciate it sincerely, but I know better, Mr. Bathurst. Good-bye." She waved her hand to him as he stepped back.

His eyes followed the departing car. Mr. Bathurst lit a cigarette. This was the second girl whom he had encountered in the case who could be described as the reverse of ordinary. And yet . . . ! Mr. Bathurst contemplated the sisterly qualities of the Colonel's lady and Judy O'Grady. It was a habit of his. He walked on to his flat, and dinner, thinking hard.

CHAPTER V
ON THE TRACK

ANTHONY Lotherington Bathurst read Sir Austin Kemble's hastily scribbled note with undisguised interest.

Dear Bathurst,

Evershed and Ashcroft have been at work as you suggested. Their news, on the whole, is good. On the 12th of March, in the morning, a first-class return ticket was issued at Paddington for East Brutton. Presumably for the 10.22 train. The booking-clerk who issued it, by name of Samuel Flood, remembers that the purchaser of this ticket was a middle-aged man of medium height. This is the only description that he will permit himself to make. Says that he can be certain of nothing more. The outward half of this ticket—number 0179—was given up at East Brutton station at 1.59. The 10.22, I may say, is due to arrive there at 1.57, but on this particular day it ran two minutes late. The ticket collector at East Brutton gives a rough description of a man surrendering it there who might well be our man. Note! He seems to have been alone. Note also! The return half of the ticket was given up at Paddington at 8.58 that evening, but, naturally, identification at this end of the man who surrendered it is impossible. Some hundred odd people came off that particular train. Also, nobody at East Brutton station can remember the man as having travelled by the return train. There you are!

In accordance with your wishes, which I have made quite clear to them, neither Evershed nor Ashcroft has made any further inquiries concerning David Somerset at East Brutton itself. Let me know what you are doing. Nothing more from any other source has so far come through. The photograph of David Somerset for which you asked is enclosed.

A.M.K.

Mr. Bathurst rubbed his cheek. Here, certainly, was information. To an extent, though, disconcerting! Despite the

Commissioner's opinion. Assuming that it were David Somerset who had travelled by the 10.22 from Paddington to East Brutton he had evidently returned from Gloucestershire on the evening of the same day. So that he had met with no foul play at the place of his assignation. Whatever it was that had happened to him, must have taken place *after* he had reached the Paddington terminus. The problem, the immediate problem, therefore, resolved itself into this. Was it certain that David Somerset's visit to East Brutton had been in connection with the affair that was at the bottom of his disappearance and the simultaneous disappearance of his son? Why hadn't Geoffrey Somerset gone with him? Or had the son gone down to Gloucestershire by car and returned to Irene Pearce in the evening? Also, if the East Brutton end of the tangle were *not* the sinister end of the business, would any good purpose be served by him, Anthony Bathurst, going to East Brutton, for the purpose of inquiries, as it had been his recent intention to do?

There was, however, another point attached to this particular difficulty. It was a distinct possibility, Mr. Bathurst considered, that David Somerset had been *accompanied* on this return journey from East Brutton. He might well have travelled down alone and returned with a companion. Stay, though! Anthony paused in the act of selecting a cigarette. What proof was there, when all was said and done, that it *was* David Somerset who had used and given up the return half of the first-class ticket numbered 0179? Anthony took a match and lit his cigarette almost unconsciously. What more simple than for anybody to take the ticket from a temporarily helpless Somerset and use it himself as his voucher for return to London?

Anthony Bathurst re-read certain parts of Sir Austin Kemble's message. Then he made up his mind and came to a decision. It was vital for him to travel to East Brutton, and he could afford to waste no time over it. He realized that he must get down there as soon as possible. He looked at his wrist-watch. Good! There was time for him to catch the 10.22. The identical train by which Somerset had travelled on the 12th of March.

There were three minutes to spare when Anthony took his seat in the corner of a first-class compartment. The train was only half-filled. He occupied himself with the morning papers until they reached Cheltenham. At two o'clock almost exactly the train ran into East Brutton station. Three minutes late on this occasion.

Mr. Bathurst alighted and casually strolled along the platform to the barrier at the end thereof. He gave up the half of his ticket to the collector on duty, but made no remark as he passed through. The Commissioner of Police's two men, Evershed and Ashcroft, had already done the necessary work here. A moment later, he stood at the top of the street where David Somerset had stood but a few days previously. Anthony thought matters over, and eventually decided to walk towards the middle of the little town. He stood at the four cross roads and then looked with interest at the sign of the "Golden Lion". More than likely, he thought, that Somerset might have called here, if indeed Somerset *were* the man who had used the ticket numbered 0179. Anyhow, the experiment of inquiry here might be well worth the trying. Naturally he chose to enter by the saloon-bar.

Mr. Bathurst ordered a tankard of bitter, and to the man who brought the drink to him he made a passing remark regarding the weather. He hated doing it, but there are times in the affairs of men when the safe and ordinary card is the one which should be played.

"You're right, sir," returned the barman, "one of the worst winters that I ever remember. Been so long, hasn't it? And we've had all kinds but one. Fog, rain, and snow, but no sunshine. Summer, or what there was of it, broke in August. On the last Friday. I remember because it was an afternoon off for me and I took a bird out. Down Cheltenham way. Spent three hours watching the rain from a railway-station waiting-room. Fair gave me the horrors, it did. If she hadn't been a nice little girl, I'd 'a' felt like doin' myself in. Thank you, sir."

Anthony regarded the man and his surroundings carefully.

"Pretty busy here?" he inquired.

"Only so-so, sir. Market days and week-ends, chiefly. Of course the motors help us. Compared with the old days. But, generally speaking, there's not a great lot doing."

As he spoke the man cast a sidelong glance at Anthony Bathurst which the latter caught before the expression faded. Mr. Bathurst decided to put the crucial matter to the test. He produced the photograph of David Somerset which Sir Austin Kemble had sent him.

"I wonder whether you could help me," he said. "I'm trying to trace somebody. Been missing since the twelfth of this month. This man. Here's a photograph. It's thought, by those of us who knew him pretty well, that he may have visited East Brutton. I suppose he didn't drop in here, by any chance?"

The barman took the photograph rather gingerly. But for a moment only. He tossed his head authoritatively.

"You're in luck, sir, and no mistake. You've come to the right shop, if I may say so. This gentleman *was* here, and it would be about the twelfth of the month. Don't I know it! I served him with a drink myself, so I ought to."

Anthony felt a thrill of triumph.

"That's excellent. It *was* a stroke of luck, then, my coming in here. Can you tell me anything else about him?"

"I can, sir. I can tell you a mouthful."

Anthony smiled.

"I'll take it, and like it."

"That gentleman whose likeness you've got there," the barman stabbed with his finger towards David Somerset's photograph, "didn't drop in here accidentally, as you might say. Oh no! He came here for a purpose. A definite purpose. You can take my word on that."

Anthony's senses responded to the situation.

"Yes?"

The barman nodded his head vigorously.

"Not a doubt of it, sir."

"What makes you so certain about that?"

"What makes me so certain about it? Why—I'll tell you. When he arrived, that's your friend, I mean, he went straight upstairs to the smoke-room. No hesitation at all. Up that way, sir. You can see where I mean from here." The barman pointed to the direction "To the smoke-room". Anthony's eyes followed the indication of his finger. "I noticed him go up there and as I was the only barman on duty, my mate, Fred, being off duty— at lunch he was—I followed him up to see what he wanted and to take his order. Well, he gave me an order, which I took up to him. Then I came straight downstairs again. As I did so, a big saloon-car drove up and stopped in the yard just outside there. I heard it come buzzing up, and natural-like I looked out of the window. We ain't so busy about midday so's we don't notice a car like that. Judge of my surprise, sir, when I saw five men get out of it. Funny-lookin' blighters too, they was. Proper foreign-looking, if you ask me."

Anthony swooped on the word.

"Foreign-looking! That's interesting. Tell me exactly, if you can, what it was about them that gave you that impression? That they were foreign, I mean."

The barman rubbed the end of his nose with the back of his hand.

"They was all short, all of 'em bar one, darkish, and their hair was done in a foreign sort of way. Do you know what I mean? Hitler would have fair licked his chops directly he caught sight of 'em. 'Ad a benefit! Do you think you get my idea, sir?"

"Yes. I think I can gather what you mean. But go on. Tell me the rest."

"They blew in here and marched straight upstairs to the smoke-room where your chum was sitting. Sitting where I'd left him. I popped up behind 'em, quiet-like, to see about drinks for 'em. I gave 'em a minute or so to settle down, as it were, and then went up nice and gentlemanly like. Just as I was about to go in, one of these foreign blokes comes out into the doorway. Seemed to appear from absolute nowhere, he did. He was wearin' gold-rimmed spectacles and had on a black dinner-jacket with a white flower stuck in it. 'Nothing yet, waiter', he says to me as soon as he catches sight of me. 'We'll ring for you when we want you. Understand?' Of course I said, 'Yes, I understand, sir', and straightway came down again. Nasty, soft, hissin' sort of voice he had. Fair gave me the creeps."

The barman stopped. Anthony Bathurst regarded him sympathetically. But the pause was of short duration.

"Now listen to the sequel, sir. About an hour later, the bell rang, and up I goes. Fred was back by that time, but I reckoned as I'd started on the job I was going to see this thing through. I got to the top of the flight of stairs, knocked on the door of the smoke-room and went in. What I saw almost took my breath away. There was half a dozen of 'em in there, seated round one of the tables. Six, that is, including the gentleman you've come inquiring about. And every man Jack of 'em was dressed in the same style of clothes. Exceptin' your pal, that is. Dinner-jacket, white waistcoat, black tie, and this 'ere same white flower stuck in the button-hole. I was fair flummoxed to see such a thing."

Anthony rubbed his hands.

"Oh—excellent! Go on. I find your story most interesting."

"Thought as how you would, guv'nor. My missus did when I told her. Well, the bloke what had spoken to me before, at the top of the stairs, gave the order. Tea and toast all round. That was it. No more—no less. Just tea and toast. I came down, gave the order to the kitchen, and took the stuff up about a quarter of an hour later."

"And they were all there when you returned?"

"Absolutely, sir. Just as they 'ad been! Not one of 'em had stirred. Leastways, not so much as you'd notice."

"*My* friend, you say, was not dressed in this dinner-jacket lark?"

"No, sir. He was just common-ordinary, same as you might be, sir."

Anthony smiled.

"Well, what happened after you took the tea and toast up?"

"Nothing, sir. Nothing that you'd write home about. I came down again."

"Did my friend seem quite comfortable, and—er—quite at his ease surrounded by these men?"

For the first time the barman showed signs of hesitation.

Anthony probed for truth. "You have your doubts of it, eh?"

"Well, now I look back on it all, sir, I think perhaps that he seemed a bit 'flushed'. As though he'd been a bit rattled over something. It's hard to explain. I saw him, you see, and I know what he looked like to me when I saw him. Bit of nasty colour in his face. My job's to make you understand what's in my mind. How shall I put it? He looked as though something had happened to him and that he was bloody glad it was all over. Yes—that's it. That's how he looked to me."

"I see. And how long did this little bunch of haircuts stay up there in the smoke-room?"

"How long?" The barman considered. "From the time they met? Oh—a good three hours—every bit of it. It was getting on for half past five before they scrammed. I saw 'em go. From 'ere. The 'head serang', the one I told you about before, came down to me in the bar here and paid the bill. Gave me a truly 'andsome tip, and about ten minutes afterwards the five of 'em climbed into the big saloon-car that was out there in the yard and cleared off. Your friend left by himself. Went off on his own up towards the station."

"*Before* the car left here, or afterwards?"

"Before, sir."

"Certain of that? Think carefully—it's important to me."

The barman nodded corroboration of his expressed opinion.

"Yes, sir. Positive, sir. I saw him wave his hand to the bunch of Dagos and set off up the High Street. I reckoned as how he was making for the station. There's a train to town about half past five."

"Did the car start off soon after that?"

"Put it at a couple of minutes afterwards and you won't be far out."

"He couldn't have got far?"

"Bless you, no, sir. Just a hundred yards or so up the High Street."

"Did the car *follow* him? I mean by that—did it go in the same direction?"

"Oh yes. It turned out of the yard here and went straight up the High Street, just as your old mate had done."

Anthony Bathurst nodded, as though he were satisfied with the barman's story.

"And that, I suppose, sums up all that you can tell me?"

"I'm afraid it does, sir."

"You've no idea of the number and registration mark of the car?"

"No, sir. I never saw it."

"My friend, we'll continue to call him that, was allowed to depart quite freely? He and the five men parted on good terms? As far as you could see, there was no interference with him? No difficulty was placed in his way?"

The barman shook his head. "No, sir, none at all. In fact, if I might say so, there seemed a far better feeling between him and the others, as he was going away, than there had been beforehand. I told you, I saw him wave his hand to the five foreign-looking fellows as he started to walk up the High Street. It was quite a friendly wave, as far as you can judge that sort of thing. You know—'cheero, you blighters'."

Anthony ordered another tankard of beer and told the barman to get a drink for himself. As the man drew the beer, Anthony tried another line of questioning.

"Ever seen any of those five men in East Brutton before?"

"No, sir. East Brutton's a respectable place." The tones of the negative were emphatic.

"You heard nothing definite of the conversation that took place upstairs?"

"No, sir. Each time I went up there, I could tell that they didn't intend that I should hear anything. You know—it got all quiet. There's only one thing, now I think of it . . ." The man stopped suddenly as though he were doubtful as to what to say. There was no rushing him on the part of Mr. Bathurst. With deliberate intent, he gave him ample time to choose the words of whatever it was he was about to say. The barman started afresh.

"There was one strange part of the affair that *did* strike me. That was this. Towards the end of the time that your friend was up there with them, there was a funny sort of smell that came floating down the stairs. I've got a pretty useful snout and I picked it up while I was standing over there." The barman pointed to the sign that showed the way to the smoke-room. "Well, I don't know what it was, but it certainly came from the room upstairs."

"Smell?" Anthony, by now, was thoroughly interested. "What was this smell like? Do you mean that there was an offensive smell?"

"No, sir. I wouldn't put it down as being like that. Not exactly." The barman seemed uncertain.

Anthony attempted to assist him. "Tell me about this smell that you noticed? Describe it in your own way. For all we know, it may be extremely important."

The man pushed his fingers through his hair and then scratched his head.

"It's not an easy task you've given me, guv'nor. That's my little bit of trouble. I only got just the fag-end of it ticklin' my nostrils, so to speak. Now, let me see. I must put my thinkin' cap on. It was a bit like fireworks on November the fifth, and yet again it wasn't. Not so good! That don't get us very far, does it?"

"Try again," suggested Mr. Bathurst. "Then it may come to you."

The man scratched his head again.

"I don't know that I . . ." Then his face cleared. As suddenly and completely as if it had been touched by a fairy wielding a magical wand. "I've got it, guv'nor!" said the barman with a triumphant grin now in possession of his face. "I knew I should if I stuck to it long enough—'chemicals'!"

Anthony nodded. The idea of this tallied with the general Somerset pattern. It was fitting. David Somerset, according to the statement made by Gerald Somerset in Sir Austin Kemble's room at Scotland Yard, was an analytical and manufacturing chemist. This visit of his to East Brutton to meet the foreign contingent of the barman's description may well have been in connection with his business.

"Yes, sir, that's what the smell was most like—'chemicals'! Not exactly 'gas', but 'fumes'. Smoky fumes. Like what we used to have at school sometimes. I'm not a good hand at describing things—but that's the nearest I can get to it."

"You've done very well. I certainly couldn't have expected anyone to have done much better than you have. Thanks a lot." Anthony slipped half a crown into the man's hand.

"Thank *you*, sir. Only too glad to have been of some assistance, sir."

"You may see me again," remarked Mr. Bathurst.

"I'll look out for you, sir. If I shouldn't be about in the bar, and you want me, ask Fred—he's bound to be knockin' about if I'm not—where Ted Clements is, then he'll come and find me for you."

In the train on the way back, Anthony wrote the following note to Sir Austin Kemble.

Have been down to East Brutton today. There is little doubt that David Somerset went down there on the day that he disappeared. I have definitely traced him to the pub. in the middle of the village. Name—"Golden Lion". Whilst there, he interviewed, or was interviewed by (the difference in the two terms will undoubtedly suggest itself to you), a company of five men. According to the only description that I can obtain of them, they were all "foreign-looking". I should say from what I have been able to gather of the interview that it concerned, in some way, an activity of Somerset's business as analytical chemist. This fact alone may provide us with a clue. There is no sign in any of this East Brutton business of the missing son, Geoffrey Somerset. The man whom I saw and who was in the bar when Somerset arrived is positive that he was unaccompanied. Query—is the boy being held somewhere, together with his father, in respect of a big business deal that is being put through by somebody? A discovery or invention? Armaments of some kind? Query again—new poison gas? This seems to me to be a highly likely contingency. If you hear of anything more, please let me know as soon as possible. Toujours!

A. L. B.

Sir Austin read this letter and immediately sent for Inspector MacMorran.

CHAPTER VI
SHOCK FOR MR. BATHURST

ANTHONY Bathurst was already at breakfast when Sir Austin Kemble was shown into the room.

"Thank you, Emily, I can find my way," said Sir Austin fussily. "I know it's on the early side for a caller, but these things can't be helped sometimes."

The Commissioner took up his usual stand in front of the fire. That is to say he hid it from everybody else. He was an old campaigner and as an officer, of course, naturally used to roughing it. Anthony waved a grape-fruit spoon at him.

"Good morning, sir."

"'Morning, Bathurst."

"Why am I honoured so early?"

Sir Austin pointed to the unopened newspaper that lay beside Anthony's plate.

"Seen this morning's paper?"

"Not yet. Why?"

"What is it you have here, the *Message*?"

Anthony nodded.

"It is. Reason? It is not quite so bad as the others. More than once its details have been correct."

"Look at the fourth column, front page. Then you'll know why I'm here."

Mr. Bathurst, seeing the expression on Sir Austin's face, picked up the newspaper and obeyed. The headlines which almost immediately caught his eye sent a chill to his heart.

"So we are too late. And I was wrong," he remarked quietly.

The Commissioner nodded gloomily. "We are, and you were."

"I'm sorry."

Anthony read the whole report.

MISSING CHEMISTS FOUND

BODIES OF FATHER AND SON DISCOVERED IN BRUTTON COPSE

IS IT MURDER AND SUICIDE?

Between the hours of four and five o'clock yesterday afternoon, a rabbit catcher, by the name of Reuben Horne, working in Brutton Copse, came across the bodies of two men lying just inside the Copse on the Heronswell side. He at once walked into East Brutton, found Police-constable Hanson, and reported the bare facts of his discovery. Police-constable Hanson forthwith proceeded to Brutton Copse, and there found the bodies of the two men in accordance with Reuben Horne's story. The elder man had died as the result of a revolver shot through the brain, and the younger from severe head wounds.

The elder man in appearance was between fifty and sixty years of age, and the younger man seemed to be between twenty-five and thirty. They answer in all details of appearance to David Somerset and Geoffrey Somerset of Urswick, Clutton Chase, near Brentwood, Essex, the two analytical chemists who have been reported as missing since Thursday, the 12th of March. David Somerset, in whose fingers were clasped a revolver from which two shots had been fired, looks to have killed his son and then to have turned the weapon on to himself. The bodies were conveyed to East Brutton later on in the afternoon, and have since, we understand, been identified by Mrs. Pamela Somerset, the wife of the elder man.

Mr. Bathurst, after reading, sat on in silence for some seconds. Sir Austin Kemble could see that he was both depressed and shaken. The Commissioner, now thoroughly warmed, moved away from the fire and seated himself in the better armchair.

"This hurts my pride, sir," said Anthony eventually. "I regret to admit it, but since it's true I may as well do so. I told David Somerset's son and Geoffrey Somerset's lady that their two men were alive. I was confident of it, too. God—the thought of my cocksureness humiliates me! What must they think of me? There's one thing, sir. You must double your bodyguard for that other son, Sir Austin—Gerald Somerset. They'll be after him now for a certainty."

Anthony pushed away his plate and rose from his chair at the table. He paced the room. Sir Austin Kemble watched him.

"If we only knew *something* of what the murdering devils are after, sir. But we don't! We grope blindly in the dark."

Sir Austin nodded. With that last expression, he was in entire sympathy.

"That's our main difficulty, Bathurst. You can rest assured that I realize that as well as you do."

The Commissioner picked up the newspaper that Anthony Bathurst had put down.

"Without definite knowledge of that kind," he continued, "it's almost impossible for us to get hold of a working hypothesis. At the moment, Bathurst, I must confess that I cannot recall any one of the cases that I've brought to you, and where you've helped me, which presented such insurmountable difficulties."

"Not insurmountable, sir. At least, we'll hope so."

Sir Austin looked up from the front page of the *Morning Message*.

"What's your opinion of this 'murder and suicide theory', Bathurst? Anything in it?"

"Fantastic rubbish, sir. If you prefer—boloney!"

The Commissioner regarded him gravely. Anthony smiled. He knew what Sir Austin was thinking.

"Oh, I know all about that, sir. I was wrong before, I know. But I'm not wrong this time. David and Geoffrey Somerset were murdered. Both of 'em. You can dismiss the suicide idea *statim*. Consider the circumstances! Two shots fired, yet one of the men has severe head wounds." He came and stood in front of the seated Commissioner and looked down at him. "Although we haven't anything positive, sir, with regard to the relationship between the elder Somerset and the men whom he visited at East Brutton, we can be pretty sure that the assignation had something to do with Somerset as a chemist. The note that I sent you should have made that plain. That fact alone must be of value to us as we proceed to investigate. It does not concern Somerset as a man, as an amorist, as a relation of any other Somerset. It touches none of these capacities, but *his professional capacity as a chemist*. And I'll tell you why, Sir Austin."

"I'm waiting to hear."

Anthony told him of the barman's experience in the "Golden Lion" at East Brutton. The Commissioner nodded.

"Smell—eh? Came down from the smoke-room upstairs, you say? Yes, I think it's a thousand to one that you're right."

"I'm glad that you agree with me, sir. You observe that there's one important point about it, *most* important, when it comes to the building up of a theory, that the *Morning Message* doesn't mention. They probably don't know yet. That's the reason behind the omission. I refer to *when* David and Geoffrey Somerset actually died. I must have that information as soon as possible." He stopped and turned away. To come back again immediately. "I suppose that the 'Yard' will carry on with the case?"

"I'll see to that. The Chief Constable has already communicated with me. Mrs. Somerset and her son put the case in our hands in the first place, you know."

Anthony Bathurst nodded with satisfaction.

"I shall be in touch with the Gloucester authorities again this morning. I think that I can arrange things from that point of view. Before I came out I left instructions with MacMorran. That suit you all right?"

Anthony nodded again as he walked to the window. He had no sooner arrived there than he turned back towards the Commissioner.

"Come over here, sir."

Sir Austin Kemble obeyed.

"I'm not surprised," he said, "not a bit. In fact, I expected him, either here or at the Yard. He's followed me here. Look behind his car. Almost to the tick. That's how we do our work, my boy."

Anthony looked and saw what the Commissioner meant. Behind the car from which young Somerset had just alighted there had flashed into sight another and bigger one. It was the Somerset bodyguard that Inspector MacMorran, on the Commissioner's orders, had arranged on behalf of Gerald Somerset.

"He'll need it, sir," declared Anthony Bathurst. "More than ever now, poor devil. You mark my words, sir."

Emily's steps were heard again in the passage outside the door of Anthony Bathurst's breakfast-room, and her tap came on that door.

"Tell Mr. Somerset to come in. As a matter of fact, we saw him arrive from the window. Thank you, Emily."

Gerald Somerset entered. Both Sir Austin Kemble and Anthony saw him and pitied him. He carried tragedy in his pleasant, cultured face. The change in it since Anthony had last seen him was too marked to be missed. Anthony waved Somerset to a chair. Gerald Somerset sat there for a minute or more with a heaving chest, struggling against the emotion that was overpowering him. Then he passed a handkerchief over his face, set his lips tight, and turned his face towards the Commissioner of Police.

"You were wrong," he stated simply. "Mr. Bathurst was wrong. Because of that . . . I think . . . this news has knocked me over. I'm sorry." He wiped his brow again with the handkerchief. He looked at Anthony.

"But East Brutton was the right place, you see. That was something." The words were flat, dull, and heavy. He shook his head. "How awful! I can't realize it. I'm shaken. My father. My brother. What are we going to do?" He leant forward in his chair and put his face in his hands.

Sir Austin nodded to Anthony, who went across to Somerset and put his hand on his shoulder.

"Pull yourself together. You must, you know. This is no time for giving way. Even if you *are* up against it. Besides, you have yourself to protect. You won't do that by chucking your hand in."

Somerset, white-faced, looked up at him.

"You are right, I know. I am sorry. But I feel like a tree that has lost all its leaves and stands stripped and bare to the menace of the wind."

Anthony deliberately steered him into practical channels.

"Now listen to me. I have been to East Brutton. *Before* this discovery was made in Brutton Copse. I traced your father to an hotel there—the 'Golden Lion'."

Somerset shook his head vaguely.

"My brother, too?" he questioned.

Anthony shook his head.

"No. That's the strange part about it. I found no trace whatever of your brother. But leave Geoffrey out of it, for the time being. Let us deal with what I did find. Your father, so I've discovered, went to East Brutton for an interview with a number of people, which I will describe as a 'business' interview. It had something to do with his work as a chemist. Of that fact I'm moderately certain. Now, can't you help us? Surely?"

Somerset again shook his head—this time hopelessly. Anthony pressed him.

"Can't you rack your brains for a clue? Can't you worry your brain to find that ray of light that *must* be there, and which, once found, must lead us to the truth? Mr. Somerset, I implore you to summon all your resources and make that vital effort for which I am asking, *now*. It may mean that we shall not only be enabled to avenge your father and your brother, but also *to save you*."

Gerald Somerset's face was strained. "I can think of nothing. I can think of no more than I could when you asked me about these things before. I *have* worried my brain. Racked it. Cudgelled it. To no purpose. I give you my word of honour that I can't think of, and I can't find, any reason which would have taken my father to East Brutton that was connected with our business. Even to save my own life, as you put it, I can't do it. You tried yourself, Bathurst. The letter-book! You had it. You went through what was there. Nothing! Nothing at all! I have found no other correspondence in the office or at home. No private stuff that my father might possibly have put through on his own. If there had been anything of that kind, that cat of a Masters would be sure to have known of it. She doesn't miss anything. But she knows no more than I do. I've tested her in many ways since you were there. She may be smart, damned smart, but she's not smart enough to put anything over on me."

Sir Austin Kemble and Anthony heard him out. There was no doubt that the man meant every word of what he said.

"Mrs. Somerset?" inquired the Commissioner.

"She knows nothing. Nothing at all. My father *never* discussed his business with her. Wouldn't. Refused to . . . always. You can ease your minds upon that point, absolutely."

Anthony intervened.

"We must examine your father's papers. Anything may eventually give us the clue for which we are seeking. Did your father experiment much?"

"How do you mean, exactly?"

"Might he have been on the verge of a new discovery? I put the idea to you tentatively."

"Not to my knowledge. But, of course, he may have been without my knowing. One can never answer a question of that kind unreservedly." His eyes were bewildered. "It's my brother being there that I can't understand. Forgive me if I keep on coming back to him. Why was Geoffrey in East Brutton? For what purpose? Was he killed in defence of my father? What in the name of evil took him there? You say that you traced my father there, but not Geoffrey. It's all a hopeless mystery to me. Who were these people that you say my father went there to interview? Have you discovered their names?" He flashed the question at Anthony Bathurst.

The latter did his best to satisfy Gerald Somerset's curiosity.

"No, their names and who they were, unfortunately, we don't know. Yet! But we know that your father met five men at East Brutton. They have been described to me as 'foreign-looking'. Beyond that, all that we know of them is this. Each one wore a dinner-jacket with a white flower in it. *Not*, I should say, 'the white flower of a blameless life'."

"Can they be traced? Is it possible, do you think? Surely it would be in these days?" Gerald Somerset's voice was tense and eager.

"It may be difficult to trace them. What clues have we to their identity? They came by car. They returned, no doubt, by car. From where they came, we haven't the slightest idea. As you aren't able to help us, Mr. Somerset, I'm afraid that the outlook is extremely black." Anthony Bathurst spoke gravely.

"I'd give my head to be able to, but I can't. It's all as strange and mysterious to me as it is to you." Gerald Somerset shook his head with a gesture of despair. Sir Austin Kemble intervened.

"There's one thing, Bathurst, arising out of all this, that strikes me, and that's this. I don't believe now that it *was* David Somerset who gave up the return half of that railway ticket at Paddington that evening. I'll lay a wager that the ticket was taken off him and used by somebody else. If foul play was intended against him, why let him return to Paddington, to bring him back again to East Brutton to kill him there? To me that idea doesn't seem to hold water. It's all contrary to reason and normal intelligence. What do you think yourself, Bathurst?"

"My views on *that* point, sir, will depend upon the medical evidence. When I get it. As I said to you just now, I very badly want to know *when* it was, within a little, of course, that David and Geoffrey Somerset died. When I know more about that I'll be in a position to give an opinion on that other point of yours, Sir Austin. Before it comes to me—I can't." He turned again to Gerald Somerset. "I suppose that you can't recall any remark or passing reference that your father may have made at any time that might throw light on the difficulty? Any chance name? Any odd place?" The young man shook his head slowly.

"I can't recall anything. Neither name nor place. If you only knew how I wish that I could."

"Your father was *not* a man who took people into his confidence, I take it?"

Gerald Somerset wrinkled his brows.

"On the whole, my father was an intensely self-reliant man. Does that answer your question?"

"It goes a long way towards answering it. Well, we must hope for the best. Trust that something may turn up unexpectedly to help us. That's the position, sir. I'm sorry that it's no better." He addressed the last statement to the Commissioner of Police.

Sir Austin Kemble nodded.

"Afraid you're right, Bathurst. As you say, we must sit tight and hope for the best."

"Why East Brutton?" asked Anthony quietly. The two others stared at him. The remark had come so unexpectedly.

"Why East Brutton for the rendezvous? Is any thing in *that* which at the moment we can't see? Why not London, Hogsnorton, Wormwood Scrubs, Land's End, John O'Groats? Why East Brutton?"

"I've never been there," said Sir Austin—"in fact, before this, I may as well confess that I hadn't heard of the place."

"It's the same with me," said Gerald Somerset. "Of course," supplemented Mr. Bathurst, as though answering his own question, "there is a Brutton Copse near East Brutton. There is that to be remembered."

"There are other copses," retorted Sir Austin. "Brutton doesn't hold a monopoly in that respect."

"True for you, sir. There may be a convenience about Brutton Copse of which we are not at the moment fully aware. I merely project it as a possibility. Did you go down with your stepmother, Mr. Somerset?"

"To identify them? Yes. I *had* to, almost. She begged me to go with her. We got back to London by the last train in the early hours of this morning."

Anthony interposed.

"The revolver, Mr. Somerset, is it your father's? Can you tell me for certain?"

Gerald Somerset hesitated. Anthony spoke with kindness. "Have no fears. Tell me all you know. Believe me, in my opinion, it won't make the slightest difference to the case whatever. Whatever you say to me."

Gerald Somerset bowed his head.

"I'm afraid that the revolver which the police found *did* belong to my father. But that isn't to say that he . . ." He broke off.

"Of course not. We shall find the explanation, no doubt."

"We don't even know that the bullet which killed my father was ever fired from that revolver."

"No. But we shall know, Mr. Somerset. We're bound to. Before very long. That and other most valuable information."

Gerald Somerset rose.

"As to myself, I take it that I am still in danger? Yes?" His lips twitched nervously.

"More than ever, I'm afraid. But we're helping you all the time, and you must take courage from that knowledge. You are better off than your father and brother were. In that respect."

"Thank you, Mr. Bathurst, and you, Sir Austin. You give me hope. Even though the hour is so dark for me and for my family."

"You, in your turn, must help *us*, though," put in Sir Austin. "You must take great care of yourself, because there is little doubt that you are threatened by a very real and imminent danger. There is no knowing how and when it may fall. Are you returning to Essex now, or going along to the Boot Lane office?"

"I was going back to the office. Your car will follow on behind me as it has been doing now for some days. Why? Would you like me to do anything else?" His face looked thin and pale.

Sir Austin glanced meaningly at Anthony.

"No," returned the latter; "as long as you watch every step that you take, you should be all right. I may come on to Boot Lane a little later. Or even in a day or two's time. Will it be convenient? At either time?"

Somerset nodded eagerly.

"Yes. I shall be there until late in the afternoon. If you aren't there by five o'clock today I shan't expect you. Shall think that you are leaving it until later."

"Until I hear from Gloucestershire, I don't know quite where I stand," remarked Mr. Bathurst, "but in all probability I shall be in East Brutton again some time tomorrow."

"I may accompany you, Bathurst," declared Sir Austin. "This case demands the best brains that we can send to it."

"Exactly, sir," murmured Anthony Bathurst. . . . "In that case, then, I think that we had better take with us Chief-Inspector MacMorran. What do you think yourself?"

"Eh?" Sir Austin stared fixedly at Anthony, but Mr. Bathurst never moved a muscle.

"Er—yes—I suppose we had," declared the Commissioner. Damn it all, there were times when Bathurst said the most extraordinary things!

Chapter VII
IN THE COPSE

ANTHONY Bathurst, Sir Austin Kemble, and Chief-Inspector MacMorran reached the village of East Brutton at approximately midday of the following day. Anthony had driven his high-powered car fiercely over many miles. They saw that East Brutton, this village on the northern border of the county of Gloucestershire, possessed one street of shops around its middle and that the rest of it consisted chiefly of clusters of half-timbered cottages.

It had probably been almost unchanged for some hundreds of years. Within the last few years, however, its peculiarly picturesque appearance and general situation had attracted a number of better-class residents, whose houses and bungalows were dotted in the adjoining woods, particularly on, the Heronswell side. These woods are locally supposed to be the extreme fringe of the ancient Bruthogne Forest, which thins away in the distance until it joins the downland. The advent of this better-class resident had meant, of course, a greater demand for the more modern shop with its conveniences, and several establishments of this type had come into quick being to meet this want. Which fact gives a fair prospect to East Brutton that it may soon grow from an old clustering village into the semblance of a modern town. It has one natural advantage. It is the centre for a considerable area of country, since Cheltenham, which may be described as the nearest place of any importance, is twelve miles away.

Anthony had chosen the road into Gloucestershire that avoids Cheltenham, taking the left-hand fork of the road at Shipton Sollars. Up to Chatcombe Pitch, dropping down for three quarters of a mile to Seven Springs, they had crossed the source of the Churn river and come to their destination.

They were met outside East Brutton station by a certain Sergeant Dredge. Sir Austin Kemble had arranged this encounter with the Gloucester police authorities. Sergeant Dredge impressed Anthony more favourably than otherwise. He was a quiet, well-preserved person. His dress was totally unlike that of most of his class. The suit that he wore was one of loose Harris tweed. He was short and stout, with a florid face, little button-shaped nose, and twinkling eyes. His legs were sturdy and powerful. In short, you would have taken him, upon immediate acquaintance, to be a local farmer, more prosperous than the majority of his kind. Certainly not a police officer. He shook hands with the Commissioner of Police immediately the latter had made himself known, and greeted MacMorran and Anthony Bathurst with sincere cordiality.

"I've spent most of my time this morning," he informed them, "dodging the Press. Been round me like wasps on a marmalade pot. Nuisance, they are, in my opinion, to everybody. Get their hoofs stuck well in—and then, where are you? This is a bit of an event for East Brutton, you know, gentlemen, and something that we're by no means used to. I've ordered lunch for all you gentlemen at the 'Golden Lion'. It's about the only decent place in the neighbourhood and I don't think it'll be too bad."

They thanked him, and Dredge got into the car for the rest of the journey to the inn, to which David Somerset had come on St. Gregory's Day. Anthony told the sergeant something of what he had already learned at the "Golden Lion". They saw the smoke-room where David Somerset had held what was probably his last interview. Dredge's good-humour and genial spirits grew, upon acquaintance, rather than decreased. He gave the company a rapid sketch of the events concerning the finding of the two Somerset bodies in Brutton Copse. Anthony noted him as a zealous and efficient officer, and even Sir Austin Kemble seemed impressed. In return, Mr. Bathurst gave Sergeant Dredge full details of the barman's story of what had happened on the 12th of March. Dredge took out his note-book and committed an occasional note to paper. More than once MacMorran prompted him.

"Remarkable," said Dredge at length. "Most remarkable—every detail of it. Nothing like it has ever come my way before. I never thought, in my wildest moments, that I should be called upon to work with such distinguished company." The sergeant beamed his delight. "Not that we're altogether behind the times down here, you know, from some points of view. Don't you think that, gentlemen. All the facts have already been collected and arranged intelligently. The revolver turns out to be the elder man's own property, and I'm not altogether averse to a suicide theory in his case. But I take it you'll go along to the spot as soon as we've finished lunch, and then you can see most things for yourselves and form your own ideas."

"Any car-tracks to be seen near this copse?" Sir Austin's tone was a trifle supercilious perhaps, but that fact had no effect upon Sergeant Dredge. He gazed at the Commissioner with the enraptured look of the small boy who watches the near approach to him of Don Bradman or John Berry Hobbs.

"I didn't notice any—but it's an idea, of course." MacMorran wagged a critical head.

"I don't much hold with your suicide idea, Sergeant Dredge. As I see things, as they've come to us at the Yard, there's black blood here, and black blood usually spells 'murder'. Anything else is clean against sound common sense."

"Here's the soup," said Anthony, "and for once it doesn't look like rain. Let's put the whole case out of our minds until after the coffee. What do you say yourself, sir?"

Sir Austin nodded his agreement.

"I'm with you, Bathurst. We shall return to it probably with clearer outlooks all round. Did you ask me what I was going to drink?"

A short run in the car after lunch brought them to Brutton Copse. Police-constable Hanson, the man to whom Reuben Horne had first taken his story, was waiting there on the road to give them the benefit of his own personal experience. Sergeant Dredge introduced the man to them and Hanson touched his helmet to the two representatives of the famous Yard.

"This other gentleman," added the valiant sergeant, "is Mr. Anthony Bathurst—the well-known investigator."

Hanson made a suitable noise. Anthony brought the car under the lee of a hedge. A low stile led to Brutton Copse, which lay about a hundred yards from the road.

"Many people come this way, officer, in the ordinary course of things?" asked Anthony.

P.C. Hanson shook his head.

"Not a great many, sir, except perhaps on Sunday afternoons. Of a week-day evening, hardly any."

The five men climbed the stile. Its indication read, "To Heronswell and Heaven Gate."

"We are at least travelling in the right direction," said Mr. Bathurst, as he came last of the five.

"And to travel hopefully," replied Sergeant Dredge, anxious to create an even better impression, "is better than to arrive. That's what has always been taught to me. Drummed into me, I might say."

The long garden of a small, empty bungalow straggled at their side. They reached long wet grass at the end of a muddy path. Sergeant Dredge pointed ahead of him.

"There's the copse—away there to the left. If you've had it in your mind that the two bodies were conveyed here in a car and then carried to that copse, I'm afraid you'll have to start thinking all over again."

Anthony jerked a finger back over his own shoulder.

"That stile, you mean, I suppose?"

"Yes, sir. And also this hurdle across the grass about twenty yards in front of us."

He was right. Anthony saw the long low hurdle that stretched across the grass right in their track. He saw, too, that there was no way of avoiding it.

The five men climbed the stile. Anthony stood a few feet away from it and pointed to his left.

"Isn't that a road, Sergeant, away there to the left? Seems to me a car could have made some way down there and then the path to your copse would be much less difficult. What do you think yourself? You know the hang of the country better than I do."

Dredge followed the direction of Mr. Bathurst's pointing finger and nodded.

"I believe you're right, sir. I hadn't thought of that road, I admit. It's a new one, not been cut more than a few months. There's new building going on and it's a recent acquisition. Yes, it's on the cards, sir."

"Good. I'm glad that you agree, Sergeant. I like to think that my theories don't topple to the ground too quickly, you know."

The Commissioner and Inspector MacMorran were some paces ahead, but the sergeant and Anthony soon caught them up. A train screamed by in the distance. The sergeant essayed an explanation.

"Just left East Brutton station, sir. Not a great distance from us, you know."

They came past the hedges that ran either side of a well-filled ditch, into the beginnings of Brutton Copse.

"We have two courses open to us here, sir," said Dredge, addressing Sir Austin Kemble: "we can either walk through to the Heronswell side by jumping this ditch, or work up more to the middle of the copse, where it bears off to Heaven Gate, and make our way through from there. Which would you prefer, sir?"

Anthony took the responsibility of decision.

"Let me make a suggestion, sir, if I may. You and the sergeant and Constable Hanson go straight along and work through the copse as he has just outlined, and MacMorran and I will get across the ditch here and make our way into the growth from the Heronswell side. Hanson and Dredge know the spot where the bodies were. When they come to the place, they and you can stay by it, while MacMorran and I will do our best to locate you. We can't very well miss you. The width of the copse isn't great and, if we don't find you at once, you can shout and let us know where you are. I've a strong fancy to work round from the other side, if it's all the same to you. That suit all of you?"

Sir Austin nodded and he and the sergeant and Constable Hanson walked off. Anthony took a flying leap across the wet ditch while MacMorran, infinitely more cautious, found a broken piece of tree and used it as a part-bridge across the open space. Once across, Anthony was able to see the lie of the country very much better.

"As I thought, Andrew," he remarked to MacMorran, "that road over yonder, which we drove past in the car, comes out not so very far from a part of the copse. We shall see, later on, how far exactly it is away. I'll lay you twenty to one, you ancient ruin, that the two Somersets, *père et fils*, came, or were brought, *that* way and not the way that we came. It's a cement road, too, if you take a look at it, and we can whistle for car-wheel traces."

MacMorran nodded, ever a man of few words. He and Bathurst gradually made their way along the side of the copse. That is to say, the copse was between them, on the Heronswell side, and Sir Austin, Sergeant Dredge, and Police-constable Hanson, on the East Brutton side. The copse was fairly thickly wooded for the time of the year. The ground was damp and marshy. Suddenly, Anthony made a detour.

"What is it?" asked MacMorran.

"Nothing. I thought it was a portion of a letter, but it was part of an old paper-bag with two peach-stones and piece of orange-peel in it. Carry on, Inspector."

They passed a little reed-girt sheet of water. Here the copse grew very thick and there was a narrow belt of sodden grass between the edge of the copse and the reeds which lined this sheet of water.

"See how that road winds nearer and nearer, friend Andrew?" declared Mr. Bathurst. "Dredge was slow on the uptake there. Surprising—considering how efficient he seems to be in most things."

They walked on again for a fair distance.

"Should be somewhere about here, I imagine," said Anthony, stopping suddenly. "Can you hear anything of the others?"

Inspector MacMorran stopped and listened. "No."

"We'll carry on for a little way longer, then."

A few yards ahead, and Mr. Bathurst gave a cry of satisfaction and rubbed his hands.

"Look! There's the road. The end of it—where the cement finishes. Barely a hundred yards away. And here, to our right, is a comparatively open space. It almost invites one to enter Brutton Copse. Come, MacMorran, you and I will take advantage of the invitation."

They made their way, stooping under low-hanging branches of small trees and round thorny bushes, already clothed for the season of spring. They found bloom and birds. MacMorran grinned at Anthony's efforts to avoid the branches.

"That's the worst of being too tall," he thrust. "Five feet nine's big enough for any man. I'm five feet nine."

"I'm inclined to agree with you," returned Anthony, "although the Brigadier Etienne Gerard, of the Hussars of Conflans, had other views, I believe, on the matter."

"We're right, Mr. Bathurst," put in MacMorran. "Here's the guv'nor with the sergeant. We've come in almost a straight line towards them since we entered."

"Exactly. I thought that we should. That was my design. It proves my contention, too. I think more than ever that the Somersets came, or were brought, the way that you and I came, and *not* the other. What do you say, Inspector?"

"Maybe you're right. I've always said you've got the knack of it." MacMorran wagged his head.

Sir Austin Kemble and Sergeant Dredge stood at the foot of a small tree. The constable stood a few yards away from them. The sergeant was pointing to the ground as Anthony and MacMorran came upon them. Dredge was talking.

"This is where the man Horne found the bodies, sir. The rabbit-poacher. According to the story that he told Hanson here, he was out after rabbits. He was using a ferret and the ferret had got lost. In trying to find it, Horne had come into the copse rather further than he usually did, he said, and was horrified to find the two bodies lying just here."

Sergeant Dredge finished speaking just as Anthony and MacMorran came up. Mr. Bathurst put a question.

"Does this man Reuben Horne, who found the bodies, visit here frequently, on his rabbit-catching expeditions? Any idea?"

Dredge looked interrogatively at Hanson. The latter nodded.

"Pretty frequently, I should say, from what he told me."

"I see. How much better I should feel if I had that doctor's report."

"You'll have that as soon as you get back, sir," answered Sergeant Dredge. "Dr. Bensusan has promised it for this afternoon very definitely. I realize that there's a good deal hanging round it."

"Which way were they lying, Constable Hanson? Describe the positions of the bodies as accurately as you can, will you? It may help me considerably."

Hanson demonstrated with hand-gesture and movement.

"Each was facing the Heronswell side of the copse, sir. This way, if I can show you what I mean."

"Who was nearer to that tree, Hanson?"

"The elder man, sir. The father." Hanson walked over to the spot. "He was lying just there, sir. Head about there." Hanson pointed. "Feet about here. The son, Geoffrey Somerset, was lying there. His head was almost touching his father's right knee. One arm was under the body, twisted-like."

With his eyes Mr. Bathurst attempted to measure the various distances that Hanson had shown him. . . .

"I see. Now let me have a look round."

He turned on his heel and walked back part of the way that he and MacMorran had just come. MacMorran heard him muttering to himself as he walked. Then he turned suddenly and called out to the constable.

"Hanson! From which side of the copse was Home working after his ferret? Did he tell you?" Hanson nodded and pointed away from Anthony. "The East Brutton side. I am sure of it. He told me that as he brought me along here."

"Good! And did you and he, and the others you brought with you afterwards, enter from the East Brutton side? Like you did this afternoon?"

"Yes, sir. Along the field. Over the stile and over the hurdle and straight up, keeping the copse on our left. Just in the same way as today."

Mr. Bathurst rubbed his hands.

"Excellent! All of it." He turned again and continued to walk away from them. MacMorran kept near him.

"Ah! What's this?" MacMorran saw him bend towards the grass. "Footmarks. Toes. Toe-marks. A man's feet." A puzzled look came over his face and he whipped out a magnifying glass. He walked away to the side. "Again here! Why? What does it mean? More marks. Ordinary. Soles. Small at that. They come and then go evidently, and come again to go again! But why not? Of course." MacMorran saw Mr. Bathurst rub his hands for the second time. "And from where did they come in the first place? From where I imagine they did?" He walked up and down in various straight and defined lines as a gardener may mow a lawn or a groundsman a cricket pitch. Sometimes he seemed to lose the tracks that he wanted, but there were other times, generally near to the edge of the copse, when he seemed entirely satisfied with what he was able to discover. Then he went further afield, and remained near the Heronswell side of the copse for some little time. Inspector MacMorran saw him slowly shake his head and begin to walk back towards him, bending here and there, as he had done before, to avoid the low branches.

When he and MacMorran rejoined the others, Sir Austin Kemble had a question for him.

"If your theory is to hold water, Bathurst, that the two men were killed somewhere else and then brought here, they would have been carried into here, would they not?"

"Undoubtedly, sir. At the moment, indeed, I find the theory most attractive."

The Commissioner regarded him dubiously.

"In that case, then, wouldn't you expect to find traces of blood somewhere in the copse? Both of the men had wounds that bled, remember."

"Doesn't follow altogether, sir, if you'll allow me to say so. That would depend, surely, upon *when* and *where* they were killed and *when* the bodies were brought here."

The Commissioner frowned.

"H'm, I suppose you're right."

"Ay," contributed MacMorran, "that's right. That's the point of it all. It's sound all the way through. You can't argue about it." He caught Anthony's eye as he spoke, and saw that Mr. Bathurst's glance was fixed upon something that was caught up on the prong of a branch some fifty yards away to the right of where they were standing. Anthony pointed to the object.

"What's that?" he said curiously. "And what's it doing up there? It looks, to me, too big and too heavy to have been blown there by the wind. We'll investigate, shall we?"

Sir Austin Kemble and Anthony led the way to the bush that the latter had pointed out.

"About the highest branch of all, I should say," remarked Anthony, "looking at it from the side that MacMorran and I look. Does that fact convey anything to you? Still, we'll see what it is before we attempt to theorize."

"It's a newspaper," said Dredge. "Rolled up into a sort of ball."

"We'll have a look at it," observed Mr. Bathurst, "although I don't suppose . . ."

Dredge stepped forward, reached up and took the paper from the branch that had caught and held it. As he had remarked a moment previously, it had been crumpled up into the shape of a ball. As boys will crumple paper into the size and shape that they can conveniently kick about. The sergeant opened it. It was a copy of the *Morning Message*, dated Thursday, the 12th of March. It was smeared in many places with grass and caked

here and there with wet mud. Anthony took it from Sergeant
Dredge and held it in front of Inspector MacMorran.

"How was this crumpled, Inspector? By human hands, of
design, or by some agency of nature, accidentally?"

MacMorran looked carefully at the newspaper.

"That's been deliberately crumpled up by somebody before
being thrown away. Not a doubt of it."

Anthony nodded.

"Exactly. That's what I think. And I'll tell you what it was
used for before it was crumpled up."

He took the paper from the Inspector. The others gathered
round him. "Look here, and here, and there! Grass and mud
stains. See the marks? Smeared, or rubbed, as it were, across the
paper? They come in smudges and smears. Look at them. And
they are here, these grass and mud stains, because this paper
was used by one or more persons to clean the soles and heels,
and perhaps even the tops, of dirtied shoes. Shoes that without
a doubt had crossed this copse from somewhere over there at
the end of the cement road, to over there where we've just been
standing, where the bodies of the two Somersets were found by
Reuben Horne, the rabbit-catcher. Afterwards it was rolled up
into a ball and thrown back into the copse, to fall and catch on
the branch where we spotted it." He handed the paper to Andrew
MacMorran. "Tell me that you agree with me, Inspector."

The Inspector examined the mud-smears with their tiny
particles of trodden grass.

"Ay. That's about the size of it. You can bet on it safely. I've
done such a thing myself before now, when I've made my shoes
over dirty. The wife's mighty particular, I might tell you, certain
days of the week." He unfolded the newspaper, smoothed out
the many creases, and brought it nearer to its original shape and
form. Parts of it, naturally, were torn and mutilated, especially
towards the edges. A newspaper receives scant ceremony when
it is used to wipe dirty shoes. Anthony saw that the Inspector
was gazing closely at the bottom of the back page.

"What is it, Andrew?" he asked him. "Any other point that
I've missed?"

"Looks to me, Mr. Bathurst," said MacMorran, "that we've struck doubly lucky. There's a name here, I fancy, that's been scrawled in rough pencil. Can you make it out, any of you? Your eyes may be sharper than mine."

The Inspector extended the newspaper in front of him. Dredge cut in quickly:

"That's the place which the newsagent uses for the name of his customer. For morning delivery, I mean. He writes either a name or an address down there for the boy, or for whoever it is that takes the paper out with him on the morning round. That's what that is all right. I've seen dozens of 'em like it."

"Dredge is correct," nodded Anthony. "It's the general custom of newsagents to do that. What's the name down there? This is interesting."

"It's faint," returned the Inspector. "Almost illegible. It was but in pencil when first written and the treatment the paper's received since hasn't improved our chance of reading it by a long chalk. Let's have that magnifying glass of yours, Mr. Bathurst. I think it'll help us here."

Anthony handed him the glass and MacMorran held it to the newspaper. Two men were either side of him.

"Well?" said Anthony. "What do you make of it?"

MacMorran nodded.

"Ay, there's a word here, or part of a word. Of course, the writing's verra careless-like. This newspaper chap would ha' made a verra good doctor, I'm thinking. But it begins with an 'A', the word does. I'll say that about it."

"Most appropriate," remarked Anthony, "as long as you don't tell me it finishes with a 'Z'."

MacMorran shook his head. He took most things seriously.

"No. There's no 'Z' here. It's an 'A', then an 'N', then a 'T', and then the rest is nothin' more than a scrawl. Here, take your glass and look at it for yourself. Looks to me as much like 'ant-eater' as anything."

"Let me look," said Sir Austin, asserting himself, "perhaps I can make something more of it."

The Inspector handed the paper and the glass to the Commissioner. Sir Austin screwed up an official eye. The men watching him saw him nod.

"I agree with you, MacMorran. The name is 'Anti'. 'Anti'-something. Or, rather, the letters make up the word 'anti'. I think that it's a safe proposition to say that. There is a bit of a scrawl after the 'i' that may mean anything, as MacMorran said. But there's no doubt concerning the 'anti'."

"May I look, sir?" said Anthony Bathurst.

Anthony used his own glass on the muddied paper. There was "anti" there all right. What names would that fit, he wondered? Very few, he considered. That is to say, if it were the name of a person. Might it not be an address, the name of a house. From what he could remember, it was the practice of newsagents to use *addresses* for the morning rounds of newspaper delivery, far more than the *names* of their customers. If, then, this were the name of a house—Mr. Bathurst's deliberations came to a sudden pause. Was not the name "Antigua" the name of Irene Pearce's house at Chiswick? Of course! Antigua— Braundway Avenue. If he were in line with the truth, this copy of the *Morning Message* might have been brought by Geoffrey Somerset from the house of Miss Pearce and been in his pocket when he had been killed. So that all that the discovery of the newspaper had done for them was to identify a person who had been, as it were, already identified.

"Yes," he said at length, "the word that we have here is 'Anti'-something. I agree. I can't make anything else out of it."

He carried the paper to the edge of the copse close to where he and MacMorran had entered. The others followed him. When he reached the margin, he turned.

"If I had wanted to rid myself of this paper, having used it to clean my shoes, I should probably have done the cleaning job somewhere about here, rolled the paper up into a lump, as this was when we found it, and then chucked it away. If I were right-handed, as nine people in ten are, I should almost certainly throw it in that direction." He pointed in the direction of the bush where the newspaper had been. Sir Austin Kemble joined him.

"We'll go back, Sir Austin, if it's all the same to you, by that cement road over there. I have little doubt that it will bring us out quite close to the spot where we left the car. I want to test that idea. If I'm right in my conjecture, it will save us climbing both a stile and a hurdle."

The five men walked over the road. As Anthony had surmised, it hit the other road a hundred yards or so lower down than the stile which had shown them the way to "Heronswell" and "Heaven Gate". They came again to the car and drove to the police-station at East Brutton. Anthony was lost in thought for the whole of the journey. A uniformed constable came to Sergeant Dredge almost immediately as they entered. Sergeant Dredge listened to what the man had to say. Then he turned to the Commissioner, and passed on the news that he had just received.

"Dr. Bensusan has given his opinion, sir, and I understand that he's positive about it, that the two men have been dead for over a week. No bullet can be found in David Somerset's brain. It has passed clean through and out. But according to the wound it might have fitted the revolver. The son's skull was fractured by a heavy blow on the head. By such a thing as a poker."

Anthony Bathurst heard the statement.

"I think, then, that they died either late on the night of the 12th of March or in the small hours of the following morning."

"That would be Friday, the thirteenth," interposed MacMorran with a nod.

"That would, Andrew," returned Mr. Bathurst. "You were always amazingly accurate."

Chapter VIII
THE TWO MEN

EMILY entered Mr. Bathurst's room almost on tiptoe. He turned and smiled at her thoughtfulness.

"It's all right, Emily," he said, reassuring her; "don't worry. I'm not doing anything in particular. What is it?"

"Mr. MacMorran, sir. He wants to know whether he can see you at once."

"Old Andrew from the 'Yard', eh? I think that we might give him audience, Emily, don't you? Yes. It's indicated. Tell him to burst right in on me. He probably wants to see me about the Somerset case."

"Very well, sir. I'll tell him at once."

Emily departed, and a matter of minutes saw Inspector MacMorran crossing the threshold. Anthony welcomed him.

"Sit down, Andrew. Candidly, I'm not surprised to see you."

MacMorran smiled his thin, dry-lipped smile.

"I thought you mightn't be. I'll be sitting here, I think, if you don't mind."

"Not a bit. Make yourself comfortable."

The Inspector took the armchair by the fire-place and rubbed his nose.

"The Commissioner sent me along. I should ha' waited a bit myself, but he insisted on my coming at once. This is by way of explanation. So that you and I know where we are."

Anthony knew his man. He waited patiently. MacMorran continued.

"The point at issue is this. Young Somerset's bodyguard served him in good stead last night, I'm thinking."

Anthony sat bolt upright.

"What's that you say? Quick! Tell me what happened?"

MacMorran's eyes glinted. Nothing pleased him better than making Mr. Bathurst sit up to take notice.

"Just this. Young Gerald Somerset was driving home last night. To his place near Ingatestone. After the funeral—he'd had to go up to the office. In accordance with instructions, our fellows were following him on his homeward journey. Quite close to him in the rear. It was pretty late, and, as you may guess, pretty dark, too. There are one or two quietish spots beyond Brentwood, let me tell you, and near one of these places a couple of men came out from the side of the road, one on either side, and waved to young Somerset's car to stop. He obeyed the signal at once. Wise of him, no doubt. He knew our fellows weren't far off, and couldn't be long before they came up with him. The men that stopped him are described as two dark, foreign-looking johnnies, each of whom carried a revolver. As they advanced towards the car, the police car swept up to them. Like hell it did. But the two fellows working the hold-up smelt a rat at once, and before our fellows could get to grips with them, or even get out of the car, took to their heels across country. *Not* along the straight road where the car could have followed them, mind you! After that, our car escorted Somerset the remainder of his way home, and saw him safely on the premises."

"That's good. Proves that our precautions were justified, then?"

"Not a doubt of it, Mr. Bathurst."

Anthony was thinking.

"Tell me, Andrew," he said eventually, "was Somerset alone in his car? Or was he driving with a companion?"

"He was absolutely alone."

"It was at a fairly lonely spot, you say?"

"Pretty lonesome. Just fields on each side of the road. Nothing much else."

"It was his customary route home, I take it?"

"Ay. When he went home by car."

"Was he carrying anything last night that he doesn't usually carry? That he hasn't, for example, ever carried before?"

"According to what he told our two fellows—no. All about him was just about as normal as it could be."

Anthony rubbed his chin. What was the reason of this attempt on Gerald Somerset, the *remaining* male Somerset, let it be noted, last evening? Was it just the sequel that he had almost been anticipating for some time—or was it prompted by any other pertinent reason? If he knew the answer to those questions he would probably hold the key to the entire problem.

"Have you seen either of *your* men since the incident, yourself?"

MacMorran nodded.

"I have that. Fellowes has been up this morning and had a word with me about it. It was reported at once, you can be sure."

"Did you question him?"

"You bet I did."

"What was his opinion of the job? Did the men appear to mean mischief towards Somerset in the sense of making a personal attack on him, or did they appear to be attempting a 'hold-up' for the purpose of obtaining something from him?"

"I asked him that, Mr. Bathurst. That idea struck me, and I put the self-same question to him. But Fellowes declined to commit himself. All he would definitely assert is this. The two chaps stopped Somerset's car, and each, with a revolver, walked towards it. Before there was time for anything to happen, and before they could sort of divine their intentions, Fellowes and Ball were up with them and the men decamped, as I told you."

Anthony shook his head doubtfully.

"Somerset must take no risks at all—that's evident. Not the slightest. He must go nowhere without protection. If necessary, Sir Austin must place a fleet of men around him. But you've made that fact clear to him, no doubt?" Anthony raised his eyebrows.

"I have, Mr. Bathurst. I'm going to suggest that we put men inside the house and in the offices as well. What do you think yourself?"

Anthony Bathurst considered the question. "Better still, get him away somewhere quietly. Smuggle him somewhere with the assistance of the 'Yard'. As soon as is possible. Like you did Sir Bernard Joyce last year when that abduction scare was on at the F.I.M.T.A. conference. Tell Sir Austin what I think, will you? It's worth consideration."

MacMorran nodded slowly.

"I will. I'm with you all the way, and then some. Seems to me, it must be healthier for young Somerset away from this locality." MacMorran rose from his armchair. "I'll be getting back, then. There's nothing else much that *can* be done at the moment, is there?"

"I'm afraid not. Thanks for coming along. Give my regards to Sir Austin." Anthony opened the door for the Inspector. "You've brought me more perhaps than you imagined, friend Andrew.

I'm not sure that I shan't drag something out of this that may put us on the road to success. At any rate, I'm going to hope so."

The two men shook hands at the door. MacMorran's mouth twisted in the way that Anthony Bathurst loved to see.

"If anybody can, you can, sir. And Sir Austin Kemble knows that as well as I do. Good-bye." He gripped Anthony's hand in his big paw and waved himself out.

Anthony returned to the fire-place. He filled his pipe, lit the tobacco, and smoked steadily. What was the pivot upon which this strange mystery was turning? What possession, or piece of knowledge, was in the hands of this ill-fated Somerset family that had caused two murders? He felt himself so completely in the dark. Beyond the incidents of the case that had occurred since he had become connected with it, he had discovered to all intents and purposes, *nothing*. Absolutely nothing! Somerset père had gone to East Brutton where he had met and been interviewed by a number of foreigners. His son, Geoffrey, had spent an evening with the girl of his choice, and had not been seen again until his body, lying by the side of his father, had been found in Brutton Copse. His other son, Gerald, the only one of the three Somersets whom Anthony Bathurst had actually seen in the flesh, was to all intents and purposes carrying his life in his hands.

What was causing the trouble? Anthony puffed steadily at his pipe. Why? Who had travelled back to Paddington with David Somerset's return-ticket, if it had not been David Somerset himself? How could it have been David Somerset, if he had died, as Anthony felt certain that he had, on the night of the 12th of March, or just afterwards? For his body had most certainly lain in Brutton Copse. *Why* had Geoffrey Somerset joined him? *Where* had he joined him? How had David Somerset *communicated* with his son? What had *made* him? If he had desired Geoffrey to be with him at East Brutton, why had he not *taken* Geoffrey with him in the first place? Surely that would have been the sensible, natural procedure? Had David Somerset *knowingly* been going into a condition of danger, would he not have been glad of the company of his son? Or of both his sons? Anthony shook his head with strong dissatisfaction. Why send for Geoffrey at the end of such a memorable day? Obviously because of something that had happened *during* the day.

At this thought, Anthony was perturbed. While we may at times smile at the categories of bygone thought, we are often forced to admire the depth and accuracy of the observation of facts, which were sought to be accounted for *in* them. The function of reason, now resisting, now aiding and abetting passion, may well be the differentiating factor between the evil and the merely erring. Great tragedies are exercises in Grief, or Jealousy, Fear, Anger, Greed, or Lust. Into which category did this case of the three Somersets fall? That was the question.

Anthony knocked out the dottle from his pipe and refilled it. The great master, Holmes, had had, during his career, what he had described as his "three-pipe problems", but this present one looked like going well beyond that. Anthony lit the tobacco of this second pipe that he had just filled. As he did so, a further idea struck him. There were two people whom he had not yet seen, who had been, each of them, in daily association with David and Geoffrey Somerset. They were Digby, the confidential clerk at the offices in Boot Lane, and Mrs. Somerset in the house at Clutton Chase. It was just on the cards, he considered, that from one of these two he might pick up something of inestimable value. But one thought-obstacle always remained in his mind. Why had David Somerset made the distinction that he appeared to have made between his two sons? He had sent for Geoffrey—not Gerald. Why? Had this choice been deliberate on David Somerset's part, or merely fortuitous? Had he just turned to Geoffrey because he happened to be close at hand? How much might reasonably depend upon the answer to that question.

The more that he reviewed the situation, the more it seemed to him that he had little or nothing upon which to work, from the standpoint of the science of deduction. That his efforts and activities, such as they might be, would have to be based more on audacity and chance-seeking than on actual plans foundationed upon sound reasoning. Eventually he brought himself to the point of deliberate decision. He would try the value of an advertisement. An advertisement in the public press. It *might* dangle a sufficiently attractive bait to land a fish. Even though the fish might be a mere minnow. A similar scheme had brought to him definite success, he remembered, when he had used it during that strange investigation of his which had been handed down to history as the *Sussex Cuckoo*. He would employ, for the purpose of the advertisement, the whole of the important London dailies. The Somerset office was in London, and there was little doubt that the men who had enticed David Somerset to East Brutton, even though their homes and antecedents might be continental, must be in regular contact and communication with London.

Mr. Bathurst considered the draft terms of his anticipated advertisement. He found suitable paper and was speedily at work upon it. . . . Some moments after, he surveyed the result of his written efforts. The advertisement that he had produced was worded as follows:

East Brutton! Will those who met at the "Golden Lion" on the 12th of March last, and who wore the sign of the white flower, communicate with, or call upon, at once, the *one who is left*. Either at the address named or at his office. If they do not, it is more than probable that everything that was accomplished at East Brutton on the 12th of March, and all sacrifices that were then and there made, will become futile. Death makes such a difference. When death is doubled, it can spell nothing but dire disaster. Not only to one side, but to ALL CONCERNED. Circumstances, over which one can have *no* control, completely alter cases. After the white flower, the white flag! What have I to do with peace? Everything! The Son and Brother.

Mr. Bathurst smiled grimly as he read what he had written, and then added his own address.

"I wonder," he muttered to himself. "You never can tell! Perhaps. Perhaps not! We shall see."

He made his way to the telephone. The message of the advertisement took him some time to deliver. This effected, he put himself in touch with Gerald Somerset at the office in Boot Lane. He spoke to him at length.

"What do you think of it?" he asked, when he reached the conclusion.

Somerset was warm in his acceptance of the idea.

"Oh—excellent, Bathurst. It's worded so that I think it's almost certain to do as you say—make them *wonder*."

"After 'wonder', will come 'doubt', Somerset. After 'doubt' will come 'apprehension'. Then 'anxiety'. Then *'fear'*. When fear enters into the arrangement I anticipate action—defensive, of course. As I see things, they *must* take it. But although it will be purely defensive, they can't take it without coming out into the open. See my idea? Well, there you are, it may or it may not come off. If things go as I have outlined to you, however, we shall start scoring."

"It's a welcome idea to me, as you may well imagine, coming on top of yesterday's affair. You've heard of that by now, of course?"

"Yes, MacMorran blew along and told me."

"Pretty steep, what?"

"You're right. But keep a good heart. You're in good hands and well looked after. Take care of yourself to the limit of your own power, and the additional help from our side should mean seeing you through safely. We're all on your side and working for you. Got that?"

Somerset murmured something down the telephone. No doubt the situation *was* different from his point of view. Anthony had other things to say. He therefore turned the subject in the direction that he desired. Gerald Somerset listened for some time before he answered. The inquiry concerned Digby.

"You can try him, of course, if you think it will help at all. I should be only too pleased. But I doubt, from what I know of him, whether he'll have anything for you."

"Very probably not. Still, I think it's worth trying. Any port in a storm, you know—and there's a storm round you all right. It's broken twice, and we mustn't let it break a third time if we can prevent it."

"I ought to tell you that I've chatted it over with him myself, more than once. I felt that I should. I told you what he told me about my father's revolver. Funny, that, you know."

"Is this Digby a reliable chap? Thoroughly and absolutely, I mean?"

"I should say so. Without the shadow of a doubt. My father thought very highly of him. He's been with the firm for a considerable number of years. That's something in his favour, isn't it?"

"Should be. I may gather something from him when we meet. That's an arrangement, then? Right. Good-bye."

Anthony replaced the receiver and went back to his chair. He felt distinctly more hopeful now than he had felt when MacMorran had been with him. Two more avenues, at least, were now opened up for exploration and perhaps one of them would prove fruitful. He filled his pipe yet again, and once more began to smoke steadily. Somewhere in front of him was the all-important clue for which he was seeking. Find it he must! Find it he would! He had already let two people down. His personal reputation was at stake and a big effort was demanded of him. Supposing David Somerset had come back to Paddington on the evening of the 12th of March and had . . .

An idea was born in Mr. Bathurst's brain.

CHAPTER IX
STAFF MATTERS AT SOMERSET

GERALD Somerset greeted Mr. Bathurst cordially. But Anthony was quick to perceive from his general manner that he was not altogether his usual self. Anthony was not allowed to remain in suspense long. Somerset told him quite frankly that the morning had opened with a surprise for him.

"Something that I feel I ought to tell you. Ten minutes or so after I arrived this morning, Bathurst, you could have knocked me down with a feather. Talk about getting me away somewhere quietly! If anybody had even hinted such a thing to me right up to yesterday I would have told him straight out to his face that I didn't believe him. But there it is—it's right enough. Read that. There's no getting away from it, as you'll see for yourself."

He handed Anthony Bathurst a letter. Mr. Bathurst took it with interest. Who knew from what unlikely spot his long looked-for clue would come? Even this might be it. The letter read thus:

> 37 Myers Terrace,
> Newbury Lane,
> Ilford, Essex.

Dear Mr. Somerset,

I write this letter to you with some reluctance. But for some days now I have been considering taking a certain step in relation to my life, and at last I have reached a decision. Will you therefore kindly accept my resignation from the staff of Somerset and Sons as from today's date? I am aware that I should give, under the terms of my service, a week's notice, but, in lieu of that, I am willing to sacrifice a week's salary. To tell the truth, the death of your father means for me that I have lost almost all my interest in the firm. You have neither the ability nor the enterprise of your father, or even of your brother. In other words, I am perfectly convinced that you and I would never hit it off together. I could never give my best to a chief whom I did not respect in every way, *and in whose ability I hadn't the most complete confidence. Perhaps you will take a grain of advice. If it is your desire that the firm should remain in being, with attendant success, take a partner as soon as you can find a suitable one. You will never win through alone. I am frank, and frankness may hurt, but I believe in it. I remain, faithfully yours,*

> *Maud F. Masters.*

Anthony Bathurst read it and then at once re-read it.

"Well," said Gerald Somerset, "what do you think of that? Pretty cool—eh? Doesn't altogether dislike herself, does she?"

Anthony smiled.

"She is a strong believer in her own efficiency. I could tell that the moment I set eyes on her. A lot of women are like her—these days. Why have you so disappointed her?"

Somerset flushed.

"The lady and I have never quite hit it, I'm afraid. In her eyes I am but the poor shadow of my father, for whom she had a most terrific admiration. I knew that. I've known it for some time. I wasn't, however, aware that she rated me as so inferior to Geoffrey. That part of the letter *did* surprise me, I'll admit. We live and learn."

Anthony smiled for the second time. He felt a certain amount of sympathy for young Somerset.

"The son of a distinguished father, Mr. Somerset, invariably goes through life with a perpetual handicap. I could name examples that come readily to my mind. I always regard the underlying idea, myself, as another angle of 'nothing's as good as it was'. It's the W.G. Grace complex. W.G. Grace jun. was doomed from the start. Your late employee, Miss Masters, feels this condition, probably, a little more acutely than most people."

Gerald Somerset shook his head rather sadly. "That's very decent of you, Bathurst, to put it like that. But you're being charitable to me. I appreciate your thoughtfulness intensely."

Anthony handed the letter back to him. Then a thought came to him.

"Where's the lady going? Any idea?"

Somerset shook his head.

"Not the foggiest."

"Matrimony?"

Somerset shrugged his shoulders.

"There's always that possibility, I suppose, when a girl resigns a position quickly, as in this case."

"Anybody in the offing, do you know?"

"Not that I know of. But I know little or nothing of Miss Masters's private affairs, so don't bank on what I say. Beyond the fact that she lives at Ilford. Somewhere near the football ground, I believe. Her people have a small villa there."

"When did she last put in an appearance here?"

"Friday last. She should have been in on Saturday, but never turned up. This morning I received this letter." He indicated the envelope. Anthony held out his hand for it.

"What's the post-mark? It would be interesting to know that."

"Ilford." Somerset handed the envelope over to him.

"H'm. Nothing in that, then. Thought perhaps it might have told us something more than that." He tossed it back on to the table. "What are you doing about it—anything?"

"One thing, and one thing only, Bathurst. Filling her place immediately. Miss Masters may be efficient, but she's not the only soapsud down the Somerset sink. The firm of Somerset and Son will survive, I hope, even such a staggering blow as this."

Anthony noted the irony.

"I hate to say it and I've resolutely set my face against mentioning such things as 'fish' and the 'sea', but nobody's indispensable, you know, bar, perhaps, Don Bradman."

"I agree with you—and we'll leave it at that. Now—how about your word with Digby?"

"Will it be convenient to see him now?"

"Yes, quite—as far as I'm concerned. I've arranged that you shall. I'll get him in here now."

Gerald Somerset pressed the bell and Anthony awaited the appearance of the late David Somerset's confidential clerk. He hadn't long to wait. Leonard Digby entered. Anthony saw a tall, thin, cadaverous-looking man with little hair and pale watery-blue eyes. He stooped badly but there was, perhaps, a certain sincerity about his face that Anthony found both appealing and attractive. Somerset introduced him. Digby bowed to Mr. Bathurst and, at a gesture, took a seat at the side of his employer's table. Somerset briefly outlined the position. Leonard Digby listened to him attentively.

"So that, if it's in your power at all, Digby," concluded Gerald Somerset, "give Mr. Bathurst the help that he desires."

"Very good, Mr. Somerset. I'll do my best." Digby turned to Anthony with a movement that seemed to suggest he was prepared for a severe examination. Anthony at once took him back to the last morning when he had seen and spoken to David Somerset. Digby nodded his understanding.

"Yes, sir. That is quite correct. Mr. Somerset, Mr. David Somerset, that is, called me into this room on the morning of the day that he disappeared, that would be the 12th of March, and informed me that he was on the point of going out. He added to that statement that he would probably be absent for some time. Let me say 'for a longer time than usual'. I think that was the exact expression which he used."

"No hint of any kind, or clue as to where he was going, or as to what was taking him away?"

"No, sir. Nothing of that kind whatever."

"Not the slightest? If you retraced your way to every word that he said to you, still not the slightest hint of anything?"

"No, sir." Digby was quietly imperturbable and unshaken. "I've been over that conversation many and many a time, word for word, trying hard to see if there *was* any special point in it that had eluded me, but without success, sir."

"Thank you. That's bad news, Mr. Digby. It's a great disappointment to me. I've been hoping against hope. Now we'll pass on to another matter. Mr. Gerald Somerset here tells me that, following upon your conversation with his father that morning, there was an unusual incident."

"Yes, sir. I told Mr. Gerald Somerset so when the bad news first reached us. There was a revolver on his father's desk."

"You had never seen a revolver there before, I take it?"

"Never, sir. In all the years that I have worked here, sir."

"Did Mr. Somerset notice that you observed it, do you think?"

"I am not sure, sir. I shouldn't like to say, either way, definitely."

"Stalemate again," thought Mr. Bathurst. "Tell me this. Were you considered to be Mr. Somerset's confidential clerk?"

"To say so would not altogether be an exaggeration."

"His right-hand man?"

Digby turned towards Gerald Somerset with an implied apology.

"If Mr. Gerald will forgive me saying so, I would answer 'yes' to that question also."

"Let me supplement that, Bathurst," cut in the man to whom the appeal had been made. "Undoubtedly! Digby means more to the business than anybody. Has done so for years. I shan't think any the less of him if he says so."

Digby's thin face flushed with pleasure. Here was a man, thought Anthony, devoted to the house and cause of Somerset. And he had more questions for him.

"Would that description, 'right-hand man', apply to matters of business only, or would it apply to *all* Mr. Somerset's connections?"

Digby looked a little puzzled.

"All connections?" he repeated after Anthony.

"Yes. I'll explain more fully what I mean. Were you Mr. Somerset's confidant as regards matters of *business* only?"

"Oh no, sir. I did many private transactions for him, as well as things to do with the office here."

"Such as?"

Digby spread out his hands.

"Little private matters like paying accounts for him, arranging certain details such as theatre seats when he wanted them, anything of that kind. You can take it, sir, that any trifling task that I could take off Mr. Somerset's hands, I did. He trained me to do these things for him right from the beginning of my service with him."

"You were familiar, then, with Mr. Somerset's private life?" Anthony realized as he spoke that he was forcing the question. Digby's answer but impressed the fact upon him.

"No, sir. I wouldn't admit that. I shouldn't care to. With certain ordinary parts of it—yes. But if I were to say that I knew all that Mr. Somerset did, and how he spent his leisure time, it would be a long way from the truth, sir. I would never make claim to such knowledge." Digby shook his head.

Anthony felt that Digby would yield him nothing against his will, persist how he might. He turned to Gerald Somerset.

"Was your father an exceptionally clever chemist? A man whom we could place much above the average in his profession?"

"Oh—undoubtedly. He had built our business up magnificently. Neither Geoffrey nor I was the equal of father. I have no illusions about that."

Anthony took his fountain-pen and toyed with it as he spoke.

"I am going to put something to you that has been in my mind for some time now. It's a leading question, I'm afraid, but as things have gone, the circumstances of the case have forced me to bring it into the open. Mr. Digby here is probably better able to answer it than you are, Mr. Somerset." He paused.

The two men watched and listened to him. Somerset anxiously, Digby with curiosity. Anthony waited a moment, and then proceeded.

"That question is this. Was Mr. Somerset on the verge of an important discovery? As a research chemist, had he succeeded in hitting on something which touched Big Finance, in any way of which you can think? Anything that might have an influence on armaments? Any new gas? Any new poison? Any new weapon, even? If either of you gentlemen who are listening to me has the *slightest* piece of knowledge in any of the directions that I have just indicated, I ask you to pass that information on to me. I assure you that I shall respect the confidence. Perhaps if you ransack your brains, and turn out the repositories of your memories, something of what I say may occur to you."

The two faces at which he looked remained blank and impassive.

"I know of nothing, as I've already said," returned Gerald Somerset.

Digby slowly shook his head to and fro with a simple dignity. "I know of nothing, either."

Anthony felt a wave of something like surprise sweep over him. He caught, for the first time, a suggestion of reserved strength in the man, and an intuition was his that in a great crisis of life, Digby might well prove to be a force far beyond the degree of his original anticipation. There came a long silence. Gerald Somerset half turned and sat back in his chair, his hands clasped behind his head and his face staring at the ceiling. Digby still retained his normal posture. His hands were white and thin, with blue veins showing on them. The lines had deepened in his face. The hollows in his cheeks had become accentuated. He was not of the type to thrive when in conflict with elemental forces. Whatever he might achieve or accomplish would be brought about by sheer projection of will power. Anthony schooled himself to remember that Digby's universe had crashed about his ears. His chief was dead, and one of his chief's sons also.

And within so short a space of time. At first, he had been dazed, no doubt, stunned and scarce knowing where to turn amid the shapeless wreckage that entangled his feet. Introspection had not yet come to him. At present, Digby could but stare dully at what he thought were the ruins of his life and attempt to fashion for himself a new, if but temporary, existence. A sudden idea flashed into Anthony's mind. There was yet a question which he hadn't put to Digby. He determined to put it to him at once.

"What do you make of Miss Masters's resignation, Mr. Digby? I presume that you have heard of it. As the senior man of the staff here, your opinion should be invaluable."

Digby looked startled, but quickly recovered himself. He shook his head.

"There's no knowing, sir, what a woman will do."

"Especially Miss Masters, eh?"

Digby gestured in acquiescence.

"Especially Miss Masters, sir."

"Were you surprised to hear that Miss Masters was leaving the service of Mr. Somerset?"

Digby appeared to hesitate.

"Not altogether, sir."

"Why—apart from the generalization that you made just now? Any particular reason?"

Again Digby hesitated. Anthony was sure of it this time.

"The deaths of Mr. Somerset and Mr. Geoffrey have made a vast difference to all of us who served them."

"Naturally. Who else, then, has resigned besides Miss Masters?"

Digby looked more pale than ever. The question was so pertinent. He glanced towards Gerald Somerset, as though he sought instructions or even help from him. But Somerset neither heeded him nor gave him help. When he saw that he must reply unaided, he accepted the situation with the best grace possible.

"Nobody, sir—that I have heard of."

Anthony followed up quickly.

"Your meaning being that Miss Masters was more affected by what has happened than anybody else on the staff was? Yes?"

"I don't know that I altogether meant that, sir."

"Well, then, what did you mean by your remark? You put forward a reason for the resignation of Miss Masters which you admit has not affected any other member of the staff. Which justifies me in asking you again—what *did* you mean?"

Digby shifted uneasily in his chair. This man who was questioning him was different from the people whom he habitually encountered. The answers that you gave him didn't satisfy him so easily. But Digby made a fight for it.

"What I meant was this. Miss Masters has resigned. Am I surprised? Not altogether. The tragic happenings of the last fortnight, I suggest, may have upset her, as indicated in her letter of resignation. That is all that I meant, sir."

Anthony felt that he *must* press this man more. Much as he disliked doing so.

"I don't think that I altogether believe you. I'm sorry—but there it is."

Digby's defences were badly shaken. The simple directness of Mr. Bathurst's attack had disarmed him thoroughly. He capitulated almost immediately, albeit with a sidelong glance towards Gerald Somerset.

"Well, sir, since you force me to say it, I don't think that Miss Masters got on well with Mr. Gerald here. If he'll pardon my saying such a thing. And I think *that's* the real reason behind her resignation, if one could but see into her mind."

Now that his confession had been made, Digby seemed to recover himself again. It is true that Gerald Somerset gave him a half-nod of corroboration which he was quick enough to see and to take unto himself for comfort. Anthony felt a tinge of keen disappointment at the result of his efforts. All his pressing of Digby had brought him no more than he had already known. Digby had merely confirmed what Miss Masters herself had stated and Somerset himself had admitted. If he took stock of himself, he would find that his gain from the interview was but little more than nothing. It is true that he had seen and been able to assess Digby better, but he had achieved little beyond that. He rose to go. Digby allowed a look of relief to cross his face. Anthony addressed Somerset.

"Any more nasty incidents? Or is the double guard doing its work too effectively?"

Gerald Somerset smiled faintly, but Anthony could read the fear and the anxiety in the young man's eyes.

"Nothing since the Brentwood affair. I'm hoping—the wish, I expect, is father to the hope—that they may not molest me any more. What do you think yourself, Bathurst?"

Anthony hesitated. He had no wish to give the man a fund of false hopes. He contented himself, therefore, by saying, "Keep your eyes open, watch your step, and take no chances. That's the best advice that I can give you." He waved a hand, and a moment later took his departure.

Gerald Somerset sat at his desk. How long would he be able to stand the strain?

CHAPTER X
MADEMOISELLE

ON THE following morning, Mr. Bathurst's advertisement duly appeared in ail the more important of the London dailies. He was destined to remember that day for a considerable time to come. Emily had received certain instructions from him, and Anthony Bathurst had made certain plans. He always described it afterwards as the day when the case took its first definite turn towards the avenue of solution. The first incident took place, to be exact, at twenty-two minutes past eight in the evening.

Soon after he had finished dinner, Emily knocked on his door, and Anthony knew, from what he had previously told her, that the moment had come and that her summons to him had to do with the East Brutton advertisement.

"Yes, Emily?" he interrogated her.

"Yes, sir. Here now. At once, sir—or shall I . . ." Emily paused. She had been surprised at what she had seen and, therefore, a trifle disconcerted.

"Who is it, Emily? A foreigner, would you say?"

The girl shook her head.

"Not exactly, sir. It's a young lady, sir. Very beautiful. But it's true, I think, that she may be foreign."

Anthony shared Emily's surprise.

"A young lady—eh? Bring her in at once."

Emily's eyes sparkled mischief. She went quickly out. Anthony made arrangements in the room. A touch here and a readjustment of chairs there. He heard Emily's voice outside.

"This way, miss. Mr. Bathurst will see you at once."

The girl who entered seemed to be dazzled by the light of the room. Anthony saw that Emily's assessment of her had been a true one. She was indeed beautiful. She was young, tall, and slender. Her hair was brown and warm, and showed, where the light caught it and danced upon it, threads of gold. Her dark eyes were large and lovely. But she was nervous, Anthony decided. There wasn't a doubt of it. In the early twenties, he judged.

"You will sit here?" He placed a chair for her. She accepted it. Then she spoke. She raised her eyebrows slightly. Her voice was crisp-cut. The inclination of her head was gracious. Her words held interest for him.

"It is, of course, the white flower? The gardenia?" The note of question sounded in her voice.

"Of course," returned Mr. Bathurst. "But not—necessarily, of a blameless life."

A delicate perfume, like the scent of wood violets, came and went in the air around her. Her eyes darkened after she had spoken, pathetic and wistful. Anthony was acutely conscious of her charm. Her foot tapped the ground.

"Well?" she asked him.

"Well?" he countered.

She drew out a copy of the *Morning Message* and pointed to the advertisement that Anthony had sponsored. He smiled at her. Charm for charm. He thrust—suddenly and unexpectedly.

"But *you* were not at East Brutton? I am sure of that."

"Yet I may represent those that were."

She said no more than that. There was a short period of silence. Anthony forced her to break it.

She spoke softly.

"You are neither the son nor the brother."

She smiled at him, smile for smile. Anthony replied quickly.

"I feel that I cannot improve upon the exact form of your own reply."

No real opening yet for either. Her eyes melted, almost beseeching his indulgence, yet retaining a hint of raillery that defied him to draw his weapons and do his worst.

"Perhaps you will outline the wishes of the . . . er . . . society? Then the way will be considerably easier for each of us, don't you think?"

She nodded with profound significance.

"It would . . . if I could. Society? You are enigmatic, as your message here is." She tapped the newspaper and gave her shoulders a tiny shrug of dissatisfaction.

"Well . . . I said 'society'." Anthony realized that he must tread carefully. His bluff had been non-productive. "Let me say, then, those that showed the white flower, the gardenia."

She shook her head.

"Still I fail to understand. Surely *you* have news for *me*? What have I to tell *you*—that you do not already know?"

"*Touché*," thought Anthony. A hit, most assuredly, and matters looking decidedly unpromising. Her voice had modulated and had become almost exultant. She drew herself up in her chair.

"You don't answer. Why?"

Anthony, it is regretted, was on the point of floundering even more seriously. In desperation, almost, he drew a bow at a venture.

"The situation, after all, is affected by the resignation, is it not? There can be little doubt about that."

Anthony watched to see the effect that this remark had upon her. There was nothing of the immature about her. Nothing of the unfinished or the tentative in her aspect. Added to her freshness, there were the strength, the poise, the assurance that we are wont to associate with a riper womanhood. Her figure was sumptuously developed despite her natural slenderness. Her face held humour, vivacity, character, and decision. Her colouring held a Southern richness. Her skin was warm white and covert rose. The brown hair was abundant and undulating. Anthony placed her more exactly now at twenty-two. But, even at that age, the astonishingly finished product. Alive, alert, distinguished, and most pre-eminently worth while. Her blood coursed quickly, he had no doubt. Her spirit burned fiercely, he felt certain. She might be generous, he thought, and loyal, because Anthony read in her face, temperament, nerve, and race-pride. All these things rushed through his brain as he waited for a reply which he confidently hoped would put added strength into his hands. But once again he was doomed to disappointment.

The girl arched her eyebrows in amiable surprise.

Her entire appearance told him unmistakably that she had utterly failed to understand his question. So, once again, he had drawn blank. He determined to give himself one last chance. He would be more particular this time, more definite. He would mention a name.

"Surely," he remarked, before she put her doubt into words, "the resignation of Miss Masters must make a difference?"

The girl opened her eyes wide in bewilderment.

"I am sorry. I do not understand you. Who is Miss Masters? I have never heard of this lady whom you mention. Please tell me why you have brought me here. Why you inserted your advertisement? Otherwise, I fear, the whole thing may be a waste of my time. Tell me at once what has happened to make the 12th of March futile?"

"How extraordinarily becoming that touch of temper makes her," he thought, his problem suddenly but a secondary consideration. "How it brings out the sparkle in her eyes." Her hair curled and rippled. Tiny blue veins showed faintly at her temples. Anthony was again acutely conscious of all these things, and thrilled in a deep sense of their nearness to him. She gave a little laugh. It was a light trill of laughter. Anthony was thrilled still more.

"The laugh," he thought, "is like rainbow-tinted spray. A jet from the fountain of the angels, each drop a flawless gem." Then he remembered again that she was awaiting a reply to her question.

"Well," he declared, "the two murders, and 'murder' is an ugly word, my dear young lady, have changed the outlook—*n'est-ce-pas*? Almost revolutionized it."

She gave him a quick shake of the head.

"All that doesn't touch the transaction at East Brutton. How can it? You know that. You know it perfectly. You *must*."

Anthony wished heartily that he did. But she didn't know all that he didn't know. Her eyes were still sparkling and spirited. Her mouth curved and her teeth looked like ivory set in the heart of a rose. He knew deep down that he must make a fight for it now, else he would lose her for ever and a day!

He therefore tried again.

"You are already using what Somerset traded with you?"

She frowned.

"To our advantage? Not altogether. It was put to one use, as you know perfectly well. It will not be put to any other. That was mutually understood. *We* shall keep our word. Listen." She cupped her chin in her hands and faced him resolutely. "Does the son and brother, whom you claim to represent, throw a wrench into the machinery, then? Is he *apart* from the family transaction?"

Anthony fenced with her. He knew that if he played his cards intelligently now, he would be on the verge of a discovery. A discovery that might well turn the issue of the day.

"He may throw the wrench . . . and he may not."

As he intended, she read mystery into the terms of his reply.

"He can, then?"

"Of course. Why not?"

"Then his father lied. That's all." Her lips flashed and her voice sounded ominous.

"Are you surprised?"

"Yes. I am. Extremely surprised. He was an Englishman. That fact meant a lot to us. Where I come from, we have learned to trust an Englishman. But *will* he?"

Anthony shrugged his shoulders and tried to look monstrous wise.

"That is up to you, is it not?"

"Oh no, my friend! Think! You cannot trifle with us like that. If the son and brother does as you suggest he *may*, we shall just have to . . . shall we say . . . take steps. That is all. It will be excessively simple, believe me. We are powerful." She rose— her cheeks flushed again and her lips half parted in emotion. Anthony challenged her. He felt that the prize was slipping from his grasp.

"Not as simple, though, as the other two."

"I cannot answer that. Who knows?"

They stood and faced each other.

"You are afraid to answer it."

Her lip curled.

"I am afraid of nothing!"

Provocation from Mr. Bathurst.

"That's how you would like to be. Is it how you really are?"

"Oh—how dare you?" She flew the flags of anger in her cheeks. Anthony struck again.

"I will repeat my statement. The third matter will not be as easy for you as the other two. And I'll also add to that statement.

I'll tell you *why* it won't be! Because this time we are fore-warned. Do you understand? On the previous occasion we were in the dark. And to be forewarned, says an English proverb, is to be forearmed. Consider the difference."

She smiled at him disdainfully, and Anthony considered her lovelier than ever.

"You can think that. I do not mind. It will make no differ-ence. I will say good-bye. I am sorry that I have been tricked into coming."

Anthony bowed. "Why?" he demanded of her.

"Why not?" she riposted.

The lady swept to the door. Exceedingly distinguished? Oh—infinitely more than that. A spirit burned within her. A fire—prismatic and aromatic. Race, nerve and sex were all there, too.

All the mystery, all the magic, all the essential, elemen-tal principles of the Supreme Feminine were there. Anthony glanced at his wrist-watch. All was well, as far as he was concerned, from the point of view of time. Emily had made the necessary arrangements by now. She had had ample time. He opened the door for his companion.

"Allow me," he said, "to show you to your car. Shall we say that honours are easy!"

His companion made no reply. From his window, therefore, he watched her go. She stood on the pavement for a minute or two before entering a taxi-cab which sidled quietly up to her. He smiled to himself as he saw what happened afterwards, and turned away from the window. All that he could do now was to wait.

He waited in his room until a quarter past eleven. Just after his clock had chimed, no less a person than Inspector MacMor-ran came to him. The look in old Andrew's eye was excessively eloquent. Anthony noticed it at once and became anxious. For he found no delight there and almost pushed the Inspector into a chair.

"Tell me the worst, Andrew. I ask for the worst—purposely. I'd love to hear the story."

"I'm not thinkin' that you'll be lovin' it after you've heard it."

Anthony was unperturbed.

"Oh? Why not?"

"Because the 'Yard' isn't goin' to show up in too good a light. That's why not."

Anthony grinned.

"My dear Andrew, this isn't the first time that I've worked with the 'Yard', is it? Lord, man—have a heart."

MacMorran smiled ruefully.

"I reckon I deserve all that. I stuck it right out in front of you, and I'd be the first to blame you if you'd missed kickin' it."

"Thank you, Andrew. The open goal, like the full toss, to leg, should always be accepted thankfully, and with a truly grateful heart. Now tell me the worst, as I asked you."

MacMorran coughed.

"When our young lady left here, she took a taxi-cab."

Anthony Bathurst nodded.

"I'm aware of that. I watched what happened from my window here. Well, go on."

MacMorran rubbed the end of his nose with his finger.

"Well, our car wasn't far away, as you also know, and we trailed off behind this young lady of yours in the taxi. There was I, with Chatterton and Evershed, thinkin' that I'm sittin' nice and pretty. Our driver knew exactly what was wanted and there was the stage all set and the bouquets for the curtain. Following anybody is one of the first of the elementary principles of the detective's art."

"You sound like Gordon Harker. Go on." Anthony grinned at him.

"Well, away we flew, and all went merry and bright. The lights held us up at one or two of the corners, but generally speakin' we did a fair bat for best part of the time. We were headin' in the direction of the East End and eventually we found ourselves runnin' down past Aldgate Station and 'The Three Nuns', towards the East India Dock Road. Suddenly, not so very far past Gardiner's corner, I saw the car in front of us draw in to the side of the road and pull up. The driver came round from the front of the car, opened the door and stood there expectantly.

But Lord bless you, not a blessed soul emerged. His face was a study. The car was stone-blind empty."

Anthony grinned again at the expression on the Inspector's face.

"Ah-ha!" he said, "and what happened after that?"

"Well, that's what I was on the point of tellin' you. I gave orders for our car to pull up just behind. Like most of his fraternity, caught in the clutch of similar circumstances, my driver friend in front fell back upon the strength of his vocabulary. He was good—believe me! A masterly performance! It will be some time before I shall hear his equal. In his time—amongst other exercises—he must have dropped wet fish on the necks of Customs officers. But you can take it from me that there wasn't the slightest sign or trace of the young lady who had left your flat here and got in that darned taxi. In other words, Mr. Bathurst, we had been sold a very substantial pup. An Alsatian!"

Anthony's face was grave. This was worse than he had anticipated. He realized how serious it might prove to be that his shot had missed fire. Before he could speak, MacMorran was in again.

"The question now arises—how was it done? How was a young girl able to get out of a car like that whilst it was in motion? That's what's eatin' me at the moment. Can't find the answer." MacMorran ran his fingers through his hair.

"Simple enough," returned Anthony.

MacMorran stared at him. There was incredulity in the stare. Anthony went on.

"Tell me this. Did you actually speak to the driver of the other car when he was reciting his thirty-nine articles?"

"Ay! But I'm not sure that I did the right thing. I've thought it over several times on my way here since."

Anthony waxed sarcastic.

"Oh—never, Andrew! You astound me! 'Pon my soul, you've handled this affair about as brainily as I handled 'The Fortescue Candle'."

MacMorran blinked at him.

"You think I did do wrong, then, in holdin' converse with that driver?"

"Oh—without a doubt."

"Why are you so certain, man?"

"He was an accomplice—that's why. Hand in glove with her. He and the girl deliberately led you to the East India Dock Road, or wherever it was, and staged that performance for your especial benefit."

MacMorran swore beautifully. Anthony shook his head despairingly.

"You're not in that driver's class, Andrew. You need a large capital 'L'. Take a course of lessons from him."

MacMorran argued.

"Why are you so *certain* that he was an accomplice? If he were, then he was also a damned good actor."

"I saw the taxi come up when Bright Eyes left my flat here. I saw the whole incident of its arrival from my window. He was waiting there for her by arrangement, and if only from the way that she got in, I'm positive that there was an understanding of some sort between them. Your story of what happened afterwards only goes to confirm that opinion."

"I'm not concerned with the way the hussy got in. I'm concerned with the way she got out."

"As I said, Andrew, an excessively simple procedure. She got into another car. Does that surprise you?"

MacMorran wrinkled his brows at Anthony's statement.

"Where?"

"At one of your traffic signal hold-ups."

MacMorran looked dubiously at him.

"I had my eyes on that car for the entire time."

Anthony shook his head. The Inspector shifted his ground somewhat.

"For ninety per cent of the time, say!"

"It was the other ten per cent that mattered. At one of the stops another car crept up in front of yours, sidled up to hers, two doors were opened when the cars were sufficiently close together, and our lady friend was transferred, self-transferred if you like, from the one that didn't count, to the one that did.

It could be accomplished almost in a second. What a girl!"
Anthony's grey eyes gleamed.

"You seem pleased about something, Mr. Bathurst. Sorry I
can't share your enthusiasm."

"Come, come. Be a sportsman, Andrew, and do the Gunga
Din stuff. Hand it to her. She bested you and she bested me. But
tomorrow, my dear young lady, has a knack of being also a day."

"That's cold comfort for me, Mr. Bathurst, however you may
feel about it."

"What does Sir Austin say?"

"I've yet to hear. 'Twill be good, I'm thinkin'. Well worth
hearin'."

"What name did the driver give you? You took his number,
of course?"

"Ay. I've got the name here." He fished in his pocket. "Here it
is. Holmes. That was the name. S. Holmes."

Anthony stared at him.

"What's the address, MacMorran? 221B, Baker Street? Don't
tell me it is, for the love of Mike. I shall go mad and bite somebody."

The Inspector stared at the paper in amazement. "You've
clicked, Mr. Bathurst. Sure enough it is. Do you know the chap,
then?"

"Oh, MacMorran, this is the greyest day of your career. That
initial 'S' you've got there, stands for 'Sherlock'. That girl of mine
as you called her just now has twisted you beautifully. Not one
pup, but the full litter—can't you see it now?"

MacMorran swore again.

"You're improving," remarked Anthony. "I doubt whether
you'll need that full course, after all."

MacMorran continued steadily on his way.

"On second thoughts, I'm sure that you won't," contributed
Mr. Bathurst.

MacMorran went from triumph to triumph. Anthony
listened in open-mouthed admiration.

IF ANTHONY Lotherington Bathurst were destined to remember for a considerable length of time the day that brought to his flat the beautiful but mysterious lady, he was destined to remember the day that followed it even more so. Sir Austin Kemble telephoned him about a quarter to five in the afternoon. Anthony, who had been out for the better part of the day, picked up the receiver, when the summons came, rather wearily. But the Commissioner's opening words dispelled his weariness and stung him into something like activity.

"That hurts me, sir," he said eventually. "I don't know how you feel about it. But it definitely hurts me. I feel humiliated about it. What's that?—you're coming over to me now? Good! I was just going out again, but I'll wait here for you."

Anthony settled himself down to wait for the Commissioner. This latest piece of news was terrible. He refused to think until he was in possession of more data. Sir Austin's car was outside the flat in quick time. Emily let the Commissioner in, and Anthony turned from his chair to see both him and Inspector MacMorran crossing the threshold.

The Commissioner got down to business immediately.

"This is a bad business, Bathurst."

"Sit down, sir, and give me all the details."

Sir Austin Kemble turned to Inspector MacMorran.

"You start, MacMorran, do you mind? You know more about it than I do. You had the first news—before I got it."

The Inspector nodded.

"Very good, sir." He then addressed Anthony. "Our first intimation at the 'Yard' was at about a quarter past one this afternoon. Young Somerset's confidential clerk 'phoned through to us. Digby, I fancy his name is. The gist of what he had to say to us was this. His guv'nor had disappeared during the morning. That was the message he gave us, exactly as we received it."

He looked at Sir Austin Kemble.

"Shall I keep on, Sir Austin—or will you?"

The Commissioner shook his head.

"You carry on, Inspector."

"Just a minute." The interruption came from Anthony. "This is important. Where were your men at the time? The men that were detailed to look after Somerset?"

"In their usual place, in his outer office. When he was on the premises, they were there. They had been there since he arrived in the morning. I arranged that with Sir Austin here."

"What happened, then?" Anthony's tones were crisp and curt.

"Digby's story was roughly this. Somewhere about eleven o'clock, he said, young Somerset came into his room, closed the door carefully, and informed him that he had just had a mysterious telephone message. 'Mysterious' was the word that was used. I sounded Digby thoroughly on the point. I guessed you'd ask me about it, so I made sure of matters beforehand." MacMorran's voice was dry-toned. Anthony noticed it and smiled at the thrust.

"Go on," he contented himself with saying.

"Digby then stated that the young guv'nor had told him that the person who had 'phoned, wanted to meet him on the steps of St. Paul's Cathedral at noon exactly, because there was vital information 'to be passed on to him'. Digby then went on to say that he advised young Somerset to take no action whatever in the matter without first informing my chaps who were in his office. Somerset, who seemed terribly worried, replied that the person who had telephoned had stipulated that on no account must he do this. Unless the matter were treated in the strictest confidence there would be no assignation. Somerset must go to the place 'absolutely alone'. Then, says Digby, after he had told him that and without telling him for certain which way he was going to act in the matter, he dashed back into his own room. *He has not been seen again.* But Digby says that Somerset seemed very much impressed by the person who had telephoned. He makes that point strongly. There you are, Mr. Bathurst. That's the full story. You have it as I had it and as I gave it to the Commissioner of Police."

MacMorran stopped and wiped his forehead with his handkerchief. With this particular audience, the recital had rather worried him. Anthony looked towards Sir Austin.

"An amazing business, it seems to me, altogether. If Somerset kept this appointment, he obviously did so by *deliberately* avoiding the use of police protection. He *kept* the terms that had been imposed upon him. That is to say, entirely at his own risk. I feel a little better now that I've heard the Inspector's version of the affair. More than a little. Considerably."

Sir Austin Kemble emitted sounds that indicated disapproval.

"Inspector MacMorran," said Anthony, "have you checked up on any part of the story yet? The telephone-call?"

"Ay. The call came from the call-box in Alma Mater Row, near the Cathedral. The operator is prepared to swear on oath that the caller was a woman."

"Confirms Somerset's report to Digby, then, doesn't it? Any attempt to check up on the assignation itself?"

"Yes. From the police-constable on duty at the nearest point. But this hasn't proved too satisfactory, from our point of view, I regret to say."

MacMorran proceeded to enlarge on his statement.

"The constable, Butt, his name is, remembers that a young man, dressed very much as Somerset is said to have been, passed him about five minutes to twelve and made his way round St. Paul's Churchyard, but I fear that this won't be of very much use to us. There must be dozens of young men dressed like Somerset, and of Somerset's build and appearance, in a busy part of London at most moments during the working day."

"Did the constable notice anybody waiting about on the steps of the Cathedral who gave an impression that he or she was waiting to keep an assignation? It's a long shot, I know, with regard to that particular place and at that time of the day, but it's just possible that somebody might have been noticed."

The Inspector shook his head.

"No. Nothing doing."

Anthony thought hard.

"I take it that Somerset, when he left the office, did not *pass* your men who you say were waiting in the outer office?"

"They have all been questioned, and are positive, both individually and collectively, that Somerset did *not* leave the office by going *past* them. The room in which they were sitting at the time is not a big one; you know it yourself, Mr. Bathurst, you've been there, and there isn't the slightest doubt that, if Somerset had left the office that way, he must have been seen by them."

"Which proves that he went out by the exit at the rear of the building and therefore, as I said just now, for some unknown reason, deliberately evaded the vigilance of the men who had been put at his disposal for the purpose of his protection."

"There seems no doubt of that whatever, Mr. Bathurst. The Commissioner and I had already agreed upon the point."

Sir Austin broke in impulsively.

"Which fact alone, my dear Bathurst, lets us out to a considerable extent."

"When Somerset went, did he take anything with him? Have you heard? Can Digby tell you anything about that?"

"I've questioned him and he tells me that Somerset went back into his room quite casually, as it were. If he went out directly after, he must have gone just as he would have done had he popped out, for example, for a morning coffee."

"Seems incredible to me," interposed the Commissioner, "that a man of his age can be abducted from a place like the steps of St. Paul's Cathedral in broad daylight."

Anthony intervened.

"There are abductions—and abductions, Sir Austin. Abduction does not always mean force or assault. Something may have been put to young Somerset, arising out of which, he was *persuaded* to accompany someone somewhere. He might have walked off quite serenely with the person who was posing as his friend but who in reality may have been his bitterest enemy."

Sir Austin demurred.

"I might accept that, if this were the first chapter of the story, instead of being the third. How could the man have *possibly* been taken unawares? Here his father and his brother have both been recently murdered. He himself has been threatened, he is under police protection, and yet you are suggesting that he is ready to walk into a trap like this without taking any precautions. Why, the man should have been on his guard every moment of the day! He'd look at everything that was presented to him with the utmost care. No—I can't believe that he'd go off anywhere with anybody like a lamb which was being led to the slaughter. It doesn't make the slightest appeal to me."

"What you say is true—but only up to a point. You're presuming things. He mightn't visualize himself as a lamb and he might not *see* the spot of slaughter that was lurking in the undergrowth. I know perfectly well that an immense amount of what you said is absolutely true and sound. But you and I are judging the facts of the case as *we* see them and as *we* know them. You are inclined to forget that the situation in which he found himself may have developed in such a way, or may have been presented to him in such a manner, that he was forced to think that what he eventually did, he was doing for the best. You don't know what dazzling pictures were decked out in front of him to cause him to take the step that he did take."

Sir Austin nodded.

"I see your point, Bathurst, but, all the same, I can't imagine Somerset falling for any simple trick as you suggest he may have done. It must have been something pretty deep and desperate. However, it's no use talking about things, we must do something. What do you advise that we do?"

Anthony rose and paced the room.

"I don't know what we can do. I am still so much in the dark. I know that certain people interviewed David Somerset at East Brutton on the 12th of March in the smoke-room of the inn known as the 'Golden Lion'. That's point number one. I presume that they wanted something that was in David Somerset's possession, and which he, evidently, was unwilling to give them. I say 'unwilling' in the light of what happened afterwards. That's point number two. I know that David Somerset and his son, Geoffrey Somerset, were found dead in a copse near East Brutton some time afterwards. That's point number three. I know that an attack has been made on the remaining son, Gerald Somerset, during the last few days, and that he was warned by all of us here that he must regard his own life as being endangered. That's point number four. I know now that there is a strong probability that he has already gone, or will eventually go, the same way as his father and brother. That's point number five."

Anthony Bathurst paused. He stood for a moment, gazing in front of him, lost in thought. Sir Austin Kemble and Inspector MacMorran each felt an atmosphere of tension. Although they would not have admitted it, or even been able to explain why it was, each experienced a sense of relief when Mr. Bathurst proceeded:

"In addition to the five points that I have enumerated, I have in my possession various other but *conflicting* data. I know that Miss Masters, the shorthand typist on the staff of Somerset and Sons, has rather suddenly tendered her resignation. I know that an exceedingly charming lady, acting as an emissary of the people who interviewed David Somerset at East Brutton, has called upon me in response to an attractively worded advertisement which I caused to be inserted in the London dailies and not only 'walked out' on me but at the same time took as many honours with her as she left behind with me. MacMorran here will also most generously subscribe to that opinion. But what I *don't* know is *what* David Somerset had that these people so badly wanted, and why it is that Gerald Somerset evidently had the same thing *but* did not know that he had it. You see, Sir Austin, the deficiency in my knowledge ties my hands so completely that I honestly don't know how I can advise you."

Inspector MacMorran punctuated these statements of Mr. Bathurst's with a series of slow nods. He spoke to Anthony Bathurst.

"A description of the girl that called upon you and then took me for that car ride has been circulated in all the likely places. Nobody seems to know her, which proves that she can't be a 'regular' or even well known, socially, as a member of one of the 'Bright Young People' sets. Having seen her once, nobody would be likely to forget her. That's the trouble." Anthony turned and looked directly at the Commissioner. Sir Austin saw from the expression on his face that he had come to a decision.

"I'll tell you what I'm going to do, sir. I'm going round to the Somerset offices again. Gerald Somerset went out from the rear of that building somewhere about midday today, and if I take another look round there I may perhaps find something to show me the way that he went. For once, at any rate, the scent should be moderately warm. What do you say, Inspector? Does the idea appeal to you? Will you come with me?"

"I will that," returned Inspector MacMorran. "For, as a matter of fact, I'd thought of doing the same thing myself."

"Report to me later," said Sir Austin Kemble, "and for heaven's sake bring me something on which I can get to work. To tell you the truth, the damn' case is getting on my nerves."

Anthony turned again to the door to close it behind the Commissioner.

"One thing I would like to know, sir," he remarked, as they descended the staircase, "and that's this. What was the real reason why Mr. Gerald Somerset didn't hit it off with Miss Maud Masters?"

Sir Austin looked at him blankly and shook his head.

"I quite agree, sir," said Mr. Bathurst warmly. "That's exactly how I feel about it."

Sir Austin frowned heavily.

CHAPTER XII
THE LAST OF THE SOMERSETS

ANTHONY'S promised visit to the offices in Boot Lane unhappily availed him nothing. As he had promised, MacMorran accompanied him. They looked carefully through Gerald Somerset's room, Miss Masters's room, saw Digby in his room, and were conducted by him to the back of the building and the door thereof through which Gerald Somerset had passed that day to keep his mysterious assignation. Their tour failed to discover the slightest hint of anything that might reasonably be regarded as suspicious. The result was, the inevitable result, that the "damn' case" affected Sir Austin Kemble's nervous system more than ever. For the next fortnight Anthony and the Inspector found a blank wall facing them in every direction to which they turned.

A month passed. Easter came and went. Not a word or a whisper reached anybody of Gerald Somerset or of Gerald Somerset's fate. The unknown lady who had called upon Anthony at his flat might never have existed, beyond his imagination, for all the tangible evidence that she subsequently gave of that existence. Sir Austin telephoned several times. Sir Austin called at Anthony's flat in person. Sir Austin sent Inspector MacMorran. To both of them Anthony expressed repeatedly the statement that events and lack of evidence had beaten him. Even an effort to find the taxi-driver with the rich vocabulary who had driven the unknown Mademoiselle to the East India Dock Road, had failed. The number-plate that the vehicle had carried had been a false one. That fact was the only one which MacMorran had been able to establish with any certainty.

On the last day of April, however, the extraordinary case took yet another even more sensational turn. A boy walking along the shore at Friningham, that morning, on a search for a pocket-knife that he had lost the night before, came upon the body of a young man lying face downwards in the sand. He at once informed the police, who came to the body as their Gloucestershire colleagues had come to the bodies of David and Geoffrey Somerset, and from the description that was already in their possession and documentary evidence in the man's pockets, found it to be the body of Gerald Somerset. He was dressed exactly as he had been when he disappeared from his offices, and his wrists and ankles were tied together by thick cord. There was no doubt from the appearance of the body that it had been in the water for some time.

The Friningham police, realizing that the case had such important antecedents, at once telephoned Scotland Yard. Sir

Austin Kemble brought the news to Anthony immediately. Mr. Bathurst listened to the story that he heard in grave silence.

"Wrists tied and ankles tied, eh?"

Sir Austin nodded.

"Yes—and I've also had this from the local police, it's not appeared in any of the papers up to now—the poor fellow had been knocked on the head and shot before they put him in the water."

"Murder, of course."

"Oh—undoubtedly."

"Been certainly identified?"

"Yes. The Friningham people saw to that, directly they suspected who it was. Mrs. Somerset has been down, went along almost at once, in fact. I believe that she took the clerk, Digby, down with her. Acted very sensibly all through. 'Phoned the Boot Lane office and fixed him up to accompany her."

"H'm! Think you and I had better go along, too, sir. Take MacMorran with us. What do you say? Run down in my car, shall we?"

"That suits me, Bathurst. If I can use your 'phone, I'll fix it right now."

"Go ahead, sir. I'll get along to the garage at once and see about the car. Tell MacMorran I shall be away within half an hour. Arrange about picking him up somewhere. I'll bring the car round to the front. That's on, then."

An hour later saw the Bathurst car flash through Ilford *en route* for the seaside town of Friningham. On they went through Romford, Brentwood, Ingatestone, the home of the Somersets, and came to Colchester. Lunch here at the Albert Hotel proved a pleasant interlude. Friningham, that select East Coast watering-place, was reached late in the afternoon.

"They're meeting us here," said Sir Austin Kemble; "I've seen to that. You want to go straight ahead to the mortuary, don't you?"

Anthony nodded.

"I want to have a look at one or two things. Think I'd better. Want to satisfy my mind. There are points about the case that are worrying me. Really worrying me. Where do you want me to pull up, sir? Any preference?"

"Outside the railway-station. I thought that would do as well as anywhere else. The mortuary is close by."

"I haven't been to Friningham," remarked Anthony, "since we looked into that strange case that is now known as 'The Five Red Fingers'. Remember, Sir Austin? When the millionaire, Julius Maitland, was found dead in the bungalow in Pin Hole Way? If my memory serve me properly, we worked on that case with a Sergeant Mansfield."

Sir Austin chuckled at Mr. Bathurst's reminiscences.

"Quite right, Bathurst. And it's Sergeant Mansfield whom you're going to meet again today. The station's on the right if you keep straight on. But you probably remember it."

Sergeant Mansfield was waiting for them as they drove up. He saluted the Commissioner and Inspector MacMorran appropriately and shook hands heartily with Anthony Bathurst.

"Glad to see you again, sir. And the years have rested lightly on you, if I may say so, sir."

"Thank you, Sergeant," returned Anthony. "That's charming of you. You don't look so bad yourself. It's almost incredible to think that it's seven years since we solved that little mystery of the dead man who spoke on the telephone, isn't it? And now we're confronted by another tangle of events. Where's the body, Sergeant? Take the Commissioner and me along to it, will you?"

"The mortuary is quite close handy, sir. If you park your car over there and then come along with me, Mr. Bathurst, perhaps the Commissioner and Inspector MacMorran would be so good as to join us."

Anthony saw to the car, came back to the Commissioner and the Inspector, and a few minutes' walking brought them to the small building where lay the body of Gerald Somerset. Sergeant Mansfield, as they entered, handed the Commissioner a paper with certain notes on it.

"There's Dr. Carey's report, sir. I brought it along for you. Body been in the water for some weeks, with a blow on the head from some blunt instrument. Besides this, the man had also been shot through the head. The cord from the wrists and ankles is over there. I hope that Dr. Carey will be along here to have a word with you very shortly. I gave him your message."

Anthony nodded. "H'm! Drowned, shot, and knocked on the head—meant making sure, didn't they!"

The four men approached the dead body on the slab. The Sergeant moved the sheet with which it had been covered. Anthony had been prepared for startling changes. He knew the effect upon the human body of prolonged immersion. But he saw at once beyond any doubt that he looked upon the face of Gerald Somerset. The features were swollen and bloated and discoloured, but here lay the man without a doubt whom he had met and with whom he had spoken during the latter days of the previous month of March. The face, neck and throat and hands, all the parts that had been uncovered in the water, seemed to have suffered most.

"What was in his pockets, Sergeant? Anything much?"

"No, sir. Two or three shillings in money—I can tell you how much exactly later on if you want me to—and a pocket-book. In the pocket-book was a visiting-card of his own, and a letter from Sir Austin Kemble."

"That's quite right. I remember. I did write to him a few days before he disappeared. With reference to the arrangements I had made about his protection. That's quite in order, Sergeant."

As the Commissioner finished speaking, a man entered the building with a quick step and an air of brisk efficiency.

"Here's Dr. Carey," said Sergeant Mansfield. "He's been as good as his word."

He introduced Dr. Carey to Sir Austin Kemble, Inspector MacMorran, and Anthony Bathurst. The doctor wasted no time over preliminaries and got down to facts immediately.

"Man was killed before he was shoved into the water." The doctor was emphatic.

"Sure of that?" said Anthony.

"Oh, positive," replied the doctor with a quick movement of the head. "He has a fractured skull and a bullet through his head.

No need to look any further. I should say that the blow on the head killed him and the shot was fired to make sure of things."

"Been dead for long?" inquired Mr. Bathurst.

Dr. Carey pursed his lips.

"Hard to say. To be exact, that is. Some weeks, though, without a doubt."

"So he was killed," thought Anthony, "either directly or soon after he was decoyed from the office in Boot Lane."

MacMorran gestured to the sergeant. The latter, understanding, drew the sheet again over the dead man's face. MacMorran turned away from the slab as though he had seen all that he wanted to see.

"Any watch on the body when it was found?" remarked Anthony.

"Yes," replied Sergeant Mansfield. "A wrist-watch. Ruined, of course, by the action of the sea water."

"What was the time that the watch showed? Any idea?"

"It had stopped at three-fifteen."

"That means nothing, of course. There wasn't much point in my asking the question. We don't know how long Somerset lay dead before his body was put into the water. We don't know either *where* it was put into the water, though I suppose that one could bank on a spot not so very far from here."

Sir Austin exhibited signs of impatience. The surroundings were far from his liking.

"If you've no more questions to ask the doctor or the sergeant, Bathurst, I think that we might as well go. I don't see that we can gain anything more here. Of all the clueless cases, this seems to me to be the worst that we've ever tackled."

Inspector MacMorran rubbed the ridge of his jaw.

"There are two lengths of cord over there, sir. We ought to be remembering them."

Anthony Bathurst motioned to Sergeant Mansfield.

"The Inspector's right. Let me have a look at those pieces of cord, Sergeant, will you?"

Sergeant Mansfield brought over the two pieces of cord as Mr. Bathurst had requested. Anthony looked at them carefully. The Commissioner of Police, with the Inspector and the sergeant, stood round him.

"Do you know what these are?" he inquired.

"Yes," returned Inspector MacMorran. "I did as soon as I set eyes on them."

"What are they, then?"

The Inspector smiled knowingly at Mr. Bathurst's last question.

"Pieces of what is usually known as 'clothes-line'. Don't you think I know all about washing day?"

Sergeant Mansfield smiled.

"I agree with you, Inspector," said Anthony. "We shall probably find clothes-line of this kind in nearly every house in the country. As far as I can see there is nothing to distinguish it from thousands of pieces that we should almost certainly find in, literally, thousands of houses."

He tossed the two pieces of cord back to Sergeant Mansfield. It was on that note that what may be termed the first inquiry into the case of the three dead Somersets concluded.

Mrs. Somerset, the widow of David, lived on in the comparative seclusion and tranquillity of Clutton Chase, near Ingatestone. Irene Pearce, the more than friend of Geoffrey Somerset, grieved for a time, and then went back to the films and made a new picture. Maud Masters, the zealous and efficient shorthand-typist of the Somerset offices in Boot Lane must have found employment elsewhere, for she disappeared from the circle of her normal acquaintance almost as completely as the firm for which she had previously worked, disappeared from commercial activity. Anthony Bathurst tried angle after angle in an attempt to find a solution. But try as he would, he could hit upon nothing that turned out to be of any real importance.

The Commissioner was persistent in his appeals to him that the truth should be extracted from the case before all the scent became too cold and everything else too late, but his appeals were unavailing.

Suddenly, however, Anthony came to a new decision. He immediately telephoned to Inspector MacMorran. MacMorran listened to what Mr. Bathurst had to say with grave composure.

"Very good, Mr. Bathurst," he remarked, after he had heard Anthony through. "I'll come along with you this evening and we'll have another look at the place. As you say, Digby won't be with us this time, and there may be something there which we missed. Right you are—seven o'clock tonight, outside number twenty-two Boot Lane."

"Inspector," returned Anthony, "I shall be there. Let's hope that it will be a case of 'third time lucky'!"

CHAPTER XIII
THE DOOR IN THE WALL

WITH the death of Gerald Somerset, the last of the three Somersets to die, the firm of chemists that had been known and had done business as Somerset and Sons, passed out of existence. Digby, remaining on the bridge until almost the last possible moment, had seen everything through that he was competent to execute, and had then found another position with a similar firm, the business address of which was but a short distance away.

Anthony met the Inspector at the time and place as he had arranged, and using the key with which the latter had furnished himself, they entered the Somerset building once again in the hope that this latest investigation would provide them with something more tangible than it had been their lot to obtain on either of the previous occasions. Although the offices had been untenanted for little more than a fortnight, it seemed to Anthony that they already possessed that atmosphere of disuse and decay which seems to belong, perhaps, to an empty city office more than to anything else.

A visit to the outer room and the room where Anthony had first interviewed Gerald Somerset yielded them nothing. The next two rooms produced no better result. One had been used, they knew, in David Somerset's time, by the two brothers, and the other room opposite had been Leonard Digby's. Anthony and the Inspector came out again into the corridor.

"Which," asked Mr. Bathurst, "was the office used by the general staff? Because we've never yet seen it."

"Probably that one, I should say," returned the Inspector. He pointed down the corridor.

"Let's see where we are and what we've covered," contributed Mr. Bathurst. "First of all, there was the small outer office where your men were on the day that Gerald Somerset disappeared. David Somerset's own room, the room used by the sons, Digby's room, and the small room that we assume was used by the efficient shorthand-typist, Miss Masters. It looks to me as though you were right and that that door down there is the door of the office where the general staff did their stuff. At any rate, we'll go down there and have a look at it."

Anthony and the Inspector made their way down the corridor. The room which they now entered would house, Anthony estimated at a quick glance, about eight people. There seemed nothing unusual about the room to excite his interest or his comment. He and the Inspector were about to make their exit when a thought struck him.

"Where does that door lead to?" he asked. He pointed across the room to a small door in the left-hand corner of the wall. "There can't be another room beyond there. There isn't enough space. I think that we ought to investigate."

MacMorran grunted. They crossed the room and tried the door. It opened. Anthony and the Inspector found themselves at the head of a flight of stone steps. Mr. Bathurst noticed that there was an electric switch conveniently to hand. He used it. They saw a stone staircase of about eighteen steps running down away to their right. At the top of the stone staircase was piled a heap of miscellaneous books and papers. They examined several of them but found nothing that seemed to be of more than ordinary importance.

"Addresses, accounts, and registers of invoices," remarked Anthony. "Nothing much more than that, I'm afraid."

The Inspector nodded his agreement.

"Come down these stairs, MacMorran, and see what's at the bottom."

On the fifth stair the Inspector suddenly stopped.

"What's the matter, MacMorran?"

Anthony saw from his companion's face that at last something had happened which was going to count in their investigation. The lines of MacMorran's face were grim.

"Why, man, look here! You're not going to tell me that you don't know what that is?"

The Inspector pointed to the stone step. Anthony's eyes followed the direction of his pointing finger. He saw a dull smear on the edge of the step.

"Unless I'm very much mistaken, Mr. Bathurst," said MacMorran, "there's been blood spilt on this step."

"I think you're right. Interesting." Mr. Bathurst passed on down the staircase. "Come to the bottom with me, Inspector. Who knows what we may find farther on?"

At the foot of the staircase, on the right-hand side, was another door. Anthony tried it. It was locked.

Anthony turned in disappointment to the Inspector. "What do we do now, friend Andrew?"

"Leave that to me, Mr. Bathurst. I came prepared for emergencies of this kind."

The Inspector took a screw-driver from his pocket and, wielding it dexterously in a series of quick manipulations, soon had the door open for them. "Good work, MacMorran," said Mr. Bathurst. They passed through into a room with a low ceiling, that had evidently been used for some time as a store-room. Shelves, well-made and recently painted, ran all round it at a convenient height, on which were, in the main, various bundles and packets of used papers.

"This store-room, Inspector," said Anthony, "brings you out at the rear of the premises. Look, that door over there must be close to the other exit door where you and I looked round that time when we came before. See where I mean?" MacMorran nodded. He walked across to the place that Anthony had pointed out. Before he came to it, Anthony, who was following him, heard him give a low whistle and saw him point again to the floor.

"Look here, Mr. Bathurst, this is where the dirty work was done. Look at the stain here on the floor! There's been more blood here, but it's dried up. How does this fit in with the rest of the story?"

"Just what I was wondering, MacMorran." Anthony leant against one of the shelves. MacMorran crossed to the farther door and opened it.

"Here you are," he said. "As I thought, it comes out just opposite to the staircase leading to Somerset's room that you and I went down that evening a month ago."

Anthony nodded almost mechanically. A new angle to the problem had been presented to him. Whose blood was this, and how had it got here in the Somerset offices? As far as he could see at the moment, this must be the spot, or near to the spot, where Gerald Somerset had been knocked on the head. In what circumstances could young Somerset have been attacked down here in the basement of his own offices? It seemed to him, as he looked at the problem at that minute, that the attack could have been made only by somebody either completely or partially in Gerald Somerset's confidence. Musing thus, he heard the Inspector close the outer door and come back into the store-room.

"I'm going back," declared Mr. Bathurst. "*We* are going back. Back to the Somerset private room. I remember seeing something in there which on the surface looked entirely commonplace but which, nevertheless, I feel we should have looked at. We will repair the omission. Come with me, MacMorran, and I'll show you what I mean."

Anthony and the Inspector went back by the way that they had come. They came again to Gerald Somerset's room. The room that had been his father's.

"That's what I mean, friend Andrew," remarked Anthony. "Unless I'm mistaken, that is young Gerald Somerset's office-coat. We should have looked at it before, you know. Experience has taught me that office-coats often hold important correspondence. Let's see if this can tell us anything."

Inspector MacMorran took down the coat from the hook where it hung and carefully went through the various pockets. Anthony watched him intensely.

"I congratulate you, Mr. Bathurst," said the Inspector eventually, "upon a brilliant piece of deduction. Every pocket is empty."

Anthony grinned.

"Bad luck! Would you have believed it? Gerald Somerset must have been a much more careful man than most city men I have known. Ah, well, we mustn't complain. We can't expect everything to go our way. We've discovered more this evening than for a good many weeks. I think we'll be getting back." He walked to the window and stood there looking out upon the river. "Yes," he said, turning, "we'll be getting back."

They retraced their steps to the front entrance of the office. Anthony pointed to the big wire-meshed post-basket attached to the door.

"Although it has gone out of business, the firm still receives correspondence, you see."

He bent down to look more closely. MacMorran, watching him, saw his body stiffen. Mr. Bathurst rose, straightened himself and spoke to the Inspector.

"Who is it, I wonder," he said quietly, "that writes personal letters to David Somerset and marks them 'Urgent'? To David Somerset, mind you, who has been dead, as all the world knows, for nearly two months."

MacMorran saw the force of the remark, and waited patiently. The two men stood there. Anthony watched the Inspector. Then prompted him.

"I suggest, with all humility, that official Scotland Yard acts. More than that—that it acts immediately."

The Inspector rubbed his ear thoughtfully. He put a question. "You mean by that, Mr. Bathurst?"

Anthony pointed again to the wire-meshed basket.

"I suggest, Inspector, that acting in your official capacity you get your hooks, as my old friend Inspector Baddeley of the Sussex Constabulary used to put it, on that letter. It's addressed to *David* Somerset, remember. Not to either Gerald or Geoffrey, mark you. The trouble seemed to start with David, you know, MacMorran. Who knows? That envelope at which we are looking may contain the vital clue for which we have been searching all this time. It would be criminal to neglect such a heaven-sent opportunity."

MacMorran continued to rub his ear.

"It's an entirely easy matter," declared Anthony. "The basket is only hooked on to the door. Look—here and there! A child could lift it off. An intelligent child. It was a job, probably, that the Somerset office-boy had to do as part of his (daily duty. Every morning. Came in at a quarter to nine, I expect, so that he could get on with his task before the others arrived. And then got an occasional Saturday morning off in lieu of the extra time. You could lift if off, you know, MacMorran! Come, man—'there is a tide in the affairs of men which, taken at the flood, leads on to fortune'."

The Inspector grinned at the quotation.

"Ay, and it's often misfortune, so I'm told. Still, on this occasion, I'll take your advice. As you say, there may be something here that's worth getting hold of. We'll have a look."

He bent down and carefully lifted off the wire-basket. He placed it on the floor in front of them. Solemnly and with infinite care, even for Inspector Andrew MacMorran, he took out the letter that might matter. Anthony then passed, he himself considered, the longest minute that he had ever passed or would ever be likely to pass. In addition, to the longest, the most agitated, the most elated, and, with all of those, the most impatient. Not sixty, but six hundred seconds seemed to tick by. He murmured to the Inspector:

"Why *do* people write? Why must they? When it is not the most sordid of trades, it usually becomes a mere fatuous assertion of one's egotism. Well—what's it all about, Andrew?"

He saw that MacMorran was shaking a dubious head. Anthony rallied him on his tardiness.

"You discipline my curiosity and you exercise my patience."

The Inspector made no reply beyond giving him the letter.

"It beats me, Mr. Bathurst. Read it for yourself." Anthony took the letter from the Inspector and read it:

March 10th.

Dear Mr. Somerset,

One cannot be too precise as to your instructions. At 2.15 p.m. in the smoke-room of the 'Golden Lion', High St., East Brutton. Inasmuch as it would be a blazing indiscretion for you to come by car, the 10.22 train from Paddington will suit you admirably. It is timed to arrive at East Brutton at 1.57, which will give you a margin of eighteen minutes to reach the rendezvous. You will find that this is ample. Actually the walk from the station will not take you more than four minutes at the outside, so that you will be in no way pressed for time and can take matters comfortably. When you reach the hotel don't ask for me by name. With so much at stake, from the point of view of each of us, you will readily see the soundness of the reason behind this precaution. When you arrive, go at once to the smoke-room. I shall be there waiting for you. I shall be wearing a dinner jacket with white vest, black bow, black studs and links, and a white gardenia. For my own part, I could never understand why His late Majesty, King George the Fifth of Blessed Memory, preferred the carnation to the gardenia for the purpose of sartorial decoration. But there you are, de gusti-bus non disputandum est. Till next Thursday, then, and in the very strictest confidence, I remain, your cheerful but unwilling victim, Adam Antine.

Anthony, reading, was stung to intense feeling. Pregnant words were in the letter, that he had seen, read, and recognized. His throat was dry with excitement. His pulses pounded.

"Well," demanded Inspector MacMorran curiously, "what do you make of it?"

"Andrew MacMorran," cried Mr. Bathurst, his voice ringing, "do you know what you've got here?"

"I think I'm only just beginning to realize it. I didn't take it all in the first time that I read it. It's the original letter to David Somerset making the appointment at East Brutton."

"Undoubtedly! Look here at the date, man! The 10th of March! David Somerset kept his appointment two days after this was written. On the 12th of March."

"And died!"

"And died, MacMorran."

"Question now, Mr. Bathurst. Two questions, rather! Who is this man Antine? And where do we find him?"

Anthony shook his head.

"Two more questions to add on to those, Inspector. More interesting than yours."

"Oh! And what are they?"

Mr. Bathurst answered softly:

"Who is *Miss* Antine? And where do we find her? I begin to see light, Andrew."

"As long as you see only light, I don't mind. I'll be satisfied with 'light'. I had a feeling that you were lettin' your eyes dwell on something more than light. For no man's mind is clear when it's blurged up with the consideration of the other sex. Not even yours, Mr. Bathurst. But tell me of your illumination."

Anthony's grey eyes twinkled at MacMorran's philosophy.

"You're an incarnate question, Andrew. Now I'll tell you something. Do you know, Inspector, if I didn't know the truth of it, if I hadn't traced David Somerset to the 'Golden Lion', East Brutton, *myself*, days and weeks before we find this letter—I should be inclined to regard it as a fake!"

MacMorran was startled.

"A fake? How do you mean?"

"A blind. A false clue to lure us away from the truth. *Planted* here for us. But why in the name of all that's wonderful, MacMorran, send this letter through the post to David Somerset *now*? Stay! Half a minute, though. What's the date of the post-mark?"

MacMorran turned over the envelope.

"The 10th of May. The murders were on the 12th of March, we think. *That is nearly two months after* the death of David and Geoffrey Somerset."

"Extraordinary," declared Anthony. "I don't get it. Why send to a man something which he must have had before?"

"Or a *copy*."

"Or a copy, as you say—let's look at it again, Inspector."

The two of them examined the letter.

"This is the original letter, in my opinion. Not a copy. It's creased a bit—look at it. Gives a general impression of having been handled before. Look at this—and that; don't you think so?"

MacMorran grunted acquiescence. Anthony compared letter with envelope.

"Yes," he said at length, "I stick to my opinion. This is the original letter that David Somerset had in March. Look here again." He held out both the letter and the envelope. "The colour's the same but the texture of the paper's different from the texture of the envelope. The envelope paper is of inferior quality. No doubt about that, is there?"

"Doesn't prove much, though, does it?"

"Only tends to confirm my theory. It certainly does that. The more I look at it the more extraordinary I think it is."

Inspector MacMorran rubbed the ridge of his jaw thoughtfully.

"Is it possible that the man Antine who we presume wrote the letter to David Somerset in the first place, *didn't know* that David Somerset was dead?"

Anthony looked at him fixedly.

"Now, that's interesting. In what circumstances could that lack of knowledge be a possibility? That's what we must look at. The news was published in the Press. It was the talk of the time, on everybody's tongue, in everybody's mind. Let's see now—where could Antine have been for the news not to have reached him? Are there any reasonable conditions under which that might have happened?"

MacMorran ticked off certain possibilities on his finger-tips.

"One—prison—he might have missed the news in the paper; two—in a hospital, seriously ill; three, abroad. Four . . ." He hesitated. "None of 'em's very convincing, is it?"

Anthony smiled at his predicament and shook his head.

"Afraid not, Andrew. Besides, I've thought of something else which makes me think, also, that your suggestion's a wrong one."

"What's that, Mr. Bathurst?"

"Why, this. And you can't refute it. The girl who called upon me at my flat, whom it pleased me to describe as Miss Antine just now—I admit that I took a longish shot over that—she knew that David Somerset was dead all right. I'm positive of that."

"Did she say so?" MacMorran eyed him curiously.

"Not in so many words."

"Why are you so positive, then? As a rule you're a man who doesn't jump to conclusions."

Anthony smiled at him again.

"Oh—I'm not jumping to conclusions, as you call it, Andrew. Far from it. The whole of our conversation left me in no doubt *that she knew*. Otherwise certain of her statements would have been entirely meaningless. Most of the edifice which she and I built up was foundationed on such knowledge. Don't run your head against it. She knew all right, believe me."

"Well, then, Mr. Bathurst, it beats me altogether. Why does Antine send this letter to David Somerset, who's had it, we say, before, and who's been dead a couple of months? Answer me that, if you can?"

"You're presuming something, you know," replied Anthony thoughtfully. "In fact, we've both been presuming something. All the time. Neither of us has been as bright as we might have been."

MacMorran regarded him almost suspiciously. He knew his Bathurst.

"Oh, and what is it that we've been presumin'?"

Anthony pressed.

"Do a bit of thinking, Mac! Use that grey matter of yours. See whether you can come to the same idea that I have."

The Inspector thought and shook his head.

"Not sure what you mean. Might not be the same as mine. Tell me."

"Why this, of course. We've been reckoning all along that Antine, who wrote the letter, has also sent it to Somerset on this second occasion. Whereas there's no evidence whatever that he sent it any more than any other person in the world. Is there now? Let's be sensible over it. We accepted it as coming from Antine simply because Antine had evidently *once* put his name to it. Now do you see to where I'm getting?"

"Ay! I took the reasonable line, though, when we first looked at it, same as you did. It's reasonable, nine times out of ten, to assume that the person that signs a letter *does* send it to the person he writes to. You can't get away from that, Mr. Bathurst, can you?"

"In the ordinary course of events—no! But this isn't an ordinary letter, MacMorran, and the events generally are the reverse of ordinary. We may not know much about the case, but we do know that. Friend Andrew, the case grows more interesting than ever. It's beginning to get hold of me."

"You think so? *More* interesting?"

"I do. And a damned sight more complicated."

"Seems to me it should be clearer. We're on to this Adam Antine fellow. When we came here, we didn't even know of his existence. He seems to have enticed David Somerset and the first son to East Brutton. We've seen the very terms of the appointment—all that black coat and white gardenia business. Secret society stuff, I expect we shall find it is, when we do get at the truth."

"Somehow I don't think so. Looking at matters all round, that is. You may be right, of course. We shall see. But in this case I don't get the Mafia, or something like it, myself." Mr. Bathurst shook his head. "No, MacMorran," he continued. "I'm sorry, but I don't think so. The people who sent for David Somerset wanted something which at that time he possessed. We suspected that before we came here. Now, with this letter in our possession, we are moderately certain of it."

He put the letter into the envelope and handed it over to the Inspector.

"Consider some of the sentences in that letter. Take three of them as examples. 'Don't ask for me by name.' 'With so much at stake from the point of view of each of us.' 'Your cheerful but unwilling victim.' 'Victim', observe, MacMorran. When that first letter was written, Somerset was 'on top'. Antine was underneath. Then, before this second affair was *posted*, the positions became reversed. There's the question for you and me—did Antine *himself* reverse them? If not Antine—then who did? There, my dear Inspector, lies our problem. And it's a pretty one. Come on." He clapped the Inspector on the back. "I'll stand you a supper. I haven't taken you to Murillo's since we cleared up that amazing case known as 'The Fortescue Candle'. *Allons!*"

The Inspector obeyed with alacrity.

CHAPTER XIV
THE BATHURST ANALYSIS

ANTHONY Bathurst jotted down significant points. He was alone. The evening was chilly and because it was May, that elf of the East Wind, a fire burned brightly in the grate. One feature of his detailed analysis occupied a great deal of his attention. Or, rather, a combination of two features. *(a)* Digby saw a revolver on David Somerset's desk on the morning of the 12th of March *for the first time.* He had been in Somerset's confidence for a considerable number of years, but had never before noticed such a thing. *(b)* Irene Pearce discovered that Geoffrey Somerset carried a revolver with him on the evening of the 12th of March, when he had called upon her at the house in Chiswick—*for the first time.* She had been on intimate terms with him for a considerable time, but had never before noticed such a thing.

Extraordinary coincidence, thought Mr. Bathurst. What reason had caused the eldest Somerset and one of the two sons to be armed on this occasion? Try as he would, he could find no answer that satisfied him. What had the girl who had answered the "Agony" meant by the expression "put to one use"? This was the phrase that she had used. Whose blood was it, assuming that MacMorran and he were right, that had been spilled on the stone steps of the staircase at the back of the Somerset offices? Why had David been shot and Geoffrey died from a fractured skull? And Gerald—Finally, who had sent Antine's letter to David Somerset two months after his death? If not this man Antine himself—who then?

Mr. Bathurst stopped his meditation suddenly.

"Antine. A-N-T—he thought of the name scribbled on the newspaper they had found in Brutton copse. The name that he had taken almost at once to be 'Antigua', the name of Irene Pearce's house. How if that name had been of a *man* and not of an *address*? "Antine" and not "Antigua"? Quite a possible solution in the light of this later development. Mr. Bathurst put down his paper and paced the room. An idea occurred to him. He went to his telephone and asked for a number.

"Give me Chiswick 8822."

Irene Pearce was in. He breathed relief. He hadn't wasted his time, at any rate. He recognized her voice as it came through to him. She appeared surprised that it was he. He made his apologies for his seeming neglect of her. The apologies were fortified by explanation. At length, Anthony came to the point behind his telephone call.

"It's about Gerald Somerset," he said. "The last of that tragic trio. Did you see him at all before the finish?"

He listened.

"You did? I'm rather glad to hear that. How long before the day they got him? Can you remember?"

He nodded as he heard her answer.

"An evening or two before? As close as that? Oh, good again! Couldn't be better—what's that? Yes . . . yes . . . tell me, of course. No—not for a minute. I shall welcome it." Anthony continued to listen. But he reluctantly admitted to himself ultimately that the girl had nothing of importance to tell him. Still, she had seen Gerald, almost up to the time of his disappearance, which was the fact that he had desired to establish. He had been in a highly nervous state, as she put it—"in fear and trembling". When she had finished, Anthony Bathurst returned slowly to his chair. Although her answer had pleased him, the pleasure was tinged with a certain amount of disappointment that a half-theory which he had been beginning to build had been summarily toppled over. At the same time, he reflected, it were better that it fall in the early stages of its erection than later, when the entire edifice was almost completed.

He ran through, in his mind, the various persons in the cast of this drama of the Somersets. The men—Digby, the mysterious Antine; the women, Miss Pearce, Maud Masters, and the unknown girl who had come to him at his flat. There was yet one woman whom so far he had not seen but whom nevertheless he intended to see. The second Mrs. Somerset. From all that he had been able to gather of her, she appeared to be a woman of sound common sense. One who was not flurried by a sudden emergency. One who was able to keep her head while those around her were losing theirs and blaming it on "hims". Anthony Bathurst turned over his problems from every point of view. An unsolved problem he rarely allowed to rest. He arranged and re-arranged his facts. In varying orders.

At length he came to the conclusion that his data were insufficient. There must be a missing link somewhere, waiting for him to pick it up. The question was, where was this link? Was it at the Boot Lane offices, was it at East Brutton, was it in Essex? Or was it even elsewhere at a place of which he, as yet, knew nothing? His thoughts returned again to the girl whom he had called whimsically to MacMorran, "Miss Antine". Somehow, he considered, he would see her again before the case was finally cleared up. Why he felt this, he would have been unable to explain. But feel it he did. The thought intrigued him. There was something about this girl that was different from all the others. Lady Fullgarney, Cecilia Cameron, and Rosemary Marquis—all of them receded into the background when this girl held the forefront of the picture. He remembered her as a vision of desirable loveliness. What an old ass MacMorran had been to lose sight of her, when he, Anthony, had put her right in front of MacMorran for the mere taking. He wondered what her first name was—Christian name he hoped. Her father's name was Adam. Was Adam a Christian name? Or Jewish? "The first Adam." Anthony's thought rioted again with whimsical wantonness. The Garden of Eden . . . they made themselves aprons

. . . the Angel with the flaming sword, the serpent, the forbidden fruit, when Adam delved and Eve span, who was, then, the gentleman? The old Adam . . . thus his thoughts . . . when Mr. Bathurst sat bolt upright in his chair.

Mr. Bathurst rubbed his hands. Mr. Bathurst's grey eyes were eager and alert. Funny how wisps of truth floated towards you sometimes when you didn't expect them. When you didn't deserve them. What a blind idiot he had been, to be sure! He almost chuckled to himself as he pulled paper towards him. The *Morning Message* should play its part again. His pen put words on paper. Anthony wrote steadily. Then he leant back in his chair and thoughtfully surveyed what he had written.

Adam Antine. All has been discovered. What was feared has now come to pass. Although your plans went through and you met your difficulty as you threatened to meet it, another and bigger difficulty has now arisen. Unless you act at once, the wrench will be thrown into the machinery. Nothing can be more certain than this! You are well aware of what it must inevitably mean. Chaos and disaster! If you would *avoid* this disaster— please communicate as you did before—same time, same place, and same messenger. Then there will be no misunderstanding.

Anthony smiled in anticipation and once again walked to the telephone. Then he paused. For some moments, before definitely committing himself, he debated within his mind whether to substitute "East Brutton" for "Adam Antine" as the opening name. Eventually he decided to make no alteration, to leave the "Agony" as he had originally worded it. He reasoned thus. The use of the name "Adam Antine" would convey to the white gardenia people and to their fair emissary that another step had been taken along the route to knowledge.

Anthony telephoned the "Agony" to the *Morning Message* and then returned to his chair. He carefully filled his pipe. At last he could visualize the real importance of the case and its true significances. He thought of David Somerset and his two sons. Truly, knowledge of any kind, and in any measure, could well be a dangerous thing! So dangerous that it had meant Death.

CHAPTER XV
PARTLY CONCERNING JOSEPH OF ARIMATHEA

ON THE day that his second Press announcement appeared, Anthony Lotherington Bathurst came to Clutton Chase, between Brentwood and Ingatestone, in the county of Essex. He drove down in excellent time, once clear of the congestion round Aldgate. Without difficulty, he found the house called Urswick, the house whose three men had died in such quick succession. It stood right away from the main road. Near it was a green wood, where the spring sunlight splashed on leaves. The size of the house surprised him. Round it was a meadow, where cattle fed on the outskirts. There was a shrubbery, a delightful garden, and even a terrace. The house itself had been built towards the far end of the meadow. Considering how close it lay to towns and even to the great City of London itself, it was marvellously peaceful. At night, thought Anthony, the silence of it all must be terrific. Much to his surprise, when he presented himself, he was conducted up a number of staircases, to a long room at the very top of the house. There he was requested to wait for a few moments.

The floor was polished, the furniture was severe, with two or three exceptions. A portrait by Brockhurst hung on one of the white-distempered walls. He turned to Mrs. Somerset when she came to him and held out her hand.

"Mr. Bathurst! I knew that poor Gerald had been to you. He discussed things with me before he went. We agreed on it. So I knew that eventually you must come down here to see me." They shook hands. She was tall but not awkwardly so. Her hair and eyes matched. The colour was yellowish-brown. There was a natural wave in her hair. Her head was small, perhaps, but beautifully set on a long but lovely neck. Her bust and shoulders were magnificent. Her skin was exquisite—warmly white like a soft white rose. "A siren," thought Anthony as he took her hand, "most certainly a siren." But he said: "You were right, Mrs. Somerset. I have come. I think that I need your help."

She suddenly walked forward to an empty part of the room and, then turning, motioned him to a chair. Anthony took it. She spoke again. He decided that he liked her voice. He noticed her hands. They were not only shapely, they were deft as well. They never hesitated or bungled. They didn't tremble. They were intelligent in their movements, sure and certain. Anthony deliberately waited for her to speak again. She looked painfully thoughtful. There was, he thought, just a faint suspicion of terror in her brown eyes.

"You have news for me, Mr. Bathurst?"

"No, Mrs. Somerset, I have come seeking much more than anything else."

She looked into his eyes with almost impertinent directness.

"Then you have come vainly. I have no help for you."

"We will not decide on that too quickly, Mrs. Somerset. I am still hoping."

She glanced at him again, less directly, and suddenly her whole manner seemed to soften.

"You will forgive me if I ask what may appear to be a personal question?"

She nodded gravely.

"Your husband has left you . . . in comparative affluence?"

"Yes," she replied in a low voice. "My husband left everything to me."

"You expected that?"

"Oh yes—he had told me that if anything happened to him . . . that would be the case." Her fingers opened and shut the lid of a silver cigarette-box that was on the table.

"And the two boys?"

"Neither boy left a will, Mr. Bathurst."

"I see. Strange—that—I think."

"Why?"

"Well—Gerald knew that his life was in danger, even if Geoffrey Somerset were taken unawares." An expression of sorrowful youth stole into Pamela Somerset's eyes, changing her mouth to softness and her cheeks to the curves of innocence.

"Yes—I see what you mean. To tell the truth, I hadn't thought of it in that way before. But there is another point of view. You mustn't overlook it. Gerald, poor boy, was dreadfully worried during those last few weeks. I don't think that such a thing as making a will ever entered his mind. It was all tragedy—such things as money and material things, well, they just weren't thought of."

Her innocence had been ephemeral. It slipped from her, and all that Anthony could see now were her delicious skin, her great romantic eyes, and her thick waving hair. He replied to her.

"Yes. That is understandable. It is, as you say, just one point of view, whereas mine was another. Now I want to ask you another question, Mrs. Somerset. Don't misunderstand me, or it."

She looked definitely dubious. As though something unpleasant was most certainly coming. Her countenance fell quite frankly. "I'll try not to." She glanced swiftly round the room. Anthony's question surprised her. It was so simple but yet so pregnant.

"Has anything happened . . . since?"

"Since?" she repeated.

"Since Gerald's body was found?"

She shook her head.

"Nothing?" he asked again.

"Nothing—of the least importance, that is. Nothing that could have any bearing on the case." Anthony shrugged his shoulders.

"How do we know what has a bearing on the case—and what hasn't? To decide that has been one of our chief difficulties."

A touch of temper showed on her face. He felt that she was annoyed with him.

"Surely that would apply to all cases of this kind?" Anthony disregarded the thrust.

"You can think, then, of absolutely *nothing* the slightest bit abnormal, or unusual, that has taken place since Gerald Somerset's body was washed ashore at Friningham? Nothing whatever? Please think carefully."

She sat silent.

"Yes," she returned at length, very slowly. "Yes. One thing. One thing only. That I can't explain. That I really haven't attempted to explain. To myself, that is . . . after all, it didn't seem important enough to worry about."

Anthony's eyes were eager. He put his eagerness into words. "And that one thing is, Mrs. Somerset?"

She rose from her chair.

"If you will come with me, Mr. Bathurst, I will show you." She invited him to the door by gesture. He followed her and she closed the door behind them. "This way, please."

She led the way down two of the staircases. They came to a room that was obviously the library. Once more he followed her. This time into the room. She took him to a square, open book-case that stood on the floor backed by a wall. The books, be it observed, were ready to hand. It had four shelves. Mrs. Somerset motioned towards the rows of books.

"Will you look at these books, Mr. Bathurst, please?"

Anthony nodded. "Yes. I'm looking at them."

He wondered what it was that she was about to show him. Was Somerset's secret in this book-case somewhere? Had it been here all the time?

"Take a book down from the top shelf, will you? Any book will do for the purpose."

Anthony obeyed her. He took Spenser's *Faerie Queene*, in a magnificent calf binding. She watched him almost nonchalantly.

"Well, what do you see?"

Anthony looked at the space made by the removal of the book that he held in his hand.

"A second row of books behind the others."

She nodded.

"That's what I mean. My husband had too many books. Too many, that is, for convenient handling. He used to buy more books than bookcases. He would try to keep pace with his books by increasing his book-cases, but he always fell behind. Well . . . this is what I'm coming to, the result was, that where he could fit in two rows of books, one row behind the other, he always did. He did so on all the shelves of this particular case."

She paused. Anthony found himself wondering again what it all meant. What was there important about two rows of books, as compared with the ordinary one, even if one row were placed behind the other? He contented himself by remarking: "I see. Well—and what after that?"

"Just this, Mr. Bathurst. I'll show you."

She moved books from the second row. "Look," she said.

Mr. Bathurst looked. She replaced the books she had moved. She moved books from the third row. "And here," she said. "Look!"

Mr. Bathurst looked again.

"Yes," he declared. "I see."

She replaced these books.

"Now, look here." She stooped and moved books from the fourth shelf. "You see? You see what I mean?"

Anthony looked and did see. For there was no second row of books here at all. Every one of them had gone.

"That's what I'm showing you. I discovered that these books had been stolen about midway between the time that Gerald was reported missing and the time when his body was found. I made the discovery by sheer accident. I wanted a certain book, came in here to look for it—and found that all these books, the second row of the fourth shelf, were gone. But how anybody could have got in here and made away with them, I don't know." Anthony was interested—albeit a trifle disappointed. He made a rapid mental calculation.

"There would be about thirty-five to forty books on that second row? Yes?"

Mrs. Somerset counted with her eyes. "Yes. There would. Just about. Because many of them were large . . . and heavy."

"Can you remember the titles of any of them? It's just possible that—"

"Yes. I can remember some of the titles. Let me see now. They were a terribly mixed lot. There was Hoare's *Italian Phrase Book. The Pulleyns of Yorkshire. The Scots Peerage. A Handbook for Travellers in Switzerland. Glastonbury Traditions Concerning Joseph of Arimathea. The Law of Patents. Some Inventions and Discoveries. The Poison Gas of the Next War. The Diamonds,* by the late J.S. Fletcher. How many's that?"

"Nine," replied Mr. Bathurst, making a note of the various titles. "Only about a quarter of them."

"How awful! I shall never be able to remember them all. But I'll try for a few more." She furrowed her brows in thought. "I must concentrate on the fiction that was in here. It's more in my own line. Morgan's *Fountain,* Tennyson Jesse's *A Pin to see the Peep Show, If Winter Comes, Sorrell and Son* and *Roper's Row, The Good Companions* and *Angel Pavement,* Feuchtwanger's *Ugly Duchess.*" She stopped again. "Sorry—but I'm about done. Can't think of any more. Odd ones may come to me—if I do think of any more, I will tell you. Is it so terribly important?"

"To know the titles of all that have been taken would undoubtedly help me. But if you can't remember—you can't."

"Do you think that it has something to do with the . . . trouble?" The brown eyes were full of the question.

Anthony finished jotting down the names of the books and nodded.

"I'm very much afraid so. I think that there is a strong balance of weight behind the opinion that your husband and his two sons were murdered because they possessed something or were the guardians of a valuable secret. That secret one of these missing books may well have held. Tell me, Mrs. Somerset, do you often leave the house?"

"Not a great deal. Sometimes I do, of course."

"There are always servants here when you are out?"

"Oh, certainly."

"Have you spoken to them about these books being taken?"

"Yes. Directly I discovered that they had gone. But none of them could help me. They knew nothing."

"Your husband kept no catalogue, I suppose, of his books?"

She shook her head. "Oh no! Although he was a great reader and always buying books, he wasn't a collector or anything like that. There was no need of a catalogue."

"No, I was afraid not. It seems to me that this case has gone against us right from the first."

Her next remark surprised him.

"Have you seen Irene Pearce recently?"

"No. But I rang her up a short time ago. Why do you ask?"

"She just came into my mind. A charming girl in every way. She was down here before my husband and Geoffrey were buried. I like her immensely. I asked her, when she was here last, to come and stay with me when conditions were happier. She said that she would, but I haven't heard from her since. She was terribly fond of Geoffrey, you know."

"Yes. I formed that impression from what I saw of her myself."

"There's one thing, Mr. Bathurst," she continued; "the police haven't worried me too much during the last week or so. At first they were always coming here. Asking questions of me and interviewing the servants. Looking at my husband's papers. For weeks there was no peace here at all."

"You mustn't think too hardly of them. They were bound to make the usual inquiries, you know. Routine work—a good deal of it."

"I suppose so."

Anthony glanced at the list of titles that he had put down—those of the stolen books.

"An idea has come to me, Mrs. Somerset. I'm hoping that it may prove helpful."

"Yes," she inquired. "What is it?"

"Is there any book in this list that you have given me, these titles that you have been able to remember, to which your husband was in the habit of referring? Let me say—regularly. Is there? Can you remember?"

She looked at him as though she were puzzled by the question.

"Regularly? That's the word that puzzles me. What do you mean exactly by 'regularly'?" Anthony smiled as he attempted to help her. "Well, shall we say, fairly constantly?"

"Yes. Then I *can* answer what you asked me." She nodded her head eagerly. "There *was* a book to which my husband came *fairly* frequently."

"Good! And the title of it was—?"

"*Some Inventions and Discoveries*. I can remember seeing him look at it several times during the last few weeks of his life."

Anthony noticed how pale she had gone. But he was eager for more information.

"I don't know the book too well, Mrs. Somerset. Do you happen to remember the name of the author?"

To his extreme satisfaction the lady did.

"Yes. Quite well. I've seen the book in my husband's hands far too frequently not to know the author. It was by Sir Lindsay Faviell—the metallurgist."

Anthony looked her straight in the eyes.

"Your husband never discussed the book with you, I suppose, Mrs. Somerset?"

She shook her head.

"Never, Mr. Bathurst. My husband never worried me with matters of that nature."

"Of what nature?"

"Well—to do with his business, really. I'm afraid that I wasn't very interested in my husband's business activities."

"You can tell me nothing special that you know was in the book, Mrs. Somerset?"

"I have never looked at it. The inside of it, I mean. I have never so much as discussed it. With anybody."

There was little help to be obtained here, thought Anthony Bathurst. Whichever way he turned in this case, he seemed to meet an insurmountable barrier.

On his journey back to town, his brain considered and reconsidered, point after point, and fact after fact which the case, in its various stages, had brought to him. But why, in the name of goodness, he asked himself unsuccessfully, when you wanted one book, collar a whole darned row? Mr. Bathurst shook his head and eventually brought his car to the door of his garage. Perhaps the morrow would bring him something more tangible.

He ran the car in and as he was coming away a voice that he had heard before sounded in his ears. He was annoyed that the sound pleased him. For the voice was the voice of the girl whom he called Miss Antine.

"Good evening, Mr. Bathurst."

"You have the advantage of me," he replied, "in more directions than one. But I will return your 'good evening'."

She laughed.

"Delicious," he thought. "More delicious than the time before." Ah, well—the case had its undoubted compensations.

Chapter XVI
FIND THE LADY

"Thank you," she replied. "After all, it's the least you can do. I've been to your flat. I was told that you were expected back to dinner. So I waited for you."

"Charming of you," murmured Anthony. "You will dine with me?"

She smiled. "I will accompany you."

"Half a loaf is known to have a certain advantage. This is the way—it's a short cut."

They came again to his flat. Emily was instructed on one matter alien to her usual duties. Dinner was served. The lady accepted Mr. Bathurst's invitation.

"I should have been content," she said, "with a pat of butter for my bread and a flagon of water."

"And I," returned Anthony, "with my guest alone."

She rested her chin thoughtfully upon her hands and flushed a little.

"That's what I call a pretty answer."

She spoke with a soothing gentleness. Her lips were parted and there was an odd intentness in her expression. Anthony noted this particularly, and that her eyes had a trick of growing even darker when she was absorbed or excited. Anthony raised a glass to her.

"Thrones may shake with wild alarms. *A toi.*"

She acknowledged the gesture gracefully.

"Thank you. Well—and what have you to tell me now?"

Anthony was prepared. Emily, prim and deliberately straight-faced, brought in the *entrée*. He waited until she had gone out again.

"Surely I made myself clear on this second occasion? All has been discovered. Even to the connection with the affair of Mr. Antine."

She looked into his eyes as though she would have read his soul. Anthony was positive that he was on the right track this time. He therefore followed up the advantage which he thought had been already established.

"*Everything* has been discovered. Even to the theft of the vital book."

He was amazed at the sudden change in her face. A light in her eyes danced and sparkled. A light that he had never envisaged before.

"You amaze me," she said.

"Why?"

"You have a quality that is usually assigned to my sex."

"I don't know whether to feel flattered or otherwise."

"I'll tell you what the quality is. It's not 'inconstancy', although it's something like it."

"Variable as the shade, or merely coy and hard to please? I'd love to know."

"You shall. It's this. One minute I feel that you know the truth. That you are sincere and genuine. The next moment you make me think just the reverse, because you show me unmistakably that you are not what you seem and are merely tricking me. Trying to trick me by nothing more than low cunning." A flush showed in her cheeks.

Anthony's face grew stern. "Whose fault is that? On whom lies that responsibility? Cunning must be met by cunning. It is foolish to wear kid gloves with murderers."

The word had an electric effect upon her. It stung her to a sudden fury. She rose quickly, came across to him and with her open hand struck him across the cheek. Anthony's lip twitched. For, the moment afterwards, a strange thing happened. She gave a little trembling cry and turned away from him. As she did so, Anthony felt that in a way she had delivered herself into his hands. She had surrendered to him the mastery. And he found himself exultant in the feeling. He watched her closely as she stood there in front of him. Shame clouded her face. There was humiliation and self-contempt in her very attitude. She tried to raise her eyes to look him in the face, but she could not. Anthony knew that the longer he maintained the silence, the greater would be his domination over her. She let her eyes fall to the ground. At last she spoke to him.

"I am sorry."

He smiled gravely.

"I am sure that you are. Won't you sit down again?"

She took the chair on which she had sat before. Anthony attacked immediately. He thought that never had he seen her look so beautiful. The flame of anger that had surged up in her, followed so soon by the submerging wave of shame, had given her the loveliness of an opening rose. The boldness of her eyes had been replaced by a softness.

For a moment, the moment before Anthony spoke, she sat quite still.

"Don't you think," said Mr. Bathurst, "that it would help us both if you told me your name? Seeing that you already know mine. I commend the idea to you almost frantically."

This question brought a new look into her face. "My name? Why should I tell you my name?"

"Why shouldn't you? You know mine."

"Not from *you*. I was forced to find it out."

Her eyes changed. They set in a fierce determination. Anthony looked at her with frank admiration. She repeated her question.

"Why should I tell you? I should have thought from your previous remark that the less you had to do with me the better you would have been pleased."

"Since then, though, we have come into a closer contact." Anthony rubbed his cheek.

"I think that you have mocked me enough. There is no reason that I can see why I should stay."

"Except this. One of the books that was stolen from the house of the Somersets in Clutton Chase was *Some Inventions and Discoveries*. There is little doubt, I take it, that it held reference to *the* discovery? What is your own opinion?"

She drew back in her chair with a start of surprise. "Who else would steal it?"

"Other than your people? I am as much in the dark as you."

The emphasis of his statement seemed to startle her afresh. He felt her glance rest upon him in puzzled questioning.

"How do I know that you are not tricking me again?" she demanded with new fire.

"Well," replied Anthony diffidently, "if you think that I am, you could always hit me again, couldn't you? For mere satisfaction. After all, I can turn the other cheek, even though Holy Scripture is silent concerning the third blow."

"Be silent," she cried with a stamp of her foot. Then she hesitated. She looked towards him and then away. He felt that he had stirred suspicion and disquiet within her.

"How do you know," she flashed at him, "that you yourself are not in grave danger? People who murder"—her lip curled at the word—"may not stop at murdering again."

"You mean that the slap on the cheek may be the forerunner . . . to a bullet in the brain . . . or a strangle-hold round the throat . . . or even to a blow on the head? Yes . . . I see your point. Harmonic progression in crime. Quite an idea, I admit."

She changed. A smile, or better, a half-smile, played round her mouth.

"You know what my advertisement said," he continued. "I mentioned the word 'disaster'. I meant every letter of that word—I did really. You and your white gardenia people are heading straight for it, you know. If you go on as you are going, it will be inevitable. I can't bear to think, even, of what will happen to you."

She leant over towards him and placed her fingers on his sleeve.

"Listen to me. I am serious in what I say. You are in great danger. If you persist as you are persisting, you are in grave peril."

"It seems, then, that there are at least two of us."

"You refuse to be warned?"

"No more than you."

"Oh—don't be so foolish! You are powerless against us. How can you as much as *touch* us?"

"Do tell me your name. I want to know what there's going to be between us on the next occasion we meet."

"Between us? I don't think that I—"

"I'll hasten to explain. Don't you remember your Count Hannibal? The choice that he gave the lady of his heart? 'Which shall it be between us, madam, a kiss or a blow? For every morning you shall come to me for one or t'other.' The late Oscar Asche played the part, I believe."

A sudden rush of red spread across her face and down her neck.

"And—what was the lady's answer? Is your memory equal to telling me that?"

"Oh, a blow," he answered her most emphatically. "No shilly-shallying! Her words were—'A blow—a blow, *a thousand times* a blow.' She certainly knew her own mind."

"She most certainly did."

"Of course, the conditions were reversed."

"Reversed?"

"Yes! The lady in that case was the recipient of the attention. Whereas with us . . ." Anthony rubbed his cheek.

She rose to go.

"Nevertheless, my answer is exactly the same as hers—"

"That's all right, then," returned Mr. Bathurst, "it is understood that I have already received my first instalment." He rubbed his cheek again.

She looked at him—disdainfully lovely. Anthony's thoughts rioted.

"Something, let us say," he continued, "on account."

"A deposit."

"Why a deposit? I could bear to know."

"A deposit is, usually, such a trifling sum. In comparison with the whole amount. Don't you think so?"

Anthony grinned.

"I suppose you're right, now I come to think of it."

"I make a habit of being right, Mr. Bathurst. Let me hasten to assure you on the point."

"I find you more attractive than ever," murmured Anthony; "a girl after my own heart."

"And I find your heart entirely uninteresting."

"Perseverance is a virtue that I have always admired, and even Rome wasn't built in a day." She controlled the smile that was beginning to play round her mouth.

"I couldn't spare anything like a day for the task."

"You disappoint me."

"I am sorry. Good-bye, Mr. Bathurst. And don't forget—'forewarned is forearmed'. You see—I give you back one of your own English proverbs."

"I happen to be Irish. And taking you in your own words, the words that you have just used to me, what are you? Don't tell me Irish, too."

She shook her head.

"It doesn't matter."

"Oh, but it does, believe me."

She turned to leave.

"I meant that it didn't matter—to you."

She was gone in a flash. But Anthony was ready. He knew that the efficient Emily hadn't let him down. MacMorran, or somebody deputed by MacMorran, would be there with the car waiting, as he had been requested, and Anthony would see that there was no slip-giving this time. Thirty seconds after he reached the pavement, MacMorran's car drew up by the kerb.

"Jump in, Mr. Bathurst. She's got less than a minute's start this time. We're all right so far, I think."

Anthony jumped.

"Good for you, Andrew. Step on the juice."

MacMorran stepped and the big car accelerated. They ran for three hundred yards, when the Inspector exclaimed:

"There she is, you see, going East just as she did before. Now keep your eyes open for that flitting act of hers."

Anthony grunted an assent.

"See that car?" exclaimed MacMorran. "That's my lady's. She was in it like lightning directly she skipped from your place. I was wondering how long I should have to wait."

"Not so long as we waited in the darkness outside L'Estrange's travelling show-ground when we looked into that strange affair of 'The Purple Calf'. Remember, Andrew?"

"I do," returned the Inspector, keeping his eye on the road. "I'll remember that to my dying day."

"Reminds me of a racing tipster I met at Ascot once. Smart chap. Started by telling the crowd that he wasn't in need of money. Said he had enough to last him for the rest of his life. If he died about half past four that same afternoon. Tickled me— that did."

MacMorran chuckled.

"Reckon it did. Hallo—see that? Look!"

The car which they were following was slowing up.

They had reached the end of the Thames Embankment.

"Watch carefully, Mr. Bathurst. It's my belief she's up to something. Be on your guard that she doesn't pull a fast one."

"She's getting out, Mac. You're right! Blackfriars Station. That's where she's making for, I'll lay any money. Drive straight past that car and then drop me a few yards ahead. I'll make a quick cut back across the road to the station. I may have a spot of luck and pick her up there again. Anyhow, I'll have a shot for it."

MacMorran dashed past the other car as Anthony had directed him, and slowing up also, in accordance with that same gentleman's wishes, brought the car to a standstill a hundred yards or so beyond John Carpenter Street and the entrance to the City of London School. Anthony was out like a shot and dashed straight across the road to Blackfriars Station. Inside the station there was no sign of the disdainful lady. Instinct told him to take a ticket that would take him west. A train, westward bound, was coming in as he descended the staircase. Anthony ran for it, and out of the corner of his eye was just able to see the person of his pursuit enter a first-class compartment. Anthony promptly entered a third just close to it. At each station to which they came, he watched carefully from his seat by the window to see whether his lady alighted. He knew she was there all right, he argued to himself, and he didn't see how she could possibly leave the train without his knowledge. He had covered all the conditions and was still satisfied.

At length his patience was rewarded. When they ran into Victoria, he saw her hurrying past his carriage. Anthony jumped out and followed her. Outside the station, she made for Grosvenor Square. Anthony, keeping her in sight all the time, maintained a respectable distance between the lady and himself. Much to his surprise, as he saw her walking ahead, a car arrived from seemingly nowhere and, sidling up to the kerb, quietly and unostentatiously, it stopped for a second, the lady entered, and the car was away again. Anthony realized that if he wished to continue the combat he must act quickly. Luckily, a taxi was conveniently to hand. Anthony hailed it and swung into it.

"Follow that limousine there in front. Anywhere and everywhere it goes. Don't lose sight of it for an instant and you'll be on a good tip."

"O.K. by me, Captain Heath," returned the driver. "The rest of the day's my own, so time ain't going to be a factor in the case."

He was away immediately and Mr. Bathurst settled down to the watch again. This time they ran in the direction of Hampstead. The car in front came to Church Row. They ran along the edge of the Heath, Anthony's car a reasonable distance in the rear. Anthony used the speaking-tube.

"I say, driver, I rather fancy my friends are going to stop before very long. When they do, take no notice at all. Drive past. I'll tell you then when to stop."

The taxi-driver lifted a hand and waved it to show Anthony that he had understood. Suddenly Anthony knew that his idea had been right. The car in front stopped. He saw a feminine form slip out and run up the white steps of a big house.

Anthony's car drove by at a good pace. Way up the road, Anthony gave his driver the signal. He almost fell out, paid the driver off and started slowly and carefully to retrace his steps. Eventually he came back to the house by the Heath into which he had seen the girl run. It was a silent, gloomy house standing in its own grounds, with a tiled verandah extending along one side of it. The verandah was lined by several windows and two doors. Anthony came to the front gate. He saw better, then, how big the house actually was. Also, he was able to see the name. "St. Mawes".

He decided to walk back. Part of the way, at least. After a time he came to a public house. The saloon-bar drew him. There were but few people in there. A prosperous-looking barmaid, with a tier of chins, smiled upon him effusively when he gave her his order. Anthony realized that she might be manna to him if she were astutely handled. He essayed one or two of the usual opening gambits. He soon knew that his optimism was justified. She was by way of being a conversationalist. Anthony played her beautifully. From weather to war, from war to politics, from politics to local matters . . . local residents . . . houses in the near vicinity. Anthony brought her to greater detail.

"There's an unusually large house . . . not far from here . . . with a tiled verandah. Let me see now, I did notice the name, a seaside place, if I remember it properly . . . now what was it?"

The fair one ogled him gladly.

"You mean St. Mawes. I know the house you mean. There's a foreign gentleman lives in it. Been there for about two years, I should think."

"Really!"

"Oh yes," she went on, "there's a six-foot wall round the back of the house. I've been round there myself and seen it. Looks as though he wants to keep himself to himself, don't it?" The tier of chins heaved and wobbled in unison.

"You speak as though he were the head of a gang of international crooks. Fill that up again, will you?" Anthony pushed his glass over to her.

"Well, you never know these days, do you? Look at the things you read in the papers. It takes my sister-in-law three hours every Sunday afternoon to get through the *News of the World*. She says she wouldn't miss it on no account. Likes a bit of dirt, she does." She filled Anthony's glass again and returned it to him.

"What makes you think that the chap at St. Mawes is a foreigner? Does he look like one?" Anthony spoke carelessly. He knew what women of this class were. He mustn't give her the slightest idea that he was pumping her.

"Several things, my dear. He *does* look like one, there's no argument about that, but that's not the only thing. He's got a foreign-sounding name. I said as much the first time that I ever heard it. Proper peculiar name."

Anthony smiled at her over the rim of his glass.

"South American Joe?"

"Oh, go on! You are a one! No, of course not. A real foreign name. Let me see if I can remember it." The fat, raddled face wrinkled in the effort. "It's a name like the seats you get at the music-hall when the boy friend's generous and doesn't mind putting his hand in his pocket."

This last statement bewildered Mr. Bathurst.

To tell the truth, he hadn't the least idea what the woman meant.

"Ah, well," he remarked with quiet diplomacy, "it doesn't matter. Especially remembering the quality of this beer."

The barmaid shook her head.

"I'm one what likes to see a thing right through. That name'll come to me all right if I stick to it long enough."

Anthony summoned a glance of admiration. The lady was receptive. She felt that a big effort was demanded of her. She rose to the occasion magnificently. She stood there behind the bar, eyes shining and with uplifted finger.

"I've got it. I knew that it would come to me. Fortolis. That's the name. Fortolis. There's a daughter there—a Miss Fortolis."

Anthony made suitable note of the fact. He now had both the name and the address. He repeated the name after her. As he did so, a dark-visaged man who had been drinking at a table a few yards away from them flashed a quick glance across the apartment and silently slipped out through the door. Anthony Bathurst noticed the movement and drew certain conclusions therefrom. The attendant behind the bar, who had proved to be so communicative, drifted away to serve another customer. Anthony drank his beer and departed. He considered that there would be no point in his staying.

CHAPTER XVII
AT CLOSER QUARTERS

HE CAME again to the edge of the Heath about nine o'clock on the following evening. For the time of the year, the weather had turned bitterly cold. The wind was so keen that Anthony wore an overcoat. He walked along the edge of the Heath again and turned up the collar of his coat, for the wind seemed to go right through him. He reached the house that he had for his objective; the residence of Mr. César Fortolis, as the telephone-directory had told him.

"I must get in," said Mr. Bathurst to himself, "with a minimum of noise. If I'm to do myself any good, once I'm there."

He had devoted many hours of thought to the problem and had decided that, if he were lucky, he might achieve more by this method than by any other. Quickly he passed through the gate and into a clump of laurels. From here, he could see the line of windows. Not a light was showing in any one of them. Walking quickly forward, he found that a row of greenhouses spread away to the right of them. Anthony went to the one nearest to the house and tried the door. As he had half-expected, it was locked.

He quickly removed a square pane of glass, and put his hand through the aperture. Finding the key, he turned it on the inside. Quickly slipping inside the greenhouse, he closed the door again behind him. The atmosphere was hot and humid. He thought immediately of some of the houses in Kew Gardens in which the exotic plants were kept. His electric torch pointed the path for him and he made his way past shrubs and flowering plants.

A moment or so brought him to the end of the greenhouse and, to his intense gratification, there, in front of him, he saw a pair of french doors, doors that communicated, no doubt, with the main part of the house itself. He put off his torch. The door opened to his handling. Anthony Bathurst paused on the threshold. His nose told him that he was close now to the occupants of the house. For it was certain that in the room which he was now about to enter, a cigar had been but recently smoked.

He stepped silently into the room. It was in darkness. He stood there and listened. There wasn't a sound. He felt almost certain that the room was empty. A second's work and the electric-torch confirmed the idea. He crossed the room in three long, silent strides and opened another door. He closed it behind him at once and found that he was in a long passage. He walked swiftly along the passage, and coming to another door on the left-hand side, opened that. In this last room to which he had come, a fire was burning. The firelight lit up the room, and as his brain registered the fact, he heard the subdued sound of voices. The room, he saw, had a bay window and, on the other side, a door that led on to the tiled verandah. Against the wall to his left stood a magnificent book-case. Anthony started to walk towards it and then heard a sudden sound away in the part of the house behind him. It was a footstep, and a footstep that was coming in his direction. Without wasting a second, he made for the heavy curtain on the right-hand side of the fire-place and took up his position behind it. But the flickering stabs of firelight, which came at irregular intervals, made him feel uneasy. As he had feared, he had not acted a moment too soon.

The footsteps came down the passage and halted at the door of the room. He heard the handle turned and the person, whoever it was, enter the room. He felt certain that the curtain behind which he was hidden must be guilty of a distinct bulge. What a pitiable end to his escapade to be caught ignominiously in this humiliating position! He braced his body to place it as near the wall as possible. He heard the person who had entered the room, start to cross it, and then stop suddenly. From the light step, he knew that it was a woman. He heard the sudden intake of her breath and he knew that she knew that there was somebody behind that curtain. He stiffened himself instinctively, both physically and mentally, for the inevitable shock of challenge. It came. He knew that it would come—but it came in a different form from that which he had been anticipating.

"Good evening again, Mr. Bathurst." The voice was the voice of the charmer.

Anthony put the best face he could upon the situation. He stepped out from behind the curtain.

"Good evening, Miss Fortolis. I've been admiring your curtains."

"Yes, of course. I guessed it was that. What a good job it wasn't the coal-cabinet that attracted you."

Anthony smiled. As the smile died on his face, her tone and attitude changed like lightning. She walked quickly to the side of the room and picked up something from the table. He saw that she held an automatic.

"Put your hands up. Turn round. March."

Anthony obeyed her. Truth to tell, his chief feeling was one of acute interest. With the gun pressed into the small of his back, Anthony was conducted along the passage for some distance until he and his companion reached another door.

"Open the door," she commanded him, "and go straight inside. I really must introduce you to the others. Why should I monopolize fortune's favours?"

"Why, indeed?" murmured Anthony. "If you want to know, I feel just as you do about it."

The two of them passed through the door into the room. It was ablaze with light. Three men were seated therein. Directly his eyes fell on them, Anthony thought of the words that the barman of the "Golden Lion", East Brutton, had used to him in the early days of the problem. "Foreign-looking men." Each one of the three was dark and swarthy. The tallest of the three sprang to his feet in amazement as Anthony entered followed by his triumphant lady.

"What is the meaning of this, Diane?" he cried.

"At last I know her name," thought Anthony, "although it may be an ill wind."

"Allow me to introduce to you all, a rather important person," returned Diane Fortolis, "for this is Mr. Anthony Bathurst. I persuaded him to accompany me here. You will observe!" She made play with her revolver.

The tall man spoke to her. His voice was harsh and discordant.

"Hers must be like her mother's," was Mr. Bathurst's second thought.

"Will you explain, Diane? I insist—please! This is, at the least, an unceremonious intrusion."

"Delighted," drawled Diane. "The explanation is absurdly simple. Mr. Bathurst has 'gate-crashed', that is all. I can't recall ever having given him an invitation to St. Mawes. And if it didn't come from me, I'm certain that it didn't come from anybody else."

Anthony saw an ugly scowl spread over the face of the shortest man.

"Where did you find him?" he rapped out curtly.

"In the library. But he wasn't looking for a book. Don't get nervy. I found him behind the big curtain by the fire-place."

"In hiding, do you mean?" demanded Fortolis. Anthony felt a good mind to answer the question himself, but on second thoughts he decided to leave matters to Diane. She was doing very well.

"Yes," she replied, "in hiding. But his feet were too big. I happened to see one of them."

Anthony grinned almost happily. Thank God Mademoiselle Diane had a sense of humour! But the scowl which grew bigger on the face of the smallest man was too ugly to be treated entirely lightly. Fortolis came to the point without further ado.

"What do you want here? Answer me at once. Why do you enter in this fashion? Are you aware that I am absolutely entitled to give you in charge?"

Anthony rubbed his cheek. The situation was developing unpleasantly. He affected, therefore, a nonchalance which he was far from feeling.

"Answering your various questions, Mr. Fortolis, (a) information; (b) I had to because you weren't in the least likely to invite me here, and (c) perfectly."

Fortolis snapped his fingers.

"T'cha!" At any rate, what he said sounded like that more than anything else. "What information do you seek here?"

"You know the answer to that question as well as I do."

"What do you mean? How is it possible? You talk in riddles."

"You give yourself away, Mr. Fortolis. You give yourself away badly. And let me warn you here and now, that our English law is not to be trifled with. If you find my meaning so obscure, as obscure as you profess to, let me ask you a question. Why did Mademoiselle Diane answer my two 'Agonies' that have appeared in the daily Press?"

"Is it, then, an offence against your English law to answer Press advertisements? I confess, if it is so, that I live and learn."

Anthony stuck out a determined jaw. Bathurst on Resolution!

"You are quibbling, Mr. Fortolis, and you know it. And while we're on the subject of English law, I'll tell you something else. You—and your companions. There is one crime that the English law never forgives. Or does it forget. It remembers that particular crime for years and years, for generations possibly, long after everybody else has forgotten it. Remembers it—to punish it and avenge it, That crime, Mr. Fortolis, to which I refer, is 'murder'. It has an ugly sound, but, believe me, an uglier punishment."

The three men ranged themselves around him, the shortest and most truculent raised his hand as though to strike. Fortolis pushed him to one side.

"Stay a moment, Max! We may be in a nasty mess—it depends what has leaked out, but let me deal with this fool. This fool who crows from the wrong side of the fence." He pushed his face close to Anthony Bathurst's. "How much do you know?"

Anthony saw Diane out of the corner of his eye. How he wished that he were more sure of his ground!

"Enough," he answered curtly.

"Shut his mouth," cried the little dark spitfire. "Dead men tell no tales! I like the sound of that. Suits me down to the ground."

Anthony flashed a reply at him.

"The three Somersets can tell no tales."

He heard Fortolis hiss softly through his teeth. He struck again as hard as he knew how.

"I want very little to complete my case. Mademoiselle Diane must have told you that I have been to East Brutton—to the 'Golden Lion'. You must know, too, in what way your own plans have miscarried."

He saw the three men eye each other anxiously. He heard the rustle of Diane's dress somewhere behind him. But he couldn't see what she was doing. He heard Fortolis cry a word in a tongue which he knew not. He thought he heard another sound behind him. He half turned to see what it might be, for the look on the face of Fortolis was far from pretty. It was the last movement that he was destined to make for some time. A blow on the back of the head sent him senseless to the floor.

"Get some cords and tie him up," commanded Fortolis.

"Slit his throat!" cried Max. "That's my advice, and have done with taking risks. Why should we run this risk? If anybody can tell me that, I'll be obliged."

"Silence, Max! Use what little brains you have. Can't you see that we're in a nasty mess all round? Every one of us? Those three dead men—who could have expected it?"

Max grumbled inaudibly. The three men tied Mr. Bathurst's wrists and ankles scientifically and effectively. Mademoiselle Diane Fortolis stood by, one hand to her mouth, and with troubled eyes. But Mr. Bathurst was unaware of this.

CHAPTER XVIII
THINGS IMPROVE

WHEN he did become aware again of Life's happenings, Mr. Bathurst found himself lying on the floor of what seemed to his first glance a room of the attic type. An intolerable aching at the back of his head reminded him painfully of the last incident through which he remembered passing. What a ridiculous position in which to be! To have brought himself into a predicament of this kind without having put up even the semblance of a fight. He would never hear the last of it from Andrew MacMorran. In addition to the pain at the back of his head, his wrists and ankles ached abominably. He was helpless, trussed like a chicken. He raised his wrists to his mouth in the hope that his teeth might, in time, work the knots loose. But he soon realized that his task was an impossible one. The cords had been tied far too tightly—knotted by a master hand. No wonder Gerald Somerset had gone to his death.

After some minutes' futile struggling, Anthony gave up the idea as a bad job. He had but one gleam of hope. Emily would report his absence to MacMorran and directly she did so the Inspector would get busy. He wished now that he had told the Inspector that he had come to St. Mawes again, instead of trying to play if off on his own bat. A dim light was burning in a corner of the attic, and when he tried to discover what time it was he realized for the first time since he had been struck down that his wrist-watch had been removed. To tie the cord round his wrists more effectively, no doubt. He had no idea how long he had been lying there unconscious. Time is a difficult factor to calculate in the condition in which he now found himself.

Suddenly, to his complete surprise, and without any preliminary sound coming to break the utter stillness, he saw the door of the room where he lay, swing slowly open. Diane Fortolis stood on the threshold. All was dark behind her, but the light from the attic was enough to tell him who it was who stood there. Her face was eagerly beautiful. Her hand, uplifted, gestured to him to be silent. Glancing back over her shoulder into the dark blanket of the stairs behind her, she advanced on tiptoe into the room towards him and whispered words: "What a fool you were to come here. What a fool—to pit your brains against men like our men. Do you know that you are in great danger? Deadly peril—almost?"

Anthony opened his lips but before he could speak she commanded him again.

"Be silent. Don't utter a single word. Don't make the slightest sound even. If you do, one of them downstairs will be certain to hear you."

Anthony was sore put to it to know what to do. He had no objection, as far as he was concerned, to the men downstairs hearing anything. There was, however, the girl's point of view to be considered. He therefore obeyed orders and kept quiet. She stood there listening. Her head was just a trifle to one side and Anthony once again thought that she looked more attractive than ever before. Then she came nearer to him.

"You can speak now. They have moved into another room. I know where they have gone and why. They will not hear."

"Why not untie me, dear lady? That would help, also, to unloose the strings of my tongue."

He saw how she hesitated.

"In addition, I happen to be in a fair amount of pain. Perhaps that possibility hadn't occurred to you."

"It is your own fault and has come of your own seeking."

Anthony managed to struggle into a sitting position by the wall of the attic. He made a reasonable attempt to shrug his shoulders.

"As you will. Forget it."

The glorious eyes softened. She came and knelt by his side.

"If I untie you, will you promise me something in return?"

"Depends what it is you want promised."

"Nothing that you can't promise easily. That you will go from here at once and never return."

"That is a poor tribute to yourself . . . Diane." To his utter amazement she blushed crimson.

"I am nothing to do with it. Will you promise what I have asked you? It is all for your own sake. Surely you can see that?"

"Alas, I am a headstrong person who likes my own way. I have not yet done what I came here to do. Therefore I cannot make you your promise. Surely *you* can see *that*?"

"It is not worth the risk that you are taking. Max Desmoulais is furious. Wants your head on a charger."

"Why, has he been dancing for you? He looks like a dancer! And an infuriated dancer—I dare not envisage such crude fierceness."

He saw her eyes flash unmistakable resentment.

"Very well, then." She moved away. "You have had your chance and refused it. Don't blame anybody but yourself for what comes to you."

"Extra to yourself, do you mean?"

But she had gone, and Anthony saw the door close behind her. Then he came to his other senses. A knife lay on the floor beside him. O, wonderful girl! So she *had* come with the intention of freeing him! More than that—she had deliberately left the knife there for him to use, despite the fact that he had declined to make her the promise for which she had asked. He took the knife between his teeth, sawed at his wrists with it and after a time the cords fell severed from them. Then he slashed at the bonds round his ankles and stood up in the room—a free man again.

Problem now—what should be his next step? He considered the situation carefully. His entry into St. Mawes had yielded him nothing. Should he postpone a further attempt to discover something until another occasion? He had learned nothing new whatever concerning the three Somersets and the fate that had befallen them. All that he had achieved had been to make a complete ass of himself. Except, though—his thoughts dwelt upon the incidents that had just occurred. A thought sequence that ended in a smile. What was the best way to get out of St. Mawes without betraying what had happened and Diane as well?

Anthony looked round the attic. There was but one window, and that at such a height as to make a drop therefrom forbidding. He crept quietly out on to the landing. He had scarcely done so when Diane Fortolis seemed to appear from nowhere and pluck almost frantically at his wrist.

"Come quickly," he heard her whisper. "They will be on us in a moment. They heard me come down the stairs after I left you. One of the wretched boards always does creak. If they go into the attic they will see that you have outwitted them. Come with me. We must be quick."

This time Anthony Bathurst found himself in agreement with her. There was certainly no time to be lost. He pulled himself together and ran with her across the landing and down a narrow winding stairway. This brought them to another wide landing and, at the moment they made it, Anthony heard the sounds of rapid footsteps and the angry murmur of men's voices. The sounds came, he judged, from the next floor beneath where he and Diane Fortolis stood.

Diane stopped suddenly as they ran and Anthony saw a flicker of fear show in her eyes. She looked quickly from side to side and then came to a decision.

"Quick! In here. With me."

Turning the handle of a door quickly, they ran into a bedroom, through the window of which Anthony could see the night hung with stars.

"My bedroom," she whispered.

"I am honoured," returned Mr. Bathurst.

"S'sh!" She placed her finger on her lips and hurried to the window. "Your chance is here. I don't trust Desmoulais. When he's in a rage he'll stop at nothing."

"So I should have believed," murmured Anthony.

He saw Diane leaning out over the window-sill.

"It isn't very high here. You should be able to drop it. The flower-beds are directly below, so your fall should be a soft one."

"'Twill be the second time, Diane."

She frowned. "What do you mean?"

"That I've fallen for you."

Both steps and voices sounded right outside the door. Anthony ran to the open window. As he did so, the door was flung open and he saw the aggressive form of Max Desmoulais, followed by that of Fortolis himself, rush forward with a revolver in his hand. Anthony measured the drop with his eyes. Twenty to twenty-five feet, he calculated. He bestrode the window-sill, waiting for a split second to hear what should pass between Diane and the two men who pursued him. He could not save himself and leave her in peril at the hands of Max Desmoulais. Still, Fortolis was her father and would, no doubt, protect her. Anthony saw her stand in Desmoulais' way and attempt to push him back. He flung her to one side on to Fortolis. But she recovered her balance quickly and caught him by the arm as he tried to rush by her.

"Are you mad, Max Desmoulais?" she cried. "You can't treat this man like this. You are in England, not abroad. Come to your senses. Put that gun away and let the man go. Do you want to get us all into trouble?"

"Out of my way!" shouted the enraged Desmoulais. "You are mad. You will ruin us. You will put a rope round the necks of each one of us. This man knows too much, I say. Let me get at him."

He pushed her heavily and rushed towards the window and Anthony. Anthony flung himself over the sill and let himself go. As he did so, he heard a shot from above, a hoarse cry from Fortolis, and then a burning pain sear the back of the fingers of his right hand. He heard again a shrill scream from the room above and then he fell smack into the flower-bed below. Diane Fortolis had been right. The earth was moderately soft, and although he was shaken in every bone of his body, he was not seriously hurt by the fall. His overcoat had helped to take some of the force of the impact of body with ground. His hand was smarting hellishly, but he picked himself up and dashed off through the various shrubs and bushes as hard as he could pelt, until he came to a long, narrow, winding path. He knew for a positive certainty that he was far from being out of the wood yet. He could still hear shouts and he fancied that he heard, also, the sound of a woman sobbing.

He turned once, as he ran, and saw stabs of light issuing from the open window from which he had just fallen. His hand was bleeding badly now and throbbing with pain. The bullet

that Max Desmoulais had fired must have ploughed the knuckles of his right hand as he had dropped from the window-sill. A
damned lucky escape—might have drilled him neatly through
the heart. He took his handkerchief and carefully wrapped it
round his knuckles. He ran for some time, then his foot tripped
over the root of a small, sturdy tree and he fell heavily.

How long he lay by this tree he never knew. But when he
began to be normal again the moon had sunk and the stars were
hidden by banks of drifting clouds. The dawn and morning were
evidently close at hand. His overcoat, trousers, and socks were
soddened by dew and the handkerchief across the back of his
hand was red and wet with blood. The hand burned and smarted
more acutely than ever.

He rose to his feet and looked round to take stock of his situation. The house known to him as St. Mawes was not visible from
where he stood. He must have travelled further from it than he
had anticipated. He surveyed himself. A ruined overcoat, a bump
on the back of the head, and a wounded hand, were the sum total
of what he could show for his night's adventure. He smiled with
rueful resignation, as he started to make his way back.

Two hours later, he had breakfasted and was just filling his
pipe when Chief-Inspector Andrew MacMorran was ushered by
Emily into the breakfast-room. "Good morning, Mr. Bathurst."

"Good morning, Inspector. Why am I honoured so early?"

MacMorran's eyes twinkled with interest.

"Do you mind?"

"Depends what's brought you along here."

"I'll answer that at once. The Somerset case. Hallo—what
have you done to your hand?"

"Grazed it on the wall of the garage. It's nothing to worry
about. The Somerset case—eh? Well, what's the latest development?"

"You listen. First of all I'll take you back to your report of a
couple of days ago. About the house on Hampstead Heath. St.
Mawes, where this man Fortolis lives."

Anthony sat straight up in his chair.

"Well, what about it? I remember it all right."

"Well—a most remarkable occurrence seems to have taken place there last night."

"How on earth do you know?"

"Telephone message to the Yard this morning. From Fortolis himself. I don't think that the gentleman's lost for it, as you might say. Doesn't in the least mind taking the war into the enemy's camp."

"Go on. This is interesting."

"Thought you'd find it so." MacMorran smiled as though in approval of his own remark.

"Fortolis has reported that his house was broken into last night, but says that he is certain it was no ordinary case of house-breaking. No article of value has been stolen, as far as he has been able to trace, but his private library was entered and many of his papers turned over as though a thorough search had been made for something. His daughter surprised the man while he was on the job, but she was alone at the time, and before she could give the alarm the man made his way out and escaped."

Anthony looked all his incredulity.

"She saw the man?"

"Oh—yes—almost caught him red-handed. Discovered him in her father's library after dinner or something. But he broke past her and got away."

"She saw him, then, well enough to describe him?"

"Yes. Fortolis has given this description of him to the Yard." MacMorran fumbled in his pocket and produced a paper. "Tall, slim and well-built. Darkish hair. Well-dressed, wore an overcoat and generally suggested a man of good social standing. Age—in the early thirties."

"H'm—dozens of men might answer to that description." Anthony stood up. "Why, hang it all, it might even be a description of myself. Don't you think so, Andrew?"

MacMorran looked him over.

"So it might. Funny how these descriptions work out on people when you apply an actual test."

A slow smile spread over Anthony Bathurst's face. MacMorran saw it and a light broke in upon him.

"Yes?" he queried tersely.

Anthony nodded.

"Yes."

The Inspector whistled.

"But why? Why alone?"

"Why not?"

"Couldn't you have taken me into your high and mighty confidence?"

"If I had—you wouldn't have come with me."

"No?"

"No. Distinctly no. You couldn't have done. I was breaking the law. That's no antic for you, Andrew. Therefore I had to chance it and work on my own."

"I suppose you're right. . . ." MacMorran nodded his head slowly and then chuckled. "I call that damned good. What did you get?"

"A bang on the nut, and this, amongst other things." Anthony extended his damaged knuckles.

MacMorran looked at him. "Your garage wall . . ."

"Was a revolver bullet that might very easily have put me out of mess."

"You don't say?"

"I most certainly do. But sit yourself down and listen, and I'll give you the full score up to the fall of the last wicket. Although, between you and me, Andrew, before you came I don't know that I'd intended to tell you anything."

MacMorran listened attentively to Anthony's description of his evening's adventure. At mention of the name Max Desmoulais he stopped Mr. Bathurst abruptly by his outstretched hand. "Desmoulais, you say? Max Desmoulais?"

"Yes. That was the gentleman's name. Gentle little fellow. Would make a thundering good man to lead the Irish pack. Why, though; do you know the sound of it?"

"I do that. We're getting nice and warm at last. But go on with your story, Mr. Bathurst."

Anthony proceeded. He saw a smile play round the Inspector's mouth.

"Eh?—but it's getting all romantic. She brought you the knife—this young leddy? It's bad."

He shook his head dolefully.

"Don't be an old ass. She saved my life, or very near it. But I haven't finished yet—you listen to the rest of the yarn."

Anthony continued until the end.

"Now, tell me, Andrew, what you know of Max Desmoulais. A continental crook, I suppose?"

The Inspector shook his head.

"No. That's just what he's not."

"What do you mean, then, about knowing him and being warm at last?"

"Just this, Mr. Bathurst. That your running into Max Desmoulais like this, tells me what this Somerset case is all about. And that's precious stones! For Desmoulais is one of the biggest names and one of the richest men that Hatton Garden knows." Anthony let go a low whistle.

"At last! MacMorran, you're a genius. You've given me the very clue that I wanted. The absolutely *vital* clue. I was right about Adam Antine. I rather fancy that my case is almost complete."

CHAPTER XIX
DIGBY AND DESMOULAIS

ANTHONY Bathurst picked up Digby's trail with comparative ease. An opportune word dropped in the receptive ear of Chief-Inspector MacMorran, and passed on by that worthy to his subordinates, was soon destined to bear fruit. Digby had found similar employment to that which he had enjoyed with the Somersets in a firm whose offices were in Ballantrae Street. MacMorran conveyed such information to Anthony a day after the latter had put the inquiry through to him.

Anthony, therefore, called upon Digby immediately afterwards. He ascertained at what time the man usually left the office for lunch and at what restaurant he took it. He joined Digby at a marble-topped table and reintroduced himself. Digby's thin face flushed with surprise when Mr. Bathurst made himself known.

"I want another word with you, Mr. Digby. I must apologize for thrusting myself upon you during your luncheon hour. You can guess what I want to speak to you about?"

Digby nodded as the tempestuous waitress threw his lunch at him ... all except one potato which went on to the floor. It was the bigger one ... not as small as the other.

"The Somerset affair, no doubt. Are there any further developments?"

Anthony shook his head.

"Not a lot. But it's about that I want to see you, as you guessed. I want to pick your brains."

Digby smiled nervously.

"I'm afraid, Mr. Bathurst, that I—"

"Oh, it's not a big job—quite an ordinary affair and all in the day's work. So you needn't get all hot and bothered. Now you can eat your lunch in comfort. I want to find out something that has to do with the late Mr. David Somerset. You were so close to him in business that you're the only man that can help me. Now, in the course of your work at the office, did you ever hear the name of Fortolis? Think carefully before you answer me, because it's important."

Digby was by now quietly eating his lunch.

"Fortolis," he repeated, as though he were weighing up the name. There was a silence of perhaps a couple of minutes. "No," he replied ultimately, "as far as I can recollect, I have never before heard the name."

"I'll try again, then. Give you another name with a similar question attached. Have you ever heard Mr. Somerset, Mr. David Somerset, mention the name of Desmoulais?" Anthony spelt it after pronunciation.

"Desmoulais," repeated Digby again. "Now where have I—"

Anthony watched him as he attempted to remember.

"Yes," said Digby, nodding his head slowly. "I have heard that name—but for the moment I can't think in what connection. Give me a minute and it may come to me."

Anthony kept silent as Digby had suggested. Digby prodded a portion of steak pie and his face cleared.

"I've got it. The guv'nor asked me to get him a number on the 'phone one afternoon, I happened to be in his room, and I remember that I found out afterwards that the number was of a person named Desmoulais. I saw it in the telephone directory."

"You mean that this telephoning incident took place in the office, don't you?"

"Oh, yes. It was all done in the office."

"You heard nothing of the actual telephone conversation?"

"Not a word, Mr. Bathurst. It was all done in Mr. David Somerset's private room."

Anthony thrust at him. "What made you search the directory afterwards to discover the name?"

But Digby was proof against the shock of the attack.

"You are wrong to say that. I didn't try to find the name. I found that name of Desmoulais quite accidentally afterwards. I can't tell you how—exactly. I just happened to be looking in the telephone directory one day, perhaps I may even have been looking for another quite different number, and I hit upon this name of Desmoulais." Digby's face was flushed again.

"I apologize, Mr. Digby," ventured Anthony. "I understand perfectly."

"You will understand, too," proceeded Digby, "that there was nothing unusual or abnormal about this incident. I frequently got numbers on the 'phone for Mr. David Somerset."

"Naturally."

"I mention that, in case you were thinking that I might have told you about it when you saw me at the office some weeks ago."

"Oh—no. I understand."

"I'm relieved to hear you say that."

Digby pushed away his luncheon plate. The waitress, observing this, came to him again and made sounds with her mouth. As a result of this second interview, Digby received a plate of stewed fruit and custard, some on the table and the remainder on his trousers. Anthony allowed him to settle down again before he subjected him to further questioning.

"How long was it before Mr. Somerset's death that this telephone conversation took place?"

"About a week, I should think. Certainly not more than a fortnight."

"How can you fix that?"

"Just by the trend of events in the office."

"Such as?"

"Well, during the last weeks of his life, Mr. David went to South Kensington on two or three occasions. About a fortnight before the tragedy, he went twice in one week. That was the week that he telephoned to this man, Desmoulais. That's how I'm able to place it."

"To South Kensington? Do you mean the Museum?"

"Yes. To the Natural History Museum."

"What was his special interest there, do you know?"

"No, Mr. Bathurst. Mr. Somerset never told me. It seemed a private hobby on his part and I respected it as such."

Anthony nodded slowly at Digby's statement.

As he did so, he noticed Digby's face change colour. His lips were parted as though he were about to speak.

"Well?" queried Anthony. "And what have you thought of now?"

"Why—one thing that I remember about Mr. David. One afternoon he came back from South Kensington and I heard him tell young Mr. Geoffrey about a wonderful instrument in which he had become interested. I'm sorry—but I forget the name. All that I can remember is that when I heard it, it made me think of the word 'microscope'."

"Microscope?"

"Yes. But it wasn't microscope—I'm sure of that."

Anthony came to meditation. Yes . . . he thought he knew now what had taken David Somerset first to the Natural History Museum at South Kensington and afterwards to the "Golden Lion" at East Brutton. This interview with Digby had been eminently satisfactory. He had been able to establish definitely, not only that there had been a connection between Desmoulais and the Somerset firm, but also what the nature of that connection had been. He thanked Digby for his information and made his way to a telephone-kiosk. His objective now was a certain jeweller in the West End, with the appropriate name of Rush, who was by way of being a special pal of his. Here, in the 'phone-box, he transacted another satisfactory piece of business, and when he returned to the flat he was informed by Emily that the booklet which had been promised him by a Mr. Hector Rush, she thought that was the name the messenger said, had duly arrived. Anthony Bathurst thanked her and settled himself down to read carefully what good old Hector Rush had sent him.

After turning several pages, Mr. Bathurst began to read with a greater zest and interest. When he came to the reference to the Natural History Museum at South Kensington, he felt that his optimism of the previous morning, which he had expressed to Inspector MacMorran, had by no means been ill-founded.

For Mr. Bathurst was reading as follows:

So difficult to detect are some of these imitations, particularly those made synthetically by chemical processes, that the diamond, pearl, and precious stone section of the trade has established a laboratory in Hatton Garden specially equipped for testing precious stones.

In addition, it has arranged classes for jewellers at which they are taught the best methods of detecting imitation stones.

Claims have been put forward from time to time that exact imitations could be made of diamonds, pearls, emeralds, rubies, and sapphires. In recent years these claims have become bolder, and it is now maintained that not even experts can distinguish between the real and the imitation article.

No gem can be considered genuine unless it is entirely produced by Nature. Any gem produced artificially, however closely it may resemble the real article of Nature, always has certain characteristics by which it can be identified.

The recent "scare" which arose when it was reported that a new process for producing diamonds had been evolved led the leading jewellers to go into the whole question of imitation stones.

Tests show, they report, that these so-called "synthetic diamonds" are not composed of diamond materials. In hardness, physical properties, and chemical composition they have nothing in common with genuine diamonds.

Apart from the "scare" in diamonds, the most vexed question in recent years in the trade has been that of cultured pearls. A very old system of the Chinese was to insert in the pearl oysters, figures of Buddha and also clay pellets which were then covered with pearl secretion, specimens of which can be seen in the Natural History Museum at South Kensington.

The Japanese improved the method by inserting mother-of-pearl beads which became covered uniformly with pearl secretion. The claim, however, that they are real pearls cannot be accepted, any more than a gilt or rolled-gold article can be accepted as a solid gold article.

It is not disputed that cultured pearls are legitimate articles of commerce, but they cannot be classified or sold as *real* pearls. As far as the legal side is concerned, it has been decided both in France and America that cultured pearls must never be sold as real pearls.

The endoscope which throws a beam of light through the hole drilled in the pearl, and X-ray machines, which are used for undrilled pearls, can distinguish a cultured pearl from a genuine pearl, and are in use at the laboratory.

"Synthetic" rubies and sapphires are the most difficult to detect, because they have the same hardness and physical properties as the natural stones. They are made by fusing together the necessary chemical ingredients under intense heat.

Careful examination under a microscope is sometimes necessary before a stone can be definitely pronounced artificial.

At the Hatton Garden laboratory, an instrument called a dichroscope has been installed to test stones of this group.

Genuine rubies show two colours when seen through the instrument—purplish red and yellowish red—in the two squares of the machine. Faked stones show the same colour in both squares.

This instrument is also used for testing emeralds. Another simple aid for testing emeralds is a colour filter. When seen through a filter, the genuine emerald appears red, while imitations retain their green colour.

Apart from synthetic stones there are other ingenious forms of imitations known as "doublets".

"Pastes" (glass imitations) are much softer and have different properties from the real stones. Thus the only other artificial stones which may occasionally deceive the unwary are certain types of "doublet" which defeat a simple hardness test.

The cheapest form of "doublet" has a thin slice of garnet at the front, fused to a glass back, coloured to imitate emerald or ruby.

More difficult to detect are the sapphire "doublets" of which there are three types. In one, two pieces of pale sapphire are cemented together with transparent material of a deep blue colour; another has a pale sapphire front cemented to an underside of blue glass; while a third has a sapphire back and front and a layer of blue glass between.

Soudee emerald "doublets" are made of carefully selected quartz. They are fused with a thin plate of green glass, and, as the harness of back and front is practically the same as real emerald, it is sometimes difficult to distinguish them when the edge is hidden in a suitable mount.

"Doublets", out of their setting, can be easily detected when viewed on edge, immersed in water. Immersion in liquid is also of assistance in detecting markings in synthetic stones.

Anthony put the booklet down and rubbed his hands. Here were precious stones indeed! All to be set in the silver sea of his creating. His eyes looked again at the printed pages and picked them out. They stood out clear, clean, hard, and sharp in his sight and also in his mind. Hatton Garden . . . diamonds . . . Natural History Museum . . . South Kensington . . . microscope . . . *dichroscope* . . . here they were there . . . each one of them.

Anthony put the book down again. The case grew clearer every minute. His telephone rang as he did so. He rose and answered it. The voice that spoke to him startled him tremendously. It was the voice of Diane Fortolis.

"I want to speak to you."

"No more than I want to speak to you."

He heard a delicious crow-gurgle come down the telephone.

"Well . . . I've something *terribly* important to tell you."

"No more important than I have to tell you."

"I know that I've an awful lot to explain to you . . . and even to apologize to you about . . . but there's something even more important than either of those. More important to me, that is. Do you think that you could bear to hear it?"

"I'll screw my courage to the sticking point. Unload!"

"Well, it's this. Max Desmoulais wants me to marry him. And my father approves. What do you think about it?"

Anthony smiled happily to himself. This was even better than he had anticipated. He carefully chose the words of his reply.

"I haven't thought about it."

Her voice changed immediately and took on an acid quality that he had not heard before.

"In that case, I'm sorry to have troubled you. Good-bye."

Anthony was in again quickly.

"Don't misunderstand me, Miss Fortolis. I didn't say that I wouldn't think about it now. By the way, how's the Yard serving you? Are you entirely satisfied with them?"

Her voice floated to him over the telephone.

"Good-bye," she said.

"Good-bye," murmured Anthony as he replaced the receiver, "but what she really means is *'au revoir'*." He thought for a minute or so and then picked up the receiver again. When he got his number, he asked for Chief-Inspector MacMorran.

CHAPTER XX
THE MILL END COFFIN-MAKER

IRENE Pearce answered the two letters that she received from Anthony Bathurst with the utmost promptitude. He noted the replies that she gave, with care and considered thought. He would have preferred, in one of the letters, to have had an entirely different answer. But there it was—Miss Pearce knew her business and her way about generally, having never been afraid to go home in the dark. Mrs. Somerset was equally frank and equally satisfactory, although he felt that her knowledge of the matter wasn't as valuable as that of Irene Pearce. For on her own admission Irene Pearce must have seen and spoken with Geoffrey Somerset a very short time before his death. This fact alone gave her a great advantage.

The official Yard inquiry had made little progress, and MacMorran, remembering Mr. Bathurst's optimism regarding the completion of the case when the Desmoulais thread was grasped, was overjoyed to receive Anthony's summons one fine morning with the intimation that a journey was intended.

Anthony brought the car round to the Yard and picked up the Inspector punctually at half past eleven.

"Whither away?" inquired MacMorran.

"Not far, Andrew. Just a little run into the county of Essex— famous for fast bowlers and cabbages. To the village of the four Somersets—you see I include the widow now. The village that lies close to the house named 'Urswick', Clutton Chase."

"Been there before, haven't you?"

"Yes—but once only. I know a great deal more today than when I went the time before."

"Pleased to hear it. Glad somebody does. And when are you goin' to spill the beans?"

"When I have delivered the enemy into your hands. Today's findings should clinch matters—beyond a doubt. That is, if I have but ordinary luck."

MacMorran grunted and the car ran on for some distance with both men silent. They passed through Stratford, Ilford and Romford.

"Not so far now, Andrew," remarked Anthony. "All this trouble started because of a clever man's brain. Then a clever woman put her wits to work and up went the balloon. Men died!"

"Women are at the bottom of everything, if you ask me," rejoined the sage MacMorran.

"Except a well, perhaps. Truth is generally accepted to hold sway down there."

"In that case, then, a woman's barred," concluded the Inspector, "because Truth and a woman have never been good stable companions. And that's a fact that you'd do well to remember."

The car made good pace through Gidea Park and Brentwood and eventually pulled up in the village street of Clutton Chase.

"Is this the house?" queried MacMorran. "What house?"

"The Somerset place?"

"No, Andrew. 'Urswick' is some distance from here. I told you."

"What are we stopping here for, then?"

"A little business inquiry, Andrew. It looks as though I can 'park' here. I'll chance it, anyway. Come on—shift your fat carcase."

Anthony piloted the Inspector down the village street of Clutton Chase. As they walked, MacMorran noticed that Mr. Bathurst was carefully noticing the various shop-fronts. They travelled up one side and down the other, until the line of shops ended. Anthony scratched his cheek. MacMorran grinned. He always enjoyed Anthony Bathurst's temporary discomfiture.

"What's the trouble?"

"Can't see what I want."

"Can I help you?"

"Afraid you can't. You can't produce something from nothing."

"Well—what the hell is it that you do want?"

"The last thing on earth that you'll want."

MacMorran's brow knitted in bewilderment.

"Can't you guess?" Anthony rallied him. "The bloke that always lets you down in the end." MacMorran looked at him. Anthony grinned. "The undertaker, of course. I'm looking for the local organizer of the rites of death."

MacMorran's look of interest became a puzzled stare.

"And what might you be wantin' an undertaker for at this time of the day? Feeling rough?"

"No, Andrew. Merely altruistic. I noticed how thin and stringy your neck had got."

"What the blazes are you—"

Anthony tucked his arm into the Inspector's. "You wait a moment or so, you old fidget—and then you'll see."

Thus linked, they approached a village policeman. Anthony verbally promoted him on the spot.

"'Morning, Sergeant! I wonder whether you could help me? Could you direct me to the local undertaker's?"

The policeman grinned.

"If you stand there in the middle of the road, you won't want directing, guv'nor! Somebody'll be takin' you there on a hurdle."

"Never mind about that. Tell me now."

The constable shook his head. "I can't."

"You can't? Why not?"

"Because there isn't such a thing in the village, sir."

"Don't they die here, then?" asked MacMorran. "Only fade away?"

The policeman's first grin returned to his face. "Some die—but the nearest undertaker's at Mill End. That's where you'll have to go to get fixed up. The family's had the trade there for generations. Name of Gildey."

"How far?" asked Mr. Bathurst.

"Stone's throw. Couple of mile at the outside. Straight up towards Ingatestone and then bear to the left. You can't miss the road. Got a car?"

"Yes."

"Do it in five minutes, then."

"Thank you, Sergeant, and here's a bit towards the summer holiday."

The man's hand went to his helmet, "Thank you, sir."

They went back to the car and were soon on the way again. Anthony began to talk.

"Listen, Andrew. Change of front from now on. Where we're going this time, you're going to be official Scotland Yard. Understand? One hundred per cent such. All brass hat and throaty voice. Get me? Undertakers, from old Chowles downwards, are fearsome things—God wot! Dark miens—sad lot. A black and sinister race, all elm and brass handles. Want careful staff work when you get to close quarters, in case they put the screw on you."

The Inspector shifted uneasily in his seat.

"Here—hold on a bit. You're givin' me the creeps."

Anthony turned the car.

"Our road, I think, and the hamlet of Mill End away there in the distance."

They discovered that Mill End had one long, straggling street. A pond, cottages, a general store, an inn, and a wheelwright's that was also the undertaker's. Anthony stopped the car. He had seen the board displayed at full length across the top of the door: "Simon Gildey, Wheelwright, Carriage Builder, and Undertaker. Established since 1722".

"There you are, Inspector," said Anthony, "there's our port of call. And there, if I mistake not, is Simon Gildey himself at work, hitting the right nail on the head. Our policeman was a false prophet. Somebody in the district *has* gone to join his rude forefathers. As every man to his rest must go . . . when Death, the umpire, raises his hand."

"All right, that's enough. You seem to relish the idea, if anything."

Simon Gildey wore a black, bushy beard. Anthony exulted. The man was so beautifully "right". He put down the tools of his trade and advanced towards them.

"Don't go in," said MacMorran; "interview him outside that shed arrangement. I never was one for the Chamber of Horrors myself."

Gildey wore a canvas apron, upon which he wiped his hands. Business was brisk, he thought to himself—"three cheers for the bodies and souls of the righteous". Particularly the bodies. To say nothing of the ungodly, when the green bay-tree dies down. MacMorran said nothing as a start. He handed Gildey a card. Gildey plucked at his face-fungus.

"Scotland Yard? What have I got to do with the likes of that?"

MacMorran nodded towards Anthony.

"Just explain, will you?"

Anthony smoothed the path of inquiry.

"Just a line of investigation, Mr. Gildey, over which we think you may be able to help us. It concerns the Somerset murders. The gentlemen who lived near here—at Clutton Chase. You knew them, no doubt?"

Gildey wagged his piratical head.

"Yes, sir. I 'ad the honour of boxin' the corpses. The cream of the Clutton Chase business comes the way of the Gildey's—it 'as done since 1722, and I think we've given all parties satisfaction. You saw the date over the door, perhaps." He pointed with unholy pride to the sign of his trade.

"Yes. We imagined that you might have been called in."

"Yes, sir. I was. At Mrs. Somerset's request, I believe it was. The corpses were brought from a mortuary down in Gloucestershire in two rough shells and the final hobsequies were left in my 'ands. I provided two 'andsome coffins, if I may say so. Fit for a Dook. Must 'ave bin a pleasure to lie in 'em—in a manner of speakin'. I said as much as I screwed 'em."

Anthony distinctly heard MacMorran shiver.

"And my charges were reasonable—Mrs. Somerset said as much when she called in to settle the account. She and Mr. Gerald Somerset walked over here one day—before 'e was killed, poor young fellow."

"You surprise me," murmured Anthony.

"Oh, I'm a master of my craft, all right. Never spare myself the spit and polish. Which is what counts. My wood'll stand almost anything. It's famous all round 'ere. The damp don't get to it. I 'ad a client last week who buried his mother. Would you believe it—but he came to me specially because the poor old girl suffered so from the rheumatics in 'er knees, and 'e wanted 'er to be comfortable."

MacMorran nudged Anthony impatiently. Gildey, the village wheelwright, was getting on his nerves.

"Good," said Anthony. "I shall certainly bear you in mind for the future. But, now tell me this. What did you do with the two shells that the bodies were in when they came from that Gloucestershire mortuary?"

Gildey looked at him with unconcealed surprise.

"What did I do with 'em, sir? Why, nothing! Mrs. Somerset first of all told me to take 'em away—but afterwards they was burnt up at the 'ouse. The gardener told me so. They was 'orrible things . . . to look at . . . and to the touch . . . a real coffin made of the proper stuff ought to be a joy to 'andle . . . and I can well understand the lady wantin' to be shot of 'em. Cheap and nasty and would 'ave given a corpse a crick in the neck to lay in 'em. Well, gentlemen, is there any more that I can do for you?"

MacMorran shook his head violently.

"You did the job right through yourself?" Anthony put the question gravely.

"Yes. Right through. Order . . . delivery and graveside etiquette. Why? Is there any more trouble knockin' about with regard to it?"

"We're not sure . . . but many thanks; whatever transpires, there will be no blame attaching to you, you can rest assured of that. Thank you, Mr. Gildey."

Anthony and MacMorran left the undertaker staring at them as they made their way back to the car. Anthony turned the car homewards.

"Well?" inquired MacMorran. "And where are we now? For I'm dashed if I know—and that's a fact."

"Where are we?" Anthony repeated his words. "In the straight, Andrew. With our mounts nicely balanced and ourselves sitting pretty."

"Sound sure of yourself, don't you?"

"If I'm wrong this time, I'll buy you that bungalow you've got your eye on down at Ferring. But don't write a book about it."

"That's a bet. I'll keep you to it. Now tell me the reasons behind this wave of optimism."

"I'll give you *facts*—not reasons. Facts'll suit you better. But, first of all, let me commend to your attention the incident of the shells from Gloucestershire."

MacMorran screwed up his face.

"Can't do it. Too difficult. Give me 'the cat saw a rat on the mat'—nothing beyond that. The shells were burned, I understood from that ancient horror that we've just interviewed. Mrs. Somerset arranged it. Under the supervision of the gardener." Anthony nodded. "I wonder."

"Anyway, what's the odds? You wouldn't keep a pair of coffin shells as keepsakes, would you? 'A present from Gloucester'. 'Think on me'. Personally, I should think burning a bright idea."

"Not bad for you, Mac. Another pyre for Dido—eh? Or Somerset 'suttee'? Still, we shall know all about it before the week's out."

"Where are we bound for now?"

"Your home from home. The Yard—and Sir Austin Kemble. This is where you and I and he get busy. How does the prospect please you?"

"Not so good. What you mean is that this is where *I* get busy."

Anthony smiled. "Andrew—I won't contradict you."

Three quarters of an hour later saw them in the presence of Sir Austin Kemble, Commissioner of Police. He listened to Anthony's story with amazement.

CHAPTER XXI
MR. BATHURST DEALS TWO ACES

MR. BATHURST told his story with dramatic effect. He came to his conclusion.

"Now, sir, I want two matters attended to. First of all, I want an order, immediately, sir, for the exhumation of the body of Geoffrey Somerset."

The Commissioner stared.

"Why Geoffrey Somerset?"

"Because Geoffrey's the crux of the question. As I see things."

Sir Austin demurred.

"H'm! You're asking me something, you know. Still—I don't see that I need—"

"Also, sir, I want Sir Roderick Hope for the job. Is it O.K., sir?"

Sir Austin Kemble showed his uneasiness.

"I can't say that I altogether like the idea. I don't want to trouble the Home Office unless I'm absolutely sure of my ground. I might cut an inglorious figure. I might be accused of—"

Anthony winked at MacMorran and interrupted: "Do you remember the case of 'The Spiked Lion', Sir Austin?"

"Perfectly."

"Was I right when I asked for the exhumations at Hurstfold and Hurrilow? Did I cause you to cut an inglorious figure in either of those cases?"

The Commissioner coughed nervously. He glanced in the direction of Inspector MacMorran.

"What Mr. Bathurst says is true, sir. He was right all along the line, sir, if you remember."

Sir Austin pulled at his upper lip.

"All right," he said eventually. "I'll do it. But I'm far from keen."

Anthony picked up the receiver and placed it in the Commissioner's hands.

"The Home Office, sir. Where they're all pathological. Get on at once, will you? They'll put you through."

Sir Austin grumbled. but took the telephone. Words came to his lips.

"The Commissioner of Police . . . speaking . . . from New Scotland Yard. . . . I want to speak to Sir Roderick Hope . . . thank you."

Three minutes later he turned to Anthony.

"There you are, you've had your way. . . . as usual with you. Now, what's the other job. you want done?"

"Co-operation with the post-office."

Sir Austin stared at him fixedly.

"In what way?"

"I want the help that only the post-office can give me. I want information from the typist that worked in the Somerset office and who has since disappeared from her usual haunts. It's vital."

"How do you want it done?"

"Remember James Canham Read, the Rochford murderer, who boarded the train at Benfleet, after killing Florence Dennis? And went into hiding?"

"Very well. What about him?"

"The post-office authorities watched every post for any letter addressed to any of his relatives or friends that came through their hands. In case it should have come from Canham Read himself. He was short of cash and was bound to write to somebody before long. I fancy he lived in Jamaica St., E. He eventually did write and the post-office picked it up. In that way he guided the police to his hiding-place. Get me? I propose to obtain Miss Masters's address by employing the same methods."

"How do we work it? Give me more details, Bathurst."

"Her people live at Ilford. The Newbury Park side, I believe. Let me see if I can remember the address . . . 37 Myers Terrace, Newbury Lane. That was it. I'm certain. I want all letters that go through to that address examined. By that means, sooner or later, when the P.O. wills, I shall find Maud Masters, the masterly! Got the idea, Sir Austin?"

"Clumsy, isn't it? Is it the only way? Can't we find a better one?"

"A far, far better thing to do? Candidly, I can't see one. But I'm all ears for anything snappy that you can suggest."

"Advertise. Broadcast for her. Flood the country with the Masters picture?"

Anthony shook his head.

"Believe me, sir—you won't get her that way. There are none so deaf as those that won't hear. When she left the firm of Somerset and Sons she knew more than she ever passed on to any of us. The post-office way's the best. It may take time—but it's sound. That's why it appeals to me."

"What do you think, MacMorran?" The Commissioner seemed a trifle anxious.

"Think it's all right, sir. It's safe—as Mr. Bathurst points out."

"Put the instruction through, then. Get the P.M.G.'s office. I'll speak to them."

MacMorran picked up the telephone. There was one thing . . . he had stood loyally by Anthony Bathurst on this occasion!

The exhumation of the body of the late Geoffrey Somerset was carried out under the conditions of the usual secrecy. Few of the villagers of Clutton Chase realized what the inhabitants of the cars that drove up to the parish church of Clutton had for their objective. Sir Roderick Hope, the Crown pathologist, was in the first car with Sir Austin, Inspector MacMorran, and Anthony Bathurst. It was close on midnight when, under the Commissioner's directions, the grave was opened and the coffin bearing the plate marked "Geoffrey Somerset" taken from the grave where he and his father had been buried, and conveyed to a small building that had been commandeered for the purpose.

Within the building, it was placed upon trestles. Sir Roderick Hope motioned to the two men who had hung about on the fringe of the crowd. They came quickly forward. MacMorran looked at Anthony, for Simon Gildey of Mill End was one of the two men. Sir Roderick Hope gave curt orders. The two men quickly opened the coffin by the flickering light of many candles.

"This is my coffin," said Simon, the wheelwright of Mill End, to his fellow workman. "I'd know it if I had no eyes." He plucked at his beard. "It's a shame to open such a beauty."

He took out his screw-driver and handed another to the man who was assisting him in his gruesome task. The screws were quickly turned by the expert toolsmen and the coffin-lid lifted off. Sir Roderick Hope and the others walked quietly towards it. But Anthony Bathurst, for a strange reason, remained where he was. He listened intently for what was to happen. If he had erred—but his intelligence came to his aid and he *knew* that he was right. He even allowed the ghost of a smile to play round his lips.

The buzz of surprise from the knot of people gathered round the head of the coffin floated down to him. He walked towards them.

"Could I have *Glastonbury Traditions concerning Joseph of Arimathea*, gentlemen?" he inquired quietly. "For I'm certain that you will find that in the coffin somewhere, *inter alia*—of course. Call it the 'Elm Library'!"

Sir Roderick Hope's face twisted into a disappointed smile.

"I'm sorry to have wasted your time, Sir Roderick, but, you see, we had to have you here in case I was wrong and there *was* a body in the coffin after all."

"Books," returned the eminent pathologist; "about fifty of 'em, I should think. You'd better go up there and pick out the one you want."

Sir Austin Kemble was far from smiling.

"What's the meaning of this piece of profanity, Bathurst?" He gestured towards the coffin-load of books. "Where's the body?"

"I think that I know, sir, but I can't prove it. Also, you would have a natural and justifiable difficulty in believing me."

Sir Austin glared, whilst Simon Gildey caressed the polished sides of the box of his craftsmanship.

"Is the other brother's body in the coffin, either, Bathurst? Gerald Somerset's body, I mean, at Friningham?"

Bathurst shook his head.

"In my opinion—it is not, sir. Neither Geoffrey's here nor Gerald's there."

Sir Austin fumed.

"Then there will have to be a second exhumation at Friningham. I shall insist on that—what a pity he wasn't buried here with the others, eh, Sir Roderick?"

"What 'others', sir?" queried Anthony imperturbably.

"Er—with his father and—er—these damned books."

"I see what you mean, sir. I wasn't quite sure." Sir Austin eyed him fixedly.

"I suppose that David Somerset's body *is* here?"

"I think you can bank on that, sir. You see, he was too old—his body wasn't of any use to them." Sir Austin stared again, before putting his arm through Sir Roderick Hope's.

"Oh, Sir Roderick, I shall have to ask the Home Office about that Friningham job. I'm afraid that it means a second exhumation order."

Sir Roderick and the Commissioner conversed rapidly. MacMorran drew Anthony Bathurst to one side.

"I'm more in the dark than ever. What's it all mean?"

"Leave it till later, Andrew. It'll wait—until when Miss Masters tells us her story—which time, I hope, will come very soon. The case will then be absolutely water-tight."

MacMorran grinned.

"Like one of old Gildey's coffins, eh? Look, he's fondling that one. By the way, the guv'nor's been on to the P.M.G. this morning. That other little job's being arranged as you wanted it."

"Good. Then the sooner we get home the better for all of us."

The Commissioner's voice called to him.

"I take it you'll be coming to Friningham with us, Bathurst?"

Anthony shook his head.

"I don't think so, Sir Austin, if it's all the same to you. As I said, you won't find Gerald Somerset in the coffin there, any more than you found Geoffrey Somerset in the coffin here this evening."

"I must make sure of that," replied Sir Austin pompously.

"I realize that, sir, and I understand your position. But if you'll excuse my coming with you, I should be grateful."

The company that had gathered for the grim proceedings broke up. The building was emptied. The exhumation of Geoffrey Somerset had been ordered by the Home Office and had taken place. The cars in procession made their way back to the places from which they had come.

Two days later, Anthony, in his own room, was summoned to the telephone. It was Inspector MacMorran speaking on behalf of the Commissioner of Police. He spoke from the seaside town of Friningham in the county of Essex.

"Sir Austin's compliments, Mr. Bathurst, but you're *wrong*! Gerald Somerset's body *is* in the coffin here. We exhumed last night."

Anthony paled a little at the Inspector's words. Then he smiled.

"If that's the case, Inspector, my case falls to pieces."

"Well, you can take it from me that it is so."

"Then all I can do is to apologize."

"I'll tell the guv'nor, Mr. Bathurst and I'll tell you this. You're a gentleman!"

"Thank you, but I wouldn't go so far as to say that, Inspector."

He put up the receiver with a thoughtful look on his face. Then returned to his chair and sat there lost in thought.

Chapter XXII
DIANE DINES

DIANE Fortolis sat opposite to Anthony Bathurst at a table at Murillo's. They dined *à deux*.

"You are early," he said as she swept to his table. "I had quite made up my mind that I should have to wait for you."

"That shows how little you know me."

"Time is a great teacher. I've taken the liberty of ordering two 'Clover Clubs'. Does that meet with your approval? By the way, when did you last see your father?"

"Does that matter?" Diane's eyes danced. "Besides, I'm a Cromwellian."

"No. Not a lot, certainly. How is he these days?"

A waiter bore down upon them carrying the cocktails.

"Thank you, Pierre," said Anthony. "I have also ordered your dinner, Miss Fortolis. I took the liberty . . . yes?"

The lady smiled graciously. There had been an occasion not long since when she had been Diane.

"I am in your hands, Mr. Bathurst."

"Charming of you. We're getting to know each other splendidly. It's an amazing thought—that I probably owe you my life."

"Is the dinner, then, in exchange for the life?"

Anthony's eyes took in her dinner-dress. She looked superb, he thought. Her dress was a study in rose. A swag of roses, in the same pastel crêpe as the dress, outlined the décolletage and shirring pulled the skirtfulness to the front and lifted it from the floor. A burnous cape was caught at the throat. The stitches of the shirring were broken to make it elastic. An Indian ruby necklace brought out the undertones of the heavy clinging rose-pink crepe.

"Well, hardly that," he answered. "Should I have worn a white gardenia?" His eyes held hers.

"In my honour?" she rallied him.

The waiter came with the hors-d'oeuvres. Diane crumbled her roll into small pieces upon the white cloth.

"Your honour, Miss Fortolis, needs no decoration."

"That's very sweet of you. Now, what shall we talk about in addition to our two selves?"

"What else is there in the world at this moment?"

"Don't be absurd."

"The truth is always unpopular. But not necessarily absurd."

She leant over towards him.

"Mr. Bathurst, tell me what you want to tell me."

"Miss Fortolis—I dare not."

She smiled deliciously.

"Then tell me what you intend to tell me."

"How do you know that it isn't the same thing?"

"Why should I tell you all my secrets?"

"Why should I tell you one of mine?"

"Perhaps—because I ask you to."

The waiter brought another course. Anthony raised his glass.

"*A toi!* That shall be the reason, then."

She raised her glass and returned the toast.

"But before I begin, tell me—how is Monsieur Max Desmoulais?"

"Why?" she replied coldly. "Does his health interest you so tremendously?"

"It didn't, once upon a time, but now it's beginning to."

"Why—again?"

"Didn't you hint at a marriage between him—and another?"

"That should do his health good."

"Yes—but not mine."

"Your health wasn't under discussion that I know of."

"How would you like to see your friend Max Desmoulais dangling at the end of a rope?"

She abruptly turned the question.

"Let us leave Max Desmoulais out of the conversation—please. Now tell me what you were going to. Do something to please me for once. Most men of my acquaintance would have done so long before this."

"Very well. But remember that I make no promises on behalf of Scotland Yard. I can't. It's not within my province or power. My connection with the official police is purely a voluntary one and I have no power to influence them in any way."

"I don't believe that, altogether, but I'll accept it for the time being."

Anthony shook his head disclaimingly.

"I can assure you that what I say is true, Miss Fortolis. By the way, I presume that the 'o' in your name is a long 'o'?"

"You are quite right, Mr. Bathurst. I should have corrected you before if it hadn't been."

"I might have known it." Anthony glanced at the clock. Diane noticed the look and wondered.

"Are you in a hurry to leave me? Because, if so . . ."

Anthony smiled that irresistible smile of his.

"I was wondering how long it would take me to tell you the story." He lifted his glass again and drank. "Starting a story of this kind is always the most difficult part. Let me see! Where shall I begin?" He looked at her quizzically. The set of her head on her shoulders couldn't be faulted. Her eyes challenged and almost mocked him.

"I am waiting," she prompted him.

"Very well. I will commence with the late David Somerset. An analytical and manufacturing chemist. Offices in London and a home in the country. In the country which is not too far from town. Not a bad life—all things considered. He was a success—that is to say, 'comfortably off'. His first wife had died leaving him with two sons. Boys of whom he was very naturally and justifiably proud. I should rather like two boys myself."

Anthony paused to see how she would take his sally.

"No doubt you will find somebody ready to supply you. Make sure that she's young and healthy before you commit yourself."

"Oh—absolutely. I agree with you. Shall I go on?"

"Please. I can't see any real reason why you should have stopped."

"David Somerset, then, had married a second time. A clever woman married a clever man. Each had the gift of personality. The personalities blended and David Somerset's brain was sharpened to a fine edge. He had a spur. Perhaps every clever man is the better for a spur. His desire was that he and his wife and two boys should have the best that life had to offer. He was already 'comfortably off', as I have put it. His great and paramount ambition was to be wealthy. So wealthy that he need not deny his wife or his two boys *anything* that the resources of science, and civilization generally, had to give them. Did you ever meet either of the two boys, Miss Fortolis?"

The question was a rapid thrust at her, but she was unperturbed.

"Never, Mr. Bathurst. We mixed in different circles. I thought you were aware of that."

"I am. But you never know where an acquaintance may spring up and be fostered. Well . . . David Somerset had long been coquetting with an idea. Not an invention altogether. Much more in the nature of a discovery. I suggest, Miss Fortolis, that David Somerset was able, when his discovery was perfected by him, and his experiments rendered successful, to produce nothing less than—diamonds. Diamonds so marvellously manufactured that not even the cleverest experts were able to distinguish between the real and the scientifically manufactured article. Even experts like your father, Cesar Fortolis, your husband-to-be, Max Desmoulais, and the man who called himself Adam Antine. I congratulate him, of course, on the happy choice of his sobriquet." He paused. "Your turn, Diane. I want your comments and criticisms."

Her eyes still teased him.

"As far as I know—you can take full marks, Mr. Bathurst. So far as you have gone. I wouldn't contradict a single statement that you have made."

The waiter arrived with the sweets. Dinner was drawing to its close.

"Good," said Anthony in reply to her. "Now . . . in the past, no gem has ever been accepted by the experts, or considered genuine, unless it had been entirely produced by Nature herself. *Any gem produced artificially, however marvellous it might be, however closely it might resemble the real article of Nature's handiwork, always* had certain . . . not imperfections, exactly . . . but characteristics by which the expert could always identify it . . . and therefore discard it, as it were, as an imitation stone. *But this could not be done with Somerset's diamonds.* Which fact has meant a trail of death."

Her face was steady now and the beauty of it quiet and wistful. Anthony took up the thread of his tale again.

"You will be able to picture what this discovery of David Somerset's meant. To the big diamond merchants, for instance. He could produce a flawless stone by a process that I suggest cost him little or nothing. If he made his discovery public property, diamonds would be as cheap as peanuts. David Somerset thought things over. Why not capitalize, if he could, the value of his tremendous discovery? There might be terms which could be agreed upon, on which he could sell to the biggest names . . . shall we say . . . in Hatton Garden? Those who afterwards wore white flowers in their buttonholes?

"I will cut this part of my story short. Negotiations, I suggest, were opened, excessively secret negotiations, which culminated in an hotel at East Brutton in Gloucestershire. David Somerset proved his claim. He performed his diamond-making experiment in the presence of the experts. The syndicate of diamond-dealers was prepared to purchase his secret. He was equally prepared to sell. I can't give you the price at which Somerset sold. We may never know. But '*you*', as opposed to '*us*', *may* know. The amount isn't of paramount importance. Anyhow, Somerset left the 'Golden Lion' at East Brutton that afternoon with an attaché-case full of bank-notes. He had stipulated in the early stage of the negotiations that if a deal were done, payment should be made in this manner. You know what happened afterwards, Miss Fortolis . . . David Somerset and his son Geoffrey, were found dead . . . murdered . . . in Brutton Copse. May I smoke? Thank you . . . and you?"

Diane Fortolis nodded, and Anthony lit the cigarettes for each of them. She smoked nonchalantly.

"Shall I still go on?" asked Anthony.

She made a slight assenting movement of the head.

"My first advertisement raised doubts in the minds of those who had paid the big price for the Somerset secret. *What was Gerald Somerset, the remaining son, going to do? Was he also in his father's confidence?* Had they purchased wastefully? I admit that I carefully and deliberately planted the doubt by the terms of my public advertisement. Candidly, it was the best stroke of work that I ever did."

"Why?" inquired Diane Fortolis innocently.

"My dear young lady, remembering all that has occurred since, how can you possibly ask that question? Even this dinner, for instance . . ."

Miss Fortolis blushed delightfully.

"I am sorry," she murmured. "My intelligence is diminishing. It must be due to the company that I keep."

"That's easily remedied, surely?"

"How?"

"Come and live with me. But let me proceed." He observed that the blush was spreading more deeply. "My advertisement in the 'Agony' Column bore fruit. Your syndicate *was* doubtful. They sent you to spy out the land. I shall never be able to repay them."

"And I shall want years for my revenge."

"But, you see, I *knew*, really *knew*, but little! I tried to bluff you into telling me more by the simple and ancient subterfuge of pretending that I knew all. I failed. For instance, you denied all knowledge of the excellent Miss Masters. I drew several bows at a venture. I failed again. You remember how our *tête-à-tête* ended? You partly saw through me—and when I tried to find out from where you came I failed for a third time. Or, rather, my auxiliaries did. Well, have I told the truth?"

Her cheeks were scarlet. "No."

"No? Wherever not?"

"I didn't partly see through you."

"You didn't?"

"No—I *completely* saw through you." Her eyes showed the satisfaction of her triumph. The orchestra seemed to sense it and share it with her.

"'I'll see you again'," commented Anthony, listening to the number played. "Clever chaps these music wallahs. Seem to have the prophetic instinct."

"Do you think so? Spring's nearly a year away, you know."

"I know—but if winter comes—well, time flies, doesn't it?"

"I think that you had better go on with your story. After I left your man down in the East End somewhere. That task was comparatively easy. We guessed that I might be followed, so we engaged two cars to assist in throwing you off the scent. Still—go on, as I asked you."

"Well, after that, the luck of the game turned my way. I got on to the mysterious Mr. Adam Antine."

She put her hand on his arm.

"I think that was marvellously clever of you. Please tell me how you found out about that."

Anthony shook his head.

"Much as I should like to bask in the sunshine of your praise, Diane, I honestly can't! I owed the discovery to pure luck. I found a letter—*the* letter, probably—signed 'Adam Antine' in the letter-box of the Somerset offices addressed to—David Somerset. Yes—to David Somerset—none other."

She knitted puzzled brows.

"When? After our first meeting?"

"Yes."

"I can't understand that."

"I couldn't—at the time. But I can now. Actually, it's been one of the vital turning-points of the case. One was able to prove conclusively so many matters arising out of it, *because* of it. I knew that by using the pseudonym that had been so deliberately chosen I should put much more wind up the white gardenias than I had been able to before. I had taken the top card, as it were, and it had turned up as the ace of trumps. *Now*, you didn't know *how* much I knew . . . and, just as I had anticipated, you came running back, all hot and bothered."

Indignation from Miss Fortolis.

"That I never did. I never *run* anywhere. Let alone to a man."

Anthony teased her.

"Don't you mean—to an ordinary man? Still, never mind, we will let it pass. At our *second* meeting, in my flat, where we fenced with each other for a hell of a time, I began more and more to see the light. Not only in your eyes, but from the problem." She was smiling now. "Since then, I, and the official police, have been able to march straight ahead." He saw her bite her lip. "We are *very* close to the final chapter and the ringing down of the curtain. One more piece of information, which may come to us now at any moment . . . and there remain but four things to be accomplished . . . arrest of the murderer . . . or murderers . . . trial of same . . . sentence . . . and execution! Hanged by the neck until dead . . . and body buried within the precincts of the prison. You see, I am confident how a jury will deal with the matter."

She was still biting her lip. Control came to her.

"What do you wish me to do? Offer you my congratulations?"

"Upon what?"

"Your brilliant handling of the case, of course. What else could there be?"

"I was wondering myself." His grey eyes smiled at her. "Still, there's no need to rush things, those other congratulations can come later. Well, what are we going to do next?"

Her eyes met his fearlessly.

"Do you know who 'Adam Antine' was? Because if it will help you, I'll tell you. It was—"

Before she could speak the name, Anthony had interposed.

"I know, Miss Fortolis. I'll write the name down for you here. My experience tells me that one never knows who's listening in a place like Murillo's."

Anthony scribbled a name on the back of a visiting-card. He handed her the card.

"Am I right?"

"You are. And I suppose you intend to hang either my father or Max Desmoulais? Is that the bright idea? Because I'm perfectly certain that you'll never hang *him*." She tapped the visiting-card on the table with her forefinger. "You'll never be able to obtain sufficient proof. He's taken good care of that. Besides, consider his position."

Anthony leant across the table.

"I intend to hang the person who murdered the Somersets. No matter who that person is."

As he spoke, a waiter came quickly towards their table.

"Monsieur Bathurst," he said, "please—you are wanted in the *foyer*. The person who wants you told me to tell you that the matter was extremely urgent."

Anthony sought permission from his companion.

"Would you mind? I'm wanted urgently. I promise faithfully that I won't be away too long."

She glanced and nodded acquiescence. Anthony walked down the restaurant behind the waiter who had delivered the message and came into the *foyer*. At once he saw who it was that had summoned him. Chief-Inspector Andrew MacMorran stood there.

Resolution and determination oozed from his finger-tips. The line of his jaw indicated the strictest attention to business. Anthony went straight to his side.

"What's afoot, Andrew?"

"I went to your flat, Mr. Bathurst. Emily, the good girl, told me that I should find you here. News of the girl Masters. From the post-office people."

Anthony gripped him by the arm.

"Oh, good, man! When?"

"This afternoon. A letter came through, so I'm told, addressed to her mother—37 Myers Terrace, Newbury Lane, Ilford. The postmark attracted the sorter's attention . . . they're all under orders about it, naturally, since the guv'nor sent word through."

"Stout fellow . . . and the postmark was . . . I could bear to know, Andrew."

Mr. Bathurst was undoubtedly excited.

"You won't feel so good when I tell you. France! South of France. Avignon."

Anthony pulled at his upper lip—his old trick when given a job of thought.

"I'm not surprised. She was well paid to clear out of England. Now, what's our best plan, Mac? Boat and train, or air? I think the latter. Yes—the latter. Arrange everything with Sir, Austin, will you? The usual formalities and so on. I'll bring Miss Pearce. In preference to Mrs. Somerset. You get Digby. I fancy that he'll be of more use than anybody. Tonight, then, at Croydon. Conditions couldn't be better. Oh, and bring your revolver."

MacMorran nodded and turned. Anthony called him back.

"By the way, Andrew, I'm dining here with Miss Fortolis. And everything's in rhythm with my heart."

He grinned as he saw the Inspector's jaw drop. MacMorran slowly shook his head.

"That's bad news. It's what I've been fearing these last three weeks."

"Why?"

"Why? Because I never like to see a good man go wrong. So long, Mr. Bathurst. See you at Croydon, then."

Anthony went joyfully back to Mademoiselle Diane.

CHAPTER XXIII
IN THE VILLA ST. MARRE

MR. BATHURST called at Antigua, Braundway Avenue, Chiswick, for Irene Pearce and quickly outlined to her why he desired her personal services. They met MacMorran and the Commissioner of Police at the Croydon Aerodrome. Sir Austin Kemble had been in touch with the *Sûreté-Générale* at Paris, and the Inspector had been to the offices of the Air Company and had hired an aeroplane.

"Where's Digby?" asked Anthony.

"Can't get him," returned MacMorran. "Been to his home and also to the place where he works now. He's supposed to be away for a few days on business. Does it matter a great deal?"

"I wanted Digby," said Mr. Bathurst. "I have such a warm corner in my heart for him. Still, what can't be cured must be endured."

He introduced Irene Pearce, and the four of them started off from the Croydon Aerodrome on an absolutely perfect night. But, as luck would have it, things ran against them. Some fifteen miles to the north of Paris, the 'plane developed engine trouble and they were forced to land. However, catching a suburban train into the capital in the early hours of the morning, they were able to leave Paris at nine o'clock by the *Rapide* to Marseilles.

Anthony and Irene Pearce, at least, will never forget that journey to the South. Woods and churches. Cities, villages, and rivers. The train roared its way on and over flat country until they came to the town of Dijon. Then on again to Valence and away again. Eventually they arrived at Avignon, that enchanting little town of narrow streets and tiny open squares.

Upon Anthony's advice, they wasted no time upon inquiries but went straight to the Hotel de l'Europe. Dinner and bed completed the day for them.

"In the morning," declared Sir Austin Kemble, "we will act. I have heard from the French police. You agree, Bathurst?"

"Most certainly, sir. Grub and a good night's rest are most strongly indicated."

Thus it went, and all inquiries were left over until the morning. When Anthony joined them in the coffee-room at breakfast they found that since rising he had been far from idle.

"News," he said, "red-hot news. Straight from the horse's mouth. The English girl has been located by me. Discreet inquiries of the hotel staff have elicited the fact that the lady whom we have come here to interview lives in a villa out at Villeneuve-les-Avignon. Near the waters of the Rhône. It's some little way from here. The actual address is the Villa St. Marre. From the description I've had from the reception-clerk, I've no doubt at all that it's the Masters girl all right. So I propose that we move over there directly after dinner tonight." He rubbed his hands. Something had evidently pleased him immensely.

The Inspector and the Commissioner were in agreement and Anthony bent over the table to have a few words with Irene Pearce. The lady in question listened attentively.

"I understand," she said eventually, "although I don't really care what happens to me, or to any of you." Anthony spoke to her again. "I am aware of that, Mr. Bathurst. I told Mrs. Somerset that when I saw her last at Clutton Chase. As a matter of fact, it's the sole reason why I am here with you now."

She rose as she spoke and left the breakfast-table. Sir Austin Kemble watched her go. He was evidently surprised. Anthony went to him and MacMorran.

"According to what I have heard this morning, sir, the Villa St. Marre stands some little distance from the banks of the Rhône. There are a terrace and shrubberies and it is surrounded by a rather unpleasant ditch. I prefer to introduce ourselves to it and its occupants in the darkness rather than by the light of day. The waiting hours will, no doubt, be trying to us, but that can't very well be helped."

Sir Austin nodded.

"We shall find something to occupy our time. Also, I have some telephoning to do. There is the question of the local police. They told me at H.Q. that I should hear from them today."

The hours dragged slowly, but evening came. Anthony gave the Inspector instructions. MacMorran left the house and, amongst other matters, hired an ancient-looking car which held the four of them. At half past eight, after dinner, they started. Darkness had swooped down upon everything. The stars looked like jewels as they dotted the sky. Anthony had a fancy that the dead David Somerset had flung them there with a lavish hand, straight-created from his own crucible.

MacMorran kept the car going at a steady rate. They crossed the long bridge that spans the river.

"How far now?" asked the Commissioner.

"About three kilometres. Not more."

"How are we handling our forces? Openly? Or are you staging a surprise? The French police will be there when we arrive," said MacMorran, "as Mr. Bathurst asked. H.Q. have agreed to our suggested line of action."

"There's one thing that's clear," replied Anthony. "Maud Masters mustn't see me. At first, that is. Or you either, Miss Pearce. What do you think? If we scare her, she won't talk."

Irene seemed listless and strangely preoccupied.

"No, perhaps she may remember me. I have been up to the office once or twice when she has been there."

Anthony watched her carefully. He was anxious—he had painful work close ahead of him. Would it be better policy to alter his plans and trust to short, sharp attack? It was quite dark now. With all the hidden horrors with which imagination can invest black night. The stars now were legion. Cattle moved close to their car, over the pasture near the roadside, occasionally an owl hooted his plaint to a moon which so far was not, and birds flew and broke and whirred their bustling wings amidst the branches of the many trees.

"Are they bound to be in the house?" inquired Sir Austin Kemble.

"Of course they aren't. But I was told that she didn't go out a great deal of an evening. Hallo! What's this?"

A car overtook and flashed by them as he spoke, a powerful Hispano-Suiza. Anthony drew back as it passed.

"I shouldn't be overwhelmed with surprise if that were they. Been out for a day's jaunt and come back for the evening. Life without serious responsibility must be a delightful proposition here, you know. Miss Masters could have chosen a worse spot."

He fell to thought again.

"Look here, Sir Austin," he said, "I've changed my ideas. I don't like the prospect of . . ." He broke off. "You've got a warrant with you, haven't you? Made out as I said?"

MacMorran nodded.

"Yes, I've taken your word once again. I've seen the French authorities and the Commissioner has had the necessary arrangements made. I trust you, like the lamb trusted Mary."

"Good! Use it when I give you word. I suggest, Sir Austin, that from now on you take charge."

"Naturally! What do I do?"

"You and Inspector MacMorran go to the front of the villa. Ask for Madame Antine." He chuckled. "A distinctly neat touch, that. I must certainly congratulate her on the choice of the name. Don't worry—you'll be on perfectly safe ground. Say that your business is both confidential and urgent. That will get you admitted to her all right. I'll leave the rest to your powers of ingenuity."

"And what are you going to do, Bathurst?"

"Miss Pearce and I will operate from the rear of the villa. If I can, and I'm confident that I can, I'll be present at the interview that you and MacMorran will conduct. Anyhow, keep it going till you get a sign from me. Here we are, I think. Stop the car here. There's no sign of that other one which passed us on the road."

MacMorran brought the car to a halt and the four people alighted.

"We'll divide our forces now," said Anthony. "As I arranged. You with me, Miss Pearce, and I promise you that you'll be quite safe—I won't let you out of my sight. Good luck, sir—and to you, Andrew. Don't forget to use your revolver—if necessary. Cheero!"

He waved his hand to them and they walked towards the front entrance. Anthony and Irene stopped where they were until the other two were out of sight.

"Now come," he said. "This is where your athletic training for the 'flicks' will come in useful. I'm going to jump a ditch and you have to perform likewise. Can you do it?"

"I'll try," she replied.

The stubbornness was still plain in the tone of her voice. They came to the ditch. Anthony jumped, but fell short. He landed into a bed of leaves, so was none the worse. Irene followed him similarly. He caught her hands and lifted her from the leaves.

"So far so good. Now we'll keep to the shadow of the trees. There's the house. Look! The birds are in their nest. Our luck has held."

Irene looked blankly at the line of lights from the illum-
ined windows. "Come on." They ran swiftly and silently until
they came to the belt of smaller trees close to the line of lighted
windows. Here the two *gendarmes* from Avignon joined
them and saluted. Whispered words and a document passed
between them. Anthony examined it and nodded assent. They
climbed on to the terrace, Irene silent still, and crept towards
the windows. One was open. Anthony slipped over the threshold into the comfort of the room and pulled Irene after him.
Sergeants Ravenal and Perrichon waited outside. Anthony and
Irene Pearce were scarcely inside the room when there came
the sound of a woman's voice. The words that she was speaking
were French.

"Quick!" whispered Anthony. "They're coming into this very
room. Behind here—and thank God for the design of the room!"

He pointed to two screens of the Chinese type—in lacquer
and embroidery. Fortunately they were unusually tall and gave
that effect of not only lowering the ceiling but also of furnish-
ing the walls. Irene Pearce stood with Anthony. Her face was
flushed and her breath came quickly. He touched her on the arm
in the hope that it would give her courage and confidence.

Four voices were now audible. The one that they had heard
when they entered, Sir Austin Kemble's, MacMorran's, and that
other which Anthony had come to France to hear. The voice
of Miss Masters, the one-time efficient stenographer on the
staff of Somerset and Sons! The four people of the four voices
entered the room. Anthony heard Sir. Austin Kemble take up
the parable.

"We are sorry to trouble you so late in the evening, Madame
Antine, but, as I attempted to explain to your maid, our business is both urgent and important. We are acting on behalf
of Messrs. Hartley, Holland, and Hill, solicitors of Basinghall
Street, London. You have been nominated as a beneficiary in a
will of one of their most wealthy and important clients."

Anthony became anxious. The Commissioner would never
get that past Maud Masters. He heard her cross the floor of the
room towards the door again. What was she doing? Ringing for

the maid again? He heard her footsteps return to the middle of the room. Irene Pearce shook her head at him hopelessly.

Miss Masters spoke.

"I don't think that I understand. None of my relations or friends knows of my marriage, so I don't see how any one of them could have left me money in a will. Would you mind giving me further particulars? Or possibly to my husband?"

There was a dangerously icy edge to her voice that told Anthony that Sir Austin Kemble's craft was already in stormy waters. Then he heard the voice of the maid again. As before, she spoke in French. Anthony held Irene by the arm and strained his ears in an effort to catch what the girl was saying. The Masters girl replied, also in French. Anthony wondered what MacMorran was thinking, chained to his seat at the Commissioner's side, in the middle of the room. As he wondered, he caught a phrase from the lips of Miss Masters, or, rather, four snatches, as it were, of one sentence.

"*Dites lui—prenez garde—le vieillard—comme au printemps. Savez-vous, Jeanne?*"

"*Oui, Madame.*"

"The old man." What was afoot now? Anthony Bathurst patted the outside of his pocket to assure himself that the revolver was to hand if wanted. Maud Masters went on talking to Sir Austin. The Commissioner embarked upon a more detailed explanation. Anthony knew that the critical moment was winging on its way . . . knew that it must arrive *soon*!

Chapter XXIV
WHAT MAUD MASTERS KNEW!

THE Commissioner of Police still talked. Madame Antine still "played" him. Anthony sensed the "edge" that she put on everything that she said. He pictured her as he had seen her in the Somerset offices. Thin, sharp-featured, and pale-blue eyes. The eyes, almost, of a sailor. He knew the game that she was now playing. How long would she keep it up? Suddenly he heard her voice change. Just for a split second. He heard that catch in a voice which means that, for that same split second, the mind of the speaker has left the subject and wandered away elsewhere. Just the swift desertion from the art of concentration. Anthony Bathurst knew whither the mind of Maud Masters had wandered. Upstairs in that villa. To *le vieillard*! He, whoever he might be, Anthony felt certain that he *knew*, must be arriving soon. Why this long delay? Could it be that the man . . . Irene Pearce was still standing there at his side like a statue carved in stone. Something was happening! The conversation in the room began to trail . . . to drag. Maud Masters had come into the open. War was unmistakably declared!

"I am not satisfied," Anthony heard her say coldly; "you must tell your story to Monsieur Antine, my husband. Here he is."

The door must have opened, for a new voice, a strange voice, said, "What is all this, my dear?"

Anthony felt Irene's arm *stiffen* in his. He saw a peculiarly wild, puzzled look take possession of her face.

"These men," replied Miss Masters, "have come here with a cock-and-bull story of a will that concerns me. Tell them to go away, Adam. The old one is a complete fool and the other might well have escaped from a mental home."

Anthony repressed a chuckle with extreme difficulty.

"What is it that you want of my wife?" asked the man who had come into the room. "Explain quickly—or get out!" The voice was harsh and guttural, strained and unnatural. Anthony whispered to Irene Pearce.

"Have you realized the truth? You agree with me?"

She nodded. Her eyes were round with fear. She trembled against him.

He repeated, "Are you sure?"

"Yes," she whispered again. "But how can it be that—"

He checked her summarily.

"Stay here. Don't move when I move and don't make a sound. Wait behind here until I call you."

He heard the man take a chair and seat himself in it. Sir Austin Kemble tried again to show justification for his presence there.

The man shook his head. "I know nothing of this firm of which you speak. Who are they? Hartley, Holland, and Hill you say the name is? Never heard of them. Don't like solicitors. Thieves, ninety per cent of 'em. Besides, how could they have known that my wife was married to me? That is known only to our two selves. I don't believe in public announcements of such things as marriage. Marriage is a private matter that affects only the two people concerned with it. Explain to me, will you . . . how your firm knew that her name was Antine?"

His hands moved restlessly up and down. If Anthony could have seen as well as heard! MacMorran came in as a support to the Commissioner. Sir Austin Kemble was so obviously nearing the end of his tether. Mr. Bathurst decided that the crucial moment had come. Action! As he stepped silently from behind the screen he saw, to his joy, that Maud Masters, to use the name by which he had known her, and her husband, were sitting with their backs to him.

"Good evening, everybody," he said pleasantly. "So pleased to see you all again."

It was as though the astral bell had sounded clearly and distinctly through the room, for there came a moment of electric stillness. Inspector MacMorran noticed the swift look of fear that darted across the face of the girl Masters. The man who was with her turned slowly in his chair. Anthony was most conscious of the man's eyes. He knew them well, those eyes. He had seen them several times before. But the hair and the face were seeming incongruities. They didn't fit. There flashed into Anthony's mind, at that moment, the realization of the truth behind the phrase that Maud Masters had used to the maid some few minutes before. *"Le vieillard"*. As he looked at the man, the whole face was so unfamiliar that a doubt crept even into his mind.

At a quick sign from Mr. Bathurst, Sir Austin and the Inspector went and stood nearer to the door. Anthony himself commanded the window entrance from the terrace. The first spoken word came from the Masters girl.

"You!" she gasped, gazing at Anthony as though spellbound.

"I can't deny it," he returned. "It's disappointing to you, no doubt."

The man's voice broke in on them.

"What does all this mean? How dare you break into my house in this fashion? It's an outrage . . . an unauthorized piece of effrontery!"

Again Anthony harboured a little devil of a doubt. But the man half rose in his chair before sinking down again, and as he did so Mr. Bathurst saw his hand stray to his knee and the fingers of the hand fidget restlessly over that knee . . . up and down . . . backwards and forwards. Anthony knew then for an absolutely cast-iron certainty that his quest was over, his quarry found, and the case of the three Somersets almost ready to be filed. A wave of relief surged through his brain. There was no fight in this man now. He could almost play cat and mouse with him. From London to East Brutton, from East Brutton to Avignon . . . the scene had shifted many times but now the curtain was close at hand. The man who had protested at the intrusion began to pull nervously at his moustache. A ghastly look had come across his face. Anthony, his triumphant conclusion paramount, turned to the screen from behind which he had so recently stepped and called, "Miss Pearce!"

Irene stepped into the circle and again Maud Masters gasped her astonishment. Irene Pearce was trembling.

"Do you know this man?" cried Anthony. "If you do, give him his name."

Maud Masters sprang to her feet, like a hunted animal she looked wildly round the room as though seeking a way of escape. Sir Austin Kemble stood bolt upright by the door. MacMorran was alert and ready to play his part. He knew that his cue was near at hand, and he knew also that he must take it "on the beat".

"Yes," faltered Irene. "I know him . . . but . . . I am not sure . . ." She stopped and still the tension grew.

"You are not sure of . . . *what*?" demanded Mr. Bathurst.

"I am not sure. . . . The face is more the face of Geoffrey . . . *but the voice and the hands are those of Gerald.*"

Anthony made a gesture of quick decision. The two French police stepped from the terrace into the room. Sergeant Ravenal rattled a sentence. Inspector MacMorran stepped forward, and interpreted.

"Gerald Somerset . . . I arrest you . . . for the murders of David and Geoffrey Somerset at 22 Boot Lane, London, on or about the 12th of March last. . . . Maud Masters . . . I arrest you as an accessory . . . after the fact . . . and I warn you that anything you say . . . will be used . . ."

MacMorran's voice trailed off almost meaninglessly. The man held out trembling wrists for the bracelets and the girl slumped into a dead faint on the floor. Anthony took Irene Pearce's arm and steadied it . . . for she, too, had both feared and trembled. Sergeants Ravenal and Perrichon clicked their heels and listened respectfully to the Commissioner's orders. The whole case had been a personal triumph for him. Sir Austin concluded. He had shown these French johnnies a thing or two. They clicked their heels again and saluted. Sir Austin was impressed with the way they collected their two prisoners. Anthony drew Irene Pearce, from the scene. He would take her back to the hotel at once. She had been unlucky. She had been intimate with the case at each end . . . from the evening that Geoffrey had left her to go to his death . . . until this last evening. It would take time for her scars to heal. She was crying when Anthony and she came again to the waiting car.

Immediately he got back to the hotel, Anthony dispatched a telegram. It was addressed to a Miss Diane Fortolis. It read as follows:

Sigh no more, lady, man was deceiver ever. Max Desmoulais need not swing, therefore wedding-bells can ring. Or, in other words, murderer in the Somerset case arrested this evening. Toujours.

Anthony.

He smiled to himself as he rang the bell for the concierge.

CHAPTER XXV
THE BATHURST BALANCING

ANTHONY Lotherington Bathurst made Sir Austin Kemble and Inspector MacMorran thoroughly comfortable. Dinner was over. Emily had drawn the curtains and the biggest glass was at the Commissioner's elbow. Anthony took a chair between his guests.

"I must confess," said Sir Austin, "that I still find myself very much in the dark. There are many points of the case that are still far from clear to me. Lighten my darkness once again, will you, my boy? MacMorran's just as anxious to hear things as I am."

Anthony lit a cigarette.

"Perhaps it will help you most, Sir Austin, if I sketch the actual facts that relate to the committing of the crime itself. I say 'crime' as opposed to 'crimes', purposely. First of all, I will deal with the discovery made by David Somerset . . . in whose clever brain the trouble started."

In a few words, Anthony told the Commissioner and MacMorran the story that he had previously related to Diane Fortolis. Of the discovery of the diamond manufacture, of the negotiations with the wealthy syndicate of Hatton Garden, of the meeting on the 12th of March in the "Golden Lion" at East Brutton, of the purchase of David Somerset's secret, and of the undertaking which he had given to the men who wore the white gardenia.

"That afternoon," said Mr. Bathurst, "David Somerset left Gloucestershire with an attaché-case packed with notes. I don't know the purchase price, but you can take it from me that it was colossal. There were men concerned who lisped in mournful millions. Somerset had bargained for the money to be paid to him in that way. *It was David Somerset who gave up the return ticket at Paddington that evening*, and he went straight, to his offices in Boot Lane. Up to then, I am certain of the truth of my story. I now enter the realm of conjecture. I think though that Gerald Somerset must have been there in the offices when his father arrived. Possibly *with* Miss Masters. These two had formed an attachment, which they hid from the head of the firm and the rest of the staff by a pretence carried out most systematically during business hours, of *disliking* each other intensely. I *think*, too, that Geoffrey was more in David's confidence than Gerald, and I fancy that the father had asked Geoffrey to come back to the office that evening, after he came away from Irene Pearce's house at Chiswick. Geoffrey went—and remember this most vital fact."

Anthony paused. Sir Austin had his glass to his lips and held it there. But not for long.

"Geoffrey had found his father's revolver on his desk in the office when he returned there that afternoon, had taken it with him to Chiswick, and had it with him when he went back to Boot Lane. There, he probably took it from his pocket and laid it down somewhere. In the light of what followed—*that* fact is most important. You will soon see what I mean."

MacMorran nodded. "I think I can see what's coming."

"Good. Now listen. Gerald, goaded constantly, I fancy, by his terribly ambitious girl friend with regard to his lack of initiative and absence of ambition, heard his father and his *favoured* brother discussing the interview at East Brutton. He made it his immediate business to discover what it was that they were talking about. He heard. He saw the wads of banknotes in the Somerset attaché-case. He saw the revolver on the desk where Geoffrey had laid it when he had come back from Chiswick. Years of bitterness and rankling jealousy took their toll of him. He saw how, instead of being almost negligible, he could become *somebody*, rich and powerful, and married to this girl of his who fascinated him. He calmly shot his father and then fired at his brother. This bullet missed and in the struggle that ensued Geoffrey was killed by a blow on the head from the revolver. Gerald then dragged the two bodies across the corridor and down the stone steps at the back of the offices into the store-room. I venture to suggest that the crime was in no way premeditated but the result of a mere minute's calculation."

The Commissioner nodded.

"Yes, I think you're right there, Bathurst. I agree with you."

"In other words, the temptation came to him very suddenly, and he was unable to resist it, and whether Maud Masters had been implicated before or not, I think that there's little doubt that she entered the scheme of things from now onwards. Arising out of the letter from Antine, that was found in David Somerset's pocket, and of the knowledge that he had been to East Brutton that very day, they decided to take the bodies there by car and put them in a likely place. Probably this journey took place on the following evening. It was not so difficult as it may seem. The store-room was locked up for a day for some excuse, and Gerald kept the key. As soon as the office was cleared, the car was brought round to the back and the bodies transferred. There wouldn't be much light prior to real darkness coming, and if they did happen to be seen, who would imagine the two men 'asleep on the back seats' to be corpses? The cement road to East Brutton copse when they came to it proved an admirable path to an equally admirable hiding-place."

Sir Austin interrupted. "But why all the trouble of going to East Brutton, when there are so many places so much nearer?"

"The explanation is this. When the bodies were found, *at East Brutton*, it only needed the production of the Antine letter to provide a partial solution of the problem of the murder. For one thing, it would most certainly divert suspicion from such a person as Gerald Somerset. What had *he* to do with East Brutton?"

The Commissioner nodded.

"I follow. Go on."

Anthony paused for a moment as though considering something.

"Well, I think that our warning him that he was in danger, as we were entitled to think he was, at that stage of the case, sowed the germ of another idea in Gerald's mind. If *he* could only 'die', he could 'live happily ever afterwards', cradled in a new identity somewhere, fortified and stimulated by the semi-fortune that had been paid for his father's discovery. To die, you see, was an infinitely more attractive proposition than to disappear. To disappear, he realized, would inevitably mean that suspicion of having had a hand in the murders would be directed against him, and he would be followed. The arrival of the two bodies from Gloucestershire, prior to the funeral at Clutton Chase, helped him to develop his idea.

"Before the funeral, he transferred the body of his brother, his twin-brother, from the coffin of Simon Gildey back to the shell in which it had come from East Brutton. Part of the contents of the library of his late father took the place of the dead Geoffrey. In other words, only one of the shells was burned. The other was, shall we say, put inside one of the biggest type of cabin-trunks, obtained by either him or his partner and adapted for the purpose and removed again to the store-room at Boot Lane. You might check up on that purchase, MacMorran. I'll guarantee that you'll find I'm not far out. In case there should be the smell of death remarked upon, by any member of the staff, he arranged for the store-room to be painted. The smell of the new paint would kill the other odour. Remember the recently painted shelves, Inspector, that we saw when we walked round the place on that third occasion? That was the idea underlying that, without a doubt. It helped to put me on the right track.

"The problem now was how long should it be before Gerald Somerset's body should be found somewhere? He arranged, I suggest, the bogus attack upon himself, put up a 'story', and paid a couple of tramps to work it for him, perhaps, and after he had taken the body, salved from the storeroom, dressed for the new part, by car to Friningham, where the sea would eventually give up its dead, sooner or later, he contrived that Miss Masters should 'phone through the St. Paul's Cathedral 'abduction' message and then heigh-ho for the South of France. To take the name of Antine was, as I said, a master touch. Or shall we say 'a mistress-touch'? I don't know how he managed with regard to passports and credentials generally, but doubtless we shall find that out."

Anthony turned to his two companions.

"More details will emerge at the trial, but there you have, I think, the principal points of what I will call the 'crime-construction' itself. Any questions?"

"Tell me how you came to the truth. For a long time, you know, you were floundering in the dark. Remember that, Bathurst?"

"That's only too true, Sir Austin." Anthony stretched his legs towards the fire. The evening had grown quite cool. Anthony harked back. "It's not easy for me to say, absolutely accurately, when I first began to get into touch. But I think that the final visit which Inspector MacMorran and I made to the Boot Lane offices, when we discovered the store-room and the bloodstain on the stone steps and smelt the paint, may be well described as my starting point. You see . . . it changed the *venue* of the murders so completely. We had all been regarding the crimes as having an East Brutton atmosphere, and suddenly I saw that the two men were in all probability killed in their own offices. It was valuable also in this way. It explained David Somerset's return ticket. He *had* returned from East Brutton."

Anthony reflected again.

"My three next advancements were *(a)* the Antine letter in the Somerset post-box; *(b)* the fact that Gerald Somerset had deliberately slipped the police on the morning of his 'abduction'—most extraordinary conduct for a man who was living in fear and trembling, and *(c)* that the body washed up on the shore at Friningham had been both shot and skull-fractured as well as drowned. I will explain how my mind worked with regard to these three points. The posting of the 'Antine' letter to a man who had been dead for some time, obviously had a *deliberate* purpose behind it. Ten to one, I thought, it had come from the murderer. As it happened, I was right. The more 'Antine' atmosphere he could place round the crime, the better for him. See my point, sir?"

The Commissioner nodded.

"Yes. He had taken it from his father's pocket, I presume?"

"Yes. Well, the second point that I just mentioned is self-explanatory. The third presented itself to me like this. Why three manners of death? To hide the true one? Probably! Which of the three had been the true one? Then the flash of knowledge came to me. Geoffrey Somerset had not been shot through the heart. But he had died from a fractured skull. Was it possible, I asked myself, that this Friningham body was not that of *Gerald* but of *Geoffrey*? In the meantime, I tested fully what I called then, the 'Antine' end of the mystery. I mean by that, the contact with the case of the Hatton Garden Syndicate which had purchased David Somerset's secret formula. I owe a lot to MacMorran here. When he told me a certain name that I had come upon, meant precious stones—'diamonds'—I began to guess why David had gone to East Brutton.

"The name 'Adam Antine' I saw as one word, and then, of course, the meaning of it stuck out a mile. 'Diamonds' were undoubtedly in the picture. 'Adamantine'. I came out of that entanglement, however, feeling more certain that the father and son had not met their deaths at the hands of Hatton Garden. So I began seriously to turn my attention to Master Gerald. Geoffrey's coffin badly wanted looking into. Both literally and figuratively. Here I remembered something else. Something absolutely vital—and I *knew* in my heart of hearts that I was safe home—high and dry."

Sir Austin was impressed.

"What was that, Bathurst?"

Anthony's eyes sparkled as he answered.

"Why, the fact that Mrs. Somerset at Clutton Chase had informed me of the strange disappearance, *theft* she called it, of a number of books from the library of her late husband. Of course—Geoffrey out—and the books in. Following that up, I took Andrew MacMorran here to interview Simon Gildey, the undertaker of Mill End. What that matinee idol told us, almost clinched the matter. There had been *four* coffins in the house called 'Urswick', or as good as coffins, pardon the euphemism, and only *two*, remember, had been required for lowering into the family vault. You remember the exhumation that took place. I plead guilty to dissembling there. You asked me if Gerald's body were in the coffin at Friningham. I told you no—I was right, strictly speaking, but I didn't reply in the way that you naturally imagined I should, because your real point was . . . 'Is the Friningham coffin *empty* like this one?'"

Anthony smiled at the expression on the Commissioner's face. Sir Austin made no remark.

"Well," continued Mr. Bathurst. "I don't know that there's very much more for me to say. You know how we succeeded in tracing the whereabouts of Maud Masters. I felt that she *must* communicate with a member of her family before long. And where Masters was, I knew there would be also the man whom I was seeking. You know the rest. Any more questions?"

MacMorran had one.

"The newspaper that was rolled up . . . that we found in Brutton Copse—"

Anthony was in like lightning.

"Had been brought by Geoffrey from Miss Pearce's house at Chiswick. It was probably taken from his pocket by our pair of birds. You know for what purpose. It was a mistake on their part to leave it where they did, but it really made no difference as things turned out."

"Tell me," said Sir Austin, "why did Fortolis and his Hatton Garden friends 'stage' the affair at East Brutton? Why the garb and the generally theatrical conditions? I must confess that that rather puzzles me."

"I think this, Sir Austin. They wanted it as far away from London as they could conveniently get . . . no whisper of the threat to the very foundations of the diamond industry must be allowed to reach Hatton Garden for obvious reasons, and they also desired to *impress* David Somerset with the gravity of their intentions. Would you care to know who 'Antine', their leader, was?"

"Certainly I should. I've been wondering."

Anthony mentioned a name . . . one of the most respected of the highest social orders. The Commissioner looked incredulous. "The Duke of . . ."

Anthony nodded.

"He has diamond interests of almost fabulous value, sir. That's the reason. Another drink, MacMorran, and you, sir, before you go."

"I've been thinking." This from the Inspector. "Where are the two bullets that were fired in the office? There was no trace of them anywhere there that we ever found."

"I know. I've thought of that. But I think that the window was partly open, and that they're probably somewhere on the Thames river-bed. Anything else?"

MacMorran shook his head. He remembered how close the water was.

Anthony walked to the telephone when his guests had gone. With smiling lips he asked for a number . . . and waited.

"Is that you, Lady Precious Stone? . . . Where shall I meet you . . . and when? You will? Good . . . so will I. Till then. . . . I'm counting the seconds."

THE END